I remembered Manderley, an intac  *annual costume ball. I stood on the second floor above the stairs waiting to be introduced, having freshened up in one of the bedrooms.*

"Miss Millie," I heard myself announced by the butler and began my trip down the long steps. Careful to pull my dress up above my silver heels lest I trip on the hem, I looked straight ahead, hoping to make a devastating impression. My dress was deep blue velvet, the skirt full around my hips dropping loosely to the floor, bursting into shades of purples and greens, mimicking the feathers of a peacock. In my hair, tucked back into a snood, two peacock feathers nested. Reaching the bottom step, I looked up to see my Edward, waiting with outstretched hand. He needed no costume, only his uniform, a testimony to his bravery.

"Have you been dancing?" he asked, his eyes taking in my costume as I took his hand. His smile captured me, and everyone else in the crowded hall passed by me unnoticed.

"Not yet."

"Waiting for me?"

"Of course."

As we moved into the ballroom, Glen Miller and his band, hired for this special night, broke into their big hit, "A Nightingale Sang in Berkeley Square." We began to dance. The other guests cleared the floor, leaving us alone as they watched the RAF pilot so handsome in his dress blues and his girl from the USO.

The Girl from the USO

by

Barbara Rebbeck

The Girl from the USO

Cover Art by *Abigail Owen*

The Wild Rose Press, Inc.
PO Box 708
Adams Basin, NY 14410-0708
Visit us at www.thewildrosepress.com

Publishing History
First Vintage Rose Edition, 2020
Trade Paperback ISBN 978-1-5092-3329-8
Digital ISBN 978-1-5092-3330-4

Published in the United States of America

Dedication

For Mom and Dad,
Another USO girl and her pilot.
For Jean, the real Maisie,
and Carol, my nursing expert.

And
For Gracie, my cat
for her patience.

Acknowledgements

Much gratitude and thanks to Laura Kelly, my TWRP editor. She told me she was good at her job, and she is. Thanks for your personal touch. Cheers to TWRP for all they do for their authors.

A thank you to Sara Coyle and her students at the Beverly Hills Academy who inspired me to write with them and for them as writer-in -residence. Also, a thank you to the now grown-up ladies who were in my language art classes at the Academy of the Sacred Heart, especially Husnah Khan and their leader then, Linda Schaffner. Thank you for staying in touch. I am also grateful for the company of authors I have met in Detroit Working Writers, Sisters in Crime, and Rochester Writers, especially Cindy Harrison. And I offer a salute to the USO and all its efforts for our military.

I also reach out with gratitude to my fans and fellow writers on Facebook and Twitter. You have kept me going with your urgings to finish the task. I particularly am grateful for the inspiration from other writers in this genre: Clare Mackintosh, Ruth Ware, and Eve Chase. I tip my hat to AJ Finn for his novel, *The Woman in the Window,* that convinced me I was headed in the right direction with my own novel.

I leave you all with this quote from Daphne du Maurier on love:

Women want love to be a novel; men a short story.

Prologue

I fled Him, down the nights and down the days;
I fled Him, down the arches of the years;
I fled Him, down the labyrinthine ways
Of my own mind, and in the mist of tears
I hid from Him, and under running laughter.

Why these lines now? Why did they keep rushing against my mind, bruising me? I recognized them as words memorized in my teens. Words from my favorite novel, *Rebecca*. A novel that had haunted me for years. But why now? I gazed around the chapel, my vision blurred by the lace veil. Alone in the front pew, I knelt, feeling hard stone beneath me in this small Cornish chapel of the great estate. How had this American girl come to know it so well? The ancient stone, so cold to the touch, the chiseled statues of saints who seemed not to care a bit for my plight. The stained glass window over the altar, dulled by the incessant rain outside, no longer held me in awe. The peacock in the glass, slumped and beaten down by the rain, looked away from me. Those proud strutting peacocks on the lawn of Sand Castles Hall seemed reduced to this dejected bird, tail dragging behind him. No sunlight shone through his colors. Just rain drummed the chapel roof. No solace reached for me, this young widow.

I could flee it no longer. The casket of my husband lay directly ahead of me. Swaddled by the British flag,

1

his medals lay upon it. My RAF pilot, flown now. My peacock of an officer, preening no longer. His blue eyes closed. His fine, curly locks hidden forever.

"Ma'am?" I startled out of my reverie, feeling the gloved hand on my shoulder.

"Yes?" I turned, my lace veil, my widow's weeds, snagging on the sleeve of my coat. "Oh, Albert. It's you."

"Yes, Her Ladyship has asked me to tell you that your bag has been sent to the train station with orders to hold it there until you decide upon which train you will depart."

"Oh."

"There is a coach that departs at six."

"Thank you."

"And Her Ladyship requests that you might return her veil."

"Of course," I replied, removing the pin that held the veil and laying it across his outstretched hands. Tears began to well in my eyes as I faced an uncertain future full out in the cold chapel. The veil lifted. "Please thank her for me," I said, my voice echoing in the still chapel. "You will see to the burial?"

"Yes, as the family wishes. I will leave you then," Albert whispered.

"Thank you," I whispered back.

I turned back to the casket, rose, and walked toward it. I reached and touched the cool, rough cloth of the flag. Red, white, and blue like the American flag, though British. The RAF flag had always looked like a bullseye target to me. They had gotten their man. Once my man. I pulled a crushed red rose from my green coat pocket and placed it on the flag just about where I imagined his quiet heart would be. "Goodbye, my English lad." I was hating. I was loving.

Alone, I walked back up the aisle, braced to face a driving Cornish rain. Not looking back, I walked out to the steps of the chapel, bowing my head against the downpour.

"Brolly?"

I squinted through the rain drops to see before me another RAF airman, this one a navigator according to the "N" on his wings on his jacket. Pulling me closer by my left arm, he covered us both with his offered umbrella.

"And you are?"

"Sorry, no proper introductions, love. Just hoping to keep you dry with my brolly."

I cringed at the familiarity of his casual "love." At least he wasn't calling me "ducks" as so many British men did. It had taken me a while to get used to that familiarity.

Balancing a cigarette in one hand, the umbrella in the other, he said, "I'm James, a friend of old Teddy. I'm here as your official RAF escort."

"My Edward?"

"Edward? Never. Teddy to me." He stood looking down at me, breathing in a puff from his cigarette.

"Edward," I said again, making my point.

"Shall we make a run for the local?" he asked, nodding his head down the road.

"The coach should be by in a few minutes," I suggested, not sure I welcomed this official intruder. A shandy, though, would taste ever so good and calming at this point.

As if commanded, the coach stopped at the end of

the lane, splashing up water. Together we huddled and ran, James gallantly pushing me onto the coach as he attempted to close the umbrella in the wind. Jumping on, he dropped coins in the driver's hand and sat across the aisle from me. We remained silent for the short ride.

The Punch & Peacock came into sight ahead of us to the left on the country lane. It was a stone pub, very old. Memories washed over me of the times spent inside, in an old wooden booth, near the huge fireplace, drinking and laughing. Mysterious names and primitive drawings were carved into the rough, wooden table. I'd never seen anything like this in the States. I swear I could walk right into the Inglenook fireplace. The aroma of the bread baking in the side oven was always heavenly. Now the old pub would be opening its arms to me for the last time.

"Shall we?" James asked, snapping open the black umbrella and reaching to help me up. I took his hand, found it quite cold, and stood up. Awkward, we hurried down the coach steps and ran for the inn. The pub sign flapped in the wind with another peacock, this one wooden, carved with feathers spread in proud purples and blues parading in the rain.

"Edward called that one, 'Pubcock,'" I shouted above the rain, pointing to the sign.

"Looks a jolly old bird," James said. "Is the specialty peacock pie?"

He pushed open the heavy door, and we almost fell into the warm room. The usual folk were not there, no one tossing darts, no one playing records on the Victrola, no one huddled by the fire, nursing ale.

"Welcome," the barkeep called. "What'll it be?"

James closed the umbrella, revealing both of us to

4

the hushed light of the pub.

"Oh, I did not see you clearly. Begging your pardon, love. We are so sorry for your loss. This war is dreadful."

Lost for words, I let James talk for us both.

"Thank you. Could you get us a bitter and a shandy, please?"

He took my hand and guided me to the table closest to the fire. I slid into the cushioned seat that backed against the wall. He sat across from me in an old leather chair that creaked as he sank into it.

"I see the fire reflected in your eyes," he said. "Gives your eyes a light they are missing otherwise."

I shivered, knowing my eyes reflected my whole demeanor, my body limp behind the table. And who was he to comment on my eyes? Too personal for this widow.

"Something to warm the cockles of your heart," the barkeep said, depositing our drinks on the table between us.

"Are you hungry?" James asked.

Looking up at the barkeep who I knew as Ian, I asked, "Do you have stargazy pie?"

"That we do, love, and it'll be on us. Specialty of the house for you. I'll just give a shout to the wife."

Before I could say my thanks, he vanished. Ian was being very formal. Perhaps wary of this stranger in blue seated across from me.

"Stargazy pie? No bangers and mash?" James asked, lighting a cig.

"Wait till you see this. Quite the Cornish dish borrowed from the tiny town of Mousehole."

"And the Cornish tale that must lurk behind it?"

I so needed the diversion of telling Cornish tales, so I began, "The fish pie with eyes that stare back at you. Originally made to celebrate a rescue from starvation in a cold December right before Christmas. After days of storms, one brave fisherman took to sea to catch fish for the town. He made it back with fish enough for all. So this pie was first made in his honor hundreds of years ago."

It seemed a distraction, a welcome one to tell this old story to this new airman. I warmed to my story, recovering somewhat from the cold sorrow of the chapel.

"And?" he said, somehow knowing I needed to tell him this fish story.

"So you take six different kinds of white fish and bake them with herbs and a lemony zest."

"Sounds harmless so far," James said, as he sipped from his glass and smiled at me.

"You layer the fish and add another layer of grated eggs. Next you smooth them over with a layer of mashed potatoes."

"Go on," he said, staring like a gazy pie into my eyes. It was good to have someone listen to me at last. I admit I was slowing down the baking recipe for dramatic effect. Now came the pie finale.

"Then you bake lots of large pilchards. We call them sardines in the States. You carefully position them on top of the potatoes with their little heads up in the air and their tails, too, to form crescents. Next step, you prepare a pie crust and carefully place it over the pilchards with slits across the dough so the heads and tails poke through. The eyeballs stare up at you and past you, gazing to the stars. Ta-da!"

He leaned back in the chair, and it creaked dramatically as he mocked me with a toothy smile. "Blimey, I guess I'll risk it for the biscuit."

I laughed with him, the shandy warming my heart. This felt good. The fear was gone for the first time in weeks, even with this stranger.

As if on cue, Ian's wife, Bette, passed by our table, carrying the pie, its fish eyes popping as she pushed it into the old bread oven beside the roaring fireplace. "Won't be long, dearie. Maisie helped me make it special for you," she said. "More drinks?"

"How about a jug of the peacock punch?" James asked. "May as well try that along with the stargazy pie."

"Coming up. It's a cracker," she said, looking closely at me. "All right, Millie? You've got a face like a wet weekend. And indeed, it is one out there."

"Yes, I'll be fine." Ian and Bette had been my loyal friends, keeping my secrets close. Even offering me shelter in one of the rooms above. Shelter for little Maisie and me. My throat caught as I thought of her. The tiny evacuee from London.

"So," James began the inevitable, "how did you and old Teddy meet? He was very secretive about you. Certainly never told us what an American beauty you are."

Blushing from the heat of the fire and his compliment, I relaxed back into the cushiony seat, sipping on my shandy. Staring at James, I wondered how much I should reveal about Edward. How much did he already know?

"The train leaves at six," I said.

"Yes, that gives us hours to share stories."

"Not sure," I said, averting my eyes.

Ian chose that moment to rescue me. "James, how about a game of darts?"

"Do you mind?" he asked, already rising from the table.

"Of course not. I'll go snuggle by the fire until the pie is ready." I crossed the room and dropped into the old sofa, careful not to spill my drink. I felt so warm, as if my heart were reawakening. My mind traveled back to that cold day in February in Detroit.

Chapter 1

I sat just inside the dorm on Alexandrine in Detroit, waiting for the bus, reading my very favorite novel, *Rebecca*. Again. The beautiful poem I had read so many times leapt out from the pages.

"I fled Him, down the nights and down the days;

I fled Him, down the arches of the years;"

Always, I was drawn in and entranced by this story of a great love. Would I ever know such love? Would there ever be a suave British Maxim de Winter in my own humdrum existence?

I looked up, hoping to see the bus. Yesterday's snow had been cleared, but slushy puddles splashed up as cars drove by and people jumped back onto the sidewalks outside the hospital across the boulevard to avoid the spray. I was a third-year nursing student at Grace Hospital, just finishing my obstetrical rotation. For three months, I had been beside doctors as they delivered tiny babies into this uncertain world. England and Germany were at war. The United States had so far resisted entering the fray, but it was rumored that FDR, our president, wanted war. That was worrying as my younger brother, Gary, would be of age to fight. I stood and walked across the lobby of the nurses' residence. It really was a virtual prison with strict rules about visitors, especially men. The old ladies, Miss Jackson, the most evil, who thought themselves wardens over us, were most unforgiving, and several young ladies had been tossed out onto Alexandrine Boulevard, forbidden to return, their nursing ambitions squelched by "unbecoming" behavior.

"That bus appears to be late today," Miss Jackson called from her desk. She was the guardian of the entranceway and knew everyone's business. A substantial woman with her hair pulled back in a severe bun, she was a formidable drawbridge for the students, her jaw flapping up and down with all the latest gossip. "What are you reading, dear Mildred?"

I cringed at my full name, always preferring "Millie." I had my great-aunt Mildred to thank for my full name, Mildred Lillian. "I'm reading *Rebecca* again. Daphne du Maurer is quite my favorite author."

"I saw the picture. Quite good," she replied. "I hear it has a good chance to win an Academy Award."

Perhaps she did have a romantic heart somewhere under her ample bosom.

"And what are your plans for the weekend?" she continued.

Nosy old bag. "Oh, nothing much. Just a quiet weekend with the family." I knew I had to show respect for her. She was the terror of every student. She could make or break you. Just last week she had informed me coldly that even though I was a senior nurse, she could still toss me out on Alexandrine at any time for the smallest infraction.

"If that Roosevelt gets his way, we may not have many more quiet days," she declared, her eyes bulging beneath her gray bangs.

"Oh, here's the bus," I said, flying out the door, almost dropping poor *Rebecca* as I struggled with my bag and little overnight case.

Avoiding puddles, I directed my little boots with the dark fur cuffs up the stairs onto the bus. My father, a no-nonsense doctor, laughed at these boots, declaring the two-inch heels useless against any onslaught of weather from a sprinkle of rain to a blizzard. But I had argued they were so attractive and matched the fur on the cuffs and collar of my dark green coat perfectly. Topped off with a tiny hat with a fur brim and dark veil, the stylish outfit was the ideal antidote to the overly starched pink cotton uniform I wore at the hospital. The dresses which fell far below our knees, almost hiding the opaque white hose and solid white shoes, were so stiff that they could be propped up in the corner of our dorm rooms so that we could actually jump into them in the early morning, clip our equally starched caps on our heads, and fly off to breakfast after a late-night study session of memorizing bones of the body or bed bath procedures.

I looked good, and that was important for my destination, far from a quiet family evening. Miss Jackson would die if she knew the truth. A few weeks ago at St. Francis Xavier Church, Father Champion had announced after his sermon a new endeavor for the war. My ears, always dulled by the monotonous drone of the Latin mass, had perked up at his words. FDR, he had told us, would be establishing a women's group called the USO, United Services Organization. Just in time, he had said, as England would be sending British personnel from the Royal Air Force for flight training on Grosse Ile. Concerned that these young men, boys really of nineteen and twenty, would need guidance in maneuvering around the possible evils they might fall upon in a strange country, the USO would function as their welcome committee to the country. We girls would form clubs at the military bases which would greet the boys, offering recreation such as dancing, card-playing, films, etc. After mass, I made a beeline to my best chum, Meg, a few pews back, and together we spoke to Father Champion and volunteered on the spot.

"We would love to help," Meg bubbled to our priest as he greeted parishioners on their way out of the church. She was my tiny friend dressed also in very impractical shoes and a new hat that covered her face with a deep blue veil. "We want to welcome those English boys."

"The RAF cadets will be coming to Grosse Ile this August," Father Champion said, looking at us both, probably wondering if these two silly girls who couldn't even wear proper boots were up to the job.

"Not until August?" Meg asked, a bit disappointed, pushing back her veil, hoping Father would read the sincerity in her brown eyes.

"Yes, but a small advance group arrives in February to check out the lay of the land," he replied, certain now that he would have no problem recruiting.

"When do we start?" I asked, one hand clutching this week's church bulletin and my prayer book and purse, the other pushing through Meg's arm.

We were starting now.

I was on my way to the Grosse Ile Naval Base for our first party. I had no idea as I pulled out my compact to check my rouge and lipstick on that bus ride to the island how much my life was about to change. Smiling, I silently thanked Aunt Mildred for all those hours playing cards across the table from me. I was ready.

****

"One stargazy pie." Ian placed the pie ever so carefully between us on the pub table. He handed James a knife and large spoon. The aroma wrapped around both of us, warming our still damp clothes and spirits.

"Magnificent, old boy," James said. "Compliments to the wife. Shall I be Mother?"

"Certainly," I said, "have at it." As many times as I'd eaten this pie, I would never forget the first time one was placed before me. I was horrified at how these fish heads, eyeballs and all, poked out from the crust. Took me several times to even think of tasting it. But now I quite liked it.

"They do seem to be staring at me," James replied. "I shall not share any secrets, my dear pilchards, no matter how you stare at me."

I looked across at him. Perhaps the punch was warming me to him, relaxing my fears of opening up to another airman. He was so like Edward, yet very different. He wore his uniform in a much more casual way than Edward had, jacket unbuttoned, tie loosened. His blond hair was very straight, sticky bits of Brylcreem waging a losing battle to keep it flat on his head after the rain. He had an aristocratic nose; one would say a Roman style. His chin jutted out, almost asking for a beard to grow and cover its sharpness. But his mouth was friendly, so easy to smile, so easy to console. He was shorter than Edward, even a bit stocky, his shirt buttons straining a bit. Blushing, I realized I was staring.

Ian laughed. I startled back to reality, aware that Ian still stood beside us. "Tuck in," he urged. "There's nothing like a stargazy pie in a pelting rain like this.

Even though there's not much up there for the fishes to see." He gestured toward the ceiling as he turned back to the bar. I lifted my glass, finishing off the punch. I had gotten used to the lack of ice in British drinks. Somehow this drink was appropriate in the chill of the downpour.

"Ian," James called after him. "Another jug, please."

Turning back to me, he looked into my eyes, his brown eyes linking with my green, but I was far away. He handed me my bowl of pie, unaware I had left him behind again.

****

This may test your belief, but I did dream of Manderley the night before I met Edward just like the second Mrs. de Winter had dreamed of the old mansion in the opening of my favorite novel. I drove up the long road through the thick foliage, which in itself was ridiculous as I couldn't drive. Funny how dreams let you do the impossible. As I approached the old mansion, now in ruins after the devastating fire, I saw her walking on the lawn. She was wearing her British tweeds, and her sturdy shoes, and an old felt hat. Still mousy-looking. Herself. I realized it was not her at all, but Joan Fontaine, of course, the actress who had played her in the movie.

I parked the car on the path by what had been the front entrance to the estate. I sat there, afraid to get out of the car. I had not been invited. I was an intruder.

She turned away from me as if she did not see me. Then she vanished into the ruins.

I summoned the courage to get out of the car and struggled through the tall grass and weeds to the left of the entrance where an old door lay collapsed on the ground. A heavy oak, it leaned against a gentle slope of the lawn. A lawn though overgrown, singed, and dry. In the dim light of sunset, I leaned over and ran my hand along the roughness of the wood. My fingers traced words I knew well: I fled Him.

A light drizzle began to plunk along the oak, wetting my fingers. I drew back and headed back to the car, the dry grass soaking up the rain and sweeping over my feet, scratching my legs.

As I crossed the lawn, I heard voices arguing from inside the ruins. Loud voices.

"I have to get away from you."

"Then go. That woman out there, snooping around, she'll drive you away."

I woke up then, shivering. I pulled the covers up to my neck in the darkness of my dorm room.

"Are you okay?" Carol, my roommate, asked from her bed across the room.

"Just a bad dream," I said.

"Was someone chasing you? You clearly said, 'I fled him'."

Chapter 2

The bus threw up gray slush at every stop along the way down Jefferson Avenue. The usual passengers climbed on, taking their usual seats, happy to be headed home on a Friday afternoon, bundled in their wintry coats, scarves, and gloves and very practical boots, stained with salt and water. Papa would be sure to point them out to me if he were here. I gazed out the window, rubbing it with my gloved finger to see clearly through the frosted pane. The bus was headed downriver, meaning we were leaving Detroit and passing through suburbs always in sight of the Detroit River. Del Ray and then Ecorse rushed by as we passed my home, my mom and dad's home really. A thick brick building with two entrances, one for the residence, the other for my dad's medical office. I loved that house where I lived with my parents and my brother, Gary, and of course, my cat, Bartholomew or Mew for short. The house had originally sat right on the river banks, but when land was needed to build a riverside esplanade and park, the city had purchased the land. With great ceremony the house was moved, lock, stock, and barrel, across Jefferson to Bourassa where it now perched. The move was legendary for not a cup or picture was wounded. Perfection. All was in its place and life went on, just a stone's throw from the river.

"Is this seat taken?"

Blushing, I realized my reverie had gone on through the last bus stop across from my house. "No, please sit down."

I scooched over, giving the lady more room as she was burdened with several packages.

"Found some good bargains. Stocking up on hosiery. You never know when we might get into that war. Things we take for granted will become scarce and rationed."

"It must be quite a different life over there," I said. "My name is Millie."

"Oh, how do you do? I'm Susan." Now she was bundled tight with bright pink wool on her head and around her neck. I couldn't see her boots, but I could be sure they were thick and practical and clumsy. "Where are you headed on this Friday afternoon?"

"Actually, I'm off to Grosse Ile, to the naval base."

"Whatever for?"

"Father Champion from St. Xavier is recruiting a group of women to help with the British troops arriving in August. Our first meeting is today."

Susan squirmed beneath her packages and asked, "Can a Protestant join? I'd love to help out."

The bus pulled over to the curb again before I had a chance to answer. The door squeaked open and up the few steps popped Meg, my very best friend. I had to giggle at her very impractical boots, heels even higher than mine. She dropped her coin in the box and politely pushed past the man who was leaving the bus to get to the seat in front of me he had just freed up.

"Millie," she said, "Aren't you just so excited?"

"You bet," I said. "I was just telling Susan here about our adventure."

"It sounds like such fun," Susan said. "I was just asking if I could join. I can't come tonight, but next time, maybe?"

"I don't see why not," Meg answered. "We'll give your name to Father Champion."

"USO girls," I said. "I've always wanted a title. You know, like The Duchess of Windsor."

Meg shook her head and said, "Oh, don't get her started on royalty. You'd think almost three years of cleaning bed pans at the hospital would have cured her of her fantasies, but she'd want nothing better than to find herself a prince or duke."

"Not true." I laughed. "An aristocrat would do just fine. As long as he came with a country estate in Cornwall, a divine plummy accent, and perhaps a mystery. A family secret."

"And we're back to *Rebecca*." Meg laughed. "Head in the clouds; that's you, Millie."

I turned back to my window in time to catch the lights of the city of Wyandotte coming on as we drove through. Wouldn't be long now.

"I'm off in Taylor," Susan said. "Susan Taylor. Please sign me up. Just remember that's Taylor from Taylor. My brother is in the Army at Fort Riley, Kansas. I'd like to think someone is cheering him up out there."

We rode along in silence for a while as the sky darkened, thickening with possible snow storms to come. Within ten minutes we pulled up to Susan's stop and she stood up, stacking her packages in her arms, her purse dangling from her arm. "Don't forget me. See you next time."

I could barely make her out as she crossed the road,

picking her way through the slushy twilight. War had a way of making instant friends of people. My brother, Gary, was suddenly with me. I knew he would enlist if war came to this country. Hadn't he begged my dad for the honor of picking Meg and me up at the base later tonight? "I only hope he will be safe," I said.

"Who?" Meg asked as she moved beside me.

"I didn't realize I said that out loud. My brother, Gary. He'd be the first to enlist if we enter the war. And FDR is starting a draft anyway."

"You got to admit he'd be dreamy in a uniform. Those dark eyes and black hair."

Just then the bus swung left and began to cross the bridge that linked downriver to Grosse Ile. It was a small island in the middle of the Detroit River. Many of the wealthy Detroit auto pioneers had first built summer homes here along the shore. In fact, our destination was a big old house once the summer home of the Olds family, Olds as in Oldsmobile. It had been donated as the new center for the base and the USO group. It was certainly worthy of the delicate boots Meg and I wore.

The bus travelled down Meridian Road and then turned into the base, well-lit in the dusk. I could see the construction that must be stop-and-go in this winter weather. My brother was up on all of the plans and had told me a new runway was being added to the original two. New barracks were in order for the RAF cadets due to arrive in August. With a sleepy population of about two thousand residents, Grosse Ile was about to burst into prominence.

"I'm so excited I could pee my panties," Meg squealed into my ear. I shook my head. It was these outbursts that made my mother wonder if Meg were

19

proper company for me, a doctor's daughter. I'd seen enough pee and worse in the last three years though, so Meg never bothered me. She was a bright light in my dark house. Aunt Lill and Grandma Stella lived next door to us and could indeed be stifling. From another lifetime, another generation, they just didn't understand.

"Here we are, ladies and sir," the bus driver said, putting on the brakes.

"Sir?" I turned around to see one soldier sitting toward the back of the bus.

He stood and moved up the aisle, stopping behind us to let us leave first. "Are you here for the USO meeting?" he asked.

"Yes, we are," I stumbled over the words.

"I'll show you the way. Might be slippery. Watch out, especially with those boots."

One for Dad, I thought and let the serviceman pass by us so we could follow.

"Good luck," the driver said. "We'll probably be seeing a lot of each other."

Meg and I balanced our way down the steps and into the hand of the soldier, one by one to plop down into yes, slush.

"Follow me," he said, walking between us. "This way."

We walked not far over to our right toward a barrack. As we neared, we could hear music playing, a big band hit. As we approached the door, the soldier pushed it open and hung back, letting us enter. The bright lights immediately calmed our nerves. Looking around, I saw about twenty guys, some playing cards, some just chatting. Some moving to the music, hoping for a dance partner. Meg pulled my arm and said, "Over there. Father Champion."

He saw us, too, and quickly covered the distance between us with a big smile on his face. "Ladies! How good to see you. How about skipping the formal meeting? We've got some pretty bored cadets here."

"Sounds good," I said, gulping back a touch of fear. My dream of the night before was there in my head all at once. *I fled him.*

"Ladies, a game of cards?"

It was a British accent calling from across the room. A rather dull, dreary room at that. Mental note to get posters on the walls soon. "You bet," Meg answered. Together we crossed the room toward the table.

"Your coats?" another man asked.

We awkwardly removed our coats, and they were whisked away and hung on a makeshift coat rack as we sat down at the table. "Colas?" Father Champion asked.

"Sure," we both said at the same time, both thirsty after the long bus ride.

"What are we playing?" I asked, looking around the table at a mix of American and British cadets. They seemed very happy indeed to see us.

"Twenty-one, or Blackjack to you Americans."

"What's in a name?" I asked, hoping I was making a clever reference to *Romeo and Juliet*. Meg laughed at me as we picked up our hands of cards from the dealer, a British airman. I knew I would have to learn what all the insignia meant on their uniforms.

"Breaking the ice with Shakespeare. Very clever lady," an American next to me said. "We're not country bumpkins, you know. We can even read." His eyes snapped as he stared at me, and then looked down at his cards.

So we began with banter and laughter, playing cards to bridge two cultures. The drinks flowed and eventually sandwiches came from somewhere. The good-natured teasing continued with taunts of "Limey" and "Yank" tossed across the table as the competitive spirit rose.

"How about some dancing?" Father Champion called out from across the room.

"Would love to, Mac," Meg said, addressing the guy sitting next to her. We were now on a first name basis. She seemed to have picked her pilot, one with a British accent. Definitely of the tall, dark, and handsome breed. A contrast to her blond curls, caught up in a snood.

Father Champion volunteered to man the gramophone, and we were off. To the hits of Tommy Dorsey and Glen Miller we danced two by two, taking turns, and then we decided on a group dance. We all sang a rousing chorus of "Boogie Woogie Bugle Boy" with an encore of "You Are My Sunshine." The men got into the music and their cares seemed to lift for just a few moments. We were their home away from home. I felt like Scarlett O'Hara surrounded by her beaux on the terrace at Tara.

Out of breath and on my way to the improvised ladies' room, I walked across to a doorway, not really sure where it led. Looking back to the dancing and paying no attention where I was going, I crashed into the arms of a stranger in blue. He pushed back, holding me in front of him, giving me a searing once-over with his blue eyes that burned through to my heart. He was simply the most handsome man I'd ever seen. His blondish-brown hair complimented his eyes. His broad smile was topped off by a thin mustache. "Don't hurt yourself." He laughed. "Would you like to dance?"

The breath knocked out of me, I rasped, "I have been dancing." Just then I heard the gang behind me start in on the tune, "Sure It's the Same Old Shillelagh."

"You silly goose, you haven't danced with me," he said, holding me at arm's length.

"And that would be different?" I managed to say, my head and heart turned upside down and inside out.

"Yes, very."

****

At the old inn we were both nursing our punch now, both a bit tipsy, the empty pie tin between us. I looked across at him as he lit up another cig, leaning back, probably unhappy with this duty he had to carry off.

"Where are you from, James?" I asked, realizing I had been ignoring him, off in my dreams, trying to make an effort.

"I'm from Ely," he said. "Ancient home of the eel, that squiggly, slippery bugger. Ever have eel pie?"

"Not really," I said. "It took me long enough to warm up to stargazy pie." I laughed.

"I grew up in a town known for its eels and its cathedral. As a lad I sang in the choir with my boy-soprano descants and attended the church school. Quite posh. Ely is not far from Cambridge and the base. Huge estates there, too."

****

Huge estates. I remembered another dream. We were invited to Manderley, an intact Manderley, before the fire, for the annual costume ball. I stood on the second floor above the stairs waiting to be introduced, having freshened up in one of the bedrooms.

"Miss Millie," I heard myself announced by the butler and began my trip down the long steps. Careful to pull my dress up above my silver heels lest I trip on the hem, I looked straight ahead, hoping to make a devastating impression. My dress was deep blue velvet, the skirt full around my hips dropping loosely to the floor, bursting into shades of purples and greens, mimicking the feathers of a peacock. In my hair, tucked back into a snood, two peacock feathers nested. Reaching the bottom step, I looked up to see my Edward, waiting with outstretched hand. He needed no costume, only his uniform, a testimony to his bravery.

"Have you been dancing?" he asked, his eyes taking in my costume as I took his hand. His smile captured me, and everyone else in the crowded hall passed by me unnoticed.

"Not yet."

"Waiting for me?"

"Of course."

As we moved into the ballroom, Glen Miller and his band, hired for this special night, broke into their big hit, "A Nightingale Sang in Berkeley Square." We began to dance. The other guests cleared the floor, leaving us alone as they watched the RAF pilot so handsome in his dress blues and his girl from the USO, proud as a peacock in her velvet gown and feathers, swirling around the floor with a nightingale serenading them.

I was living a dream. And as the song said, "There was magic abroad in the air."

Chapter 3

"He's a Protestant. That says it all."

"He's English."

"You know nothing about his family."

Those three quick verdicts condemned my Edward. My family was having none of him. The more I tried to defend him, the more they attacked. The three women who had brought me up were three harpies attacking with a vengeance. My father remained quiet, my only hope. And my brother Gary, maybe.

Sunday night my dad drove me back to the dorm. The women opted to stay behind, still shrieking away, lapsing into French at points. In the car we spoke of other things. The February slush. The groundhog seeing his shadow in Pennsylvania, signaling six more weeks of winter and how silly that custom was. How my work at the hospital was going. Where I might work after graduation. On and on, avoiding the obvious. As we pulled up in front of the dorm, I jumped out, dodging puddles and turned to wave as I headed up the steps.

"Millie," my dad called out, cranking down the window, "let them cool down a bit. You know how they can be."

Turning back to the car, I said, "Oh, Dad. I hope so." Bang out of order. That's what Edward would say. Sometimes I wondered how my dad could survive the constant henpecking by the three old birds. His radio room was his sanctuary. His league of friends he reached out to across the country on the air waves was a welcome contrast to the clucking in his ear in his own home. I blew him a kiss and hurried up the steps to get out of the cold. The lights of the hospital lit my way. I could hardly wait to tell Carol the events of Friday night. True, I hadn't heard a word from Edward all weekend, but after all, he was in the RAF and not free to follow me about. The heavy door swung shut behind me as I vanished into my life as a nurse.

"Your Edward?" Carol asked after I had spilled the glorious details. "You've only just met." We were lounging on our beds, having raided the kitchen icebox for bowls of ice cream.

"Not you, too. Don't you believe in love at first sight? You sound like my mother...my grandmother... my aunt," I said, hoping for support, not more doubt. I scooped chocolate ice cream into my mouth, savoring its comfort.

"Oh, tosh. You may never hear from him again. Besides, what's he doing here so soon? I thought the British were coming in August." Carol deposited her empty bowl on the bedside table and turned over, bare feet in the air and her head in her hands.

"Yes, they are, but he's part of an advance group, checking things out, monitoring the construction. That kind of thing." I hoped to impress her with more details.

"Getting first pick of the USO girls," she warned, rolling over and fluffing her pillow. Sinking back, she waited for my reply.

"Chasing skirts, I believe they call it. And I am one skirt loving the chase." I was not about to let her win this battle.

"I may just have to join the USO. Time for a shower and then bed. I have the early shift tomorrow on the pediatric ward. Lots of little sick kids caught in the flu season. At least the little tykes are easy to lift, not like being on the men's ward."

Carol had it tougher than me. I had the full support of my family. They gave me plenty of cash so I didn't have to pull the extra shifts she did. She'd been working since our first year and often seemed just exhausted. Nursing was hard work. Carol predicted she would die young with a disintegrating spine from all the lifting of patients and pushing and pulling of gurneys. Her parents seldom saw her as she worked every weekend. I was lucky. I owed my family.

"Let's stand those pinkies up in the corner. I'm ready for bed, too. Had a dream about dancing at Manderley last night. Who knows where I'll be tonight?"

We managed to balance our uniforms beside each other on the floor. They would stand at attention all night until we leapt into them in the morning. Carol jumped into bed first, drama in mind. "Ah, let me play Mrs. Danvers before your mother grabs the role. Remember when she first met the second Mrs. de Winter and in her eerie, creepy voice told her, 'Don't flatter yourself he's in love with you, my dear. Poor fellow, he's lonely...' Those guys at the base must be very lonely so far from England. Just a word of caution."

"For your information it was her employer, Mrs. Van Hopper, who said that, not Mrs. Danvers. I've had it up to here. Can the criticism, please." I slid my finger across my neck as I pulled the pillow over my head to block out her warnings. "Good night."

"Excuse me, if I haven't got *Rebecca* memorized like you. Sweet dreams." Carol was in a huff now, her advice unheeded. The morning would bring peace between us. We always made up.

The next morning I reported for special duty in a private room. One of Detroit's wealthy auto families was expecting an heir. The wife, name withheld for privacy, was in early labor when I took over for the night nurse. She had been in the hospital since about three a.m. She would be my only patient for the day. Her husband was nowhere to be seen. She was an attractive blonde, still wearing bright red lipstick, her hair pulled back by a simple headband. Needless to say her diamond ring could knock your eye out with its brilliance. She was alone and complaining loudly as the night nurse filled me in on her progress and left, her face signing off with a "good luck" wish.

"Where is my doctor? I need him NOW. He must do something about this pain."

"I don't think he's reported in for duty today yet. You are in the early stages of labor. He'll be in later."

"You don't understand. I don't want a nurse. I want the doctor. NOW!"

This was going to be a day from hell.

"Get me a mirror. Do I need more lipstick?"

"Actually the doctor will prefer you not wear lipstick."

"Get me some water."

"I can get you some ice chips."

"Ice chips? Are you a real nurse?"

"I graduate soon."

"You graduate soon? I'm alone with only a student

nurse? Oh, no. Not me."

"I can assure you I…" I stopped, knowing I was not supposed to argue with a patient.

Just then she was gripped with a labor pain, and she gasped, holding the bedrails. I moved to her side, urging her to breathe, reaching for her hand.

"Don't touch me," she said through gritted teeth.

And so went my day until a baby boy entered the world just before my shift was up. My ears ringing with criticism, I left her room and walked down the backstairs to the locker room to get my coat. I pulled it on, not bothering to button it for the short trip to the dorm. Tonight, I was taking the bus home again because the Lux Radio Hour was airing a radio play of *Rebecca,* starring Ronald Colman and Ida Lupino. We were all going to listen to it together. I didn't have to be back at the hospital until the afternoon shift tomorrow. Maybe the play would be a distraction from further discussion of my RAF acquaintance. Edward would be left behind as Ronald and Ida took the stage over the radio air waves.

Head in the clouds and distracted, I crossed the street and started up the dorm steps. "Millie," a familiar accent brought me back to earth.

"Edward?" I ran up the steps when I realized it was him seated on the rusted bench outside the main door. "What are you doing here?" I stood above him as he remained seated.

"I have the evening off, so I hitchhiked into Detroit to find you." He shivered in his uniform. "Not used to this bloody cold," he said, puffing on his cigarette.

"Hitchhiked from Grosse Ile?" I couldn't believe that.

"I've discovered quite a few doctors live on the island. They're more than willing to help out a lonely flight sergeant. But I'm as cold as poor Willie." He looked up plaintively at me, dragging on his cig.

"Willie?" Another of his British sayings. "But I'm going home to Ecorse tonight," I said, determined not to miss *Rebecca*. Not for anyone, even Edward.

"As good a place as any to go," Edward said, dropping his cigarette to the ground.

"Well, come in. Wait in the parlor until I can change and…"

Yes, that would be the plan. He rose from the frigid bench, crushed the cigarette into the concrete, and opened my unbuttoned coat, only to laugh at my very pink uniform. "So you have a uniform, too. At least mine sets off my blue eyes. If you were British, yours would make your English rose complexion blush."

Embarrassed, I turned and hurried up the steps, gesturing for him to follow.

Edward was not alone long in the lobby. Girls and faculty flocked around him as he held court as I slipped upstairs, changed clothes, and hurried back downstairs. There he sat, sipping tea, regaling his newfound fans with tales of jolly old England. Laughing, I saw Carol, her mouth hanging open, listening. She, too, was caught in his web.

"Fair ladies," he said, rising from the overstuffed velvet chair, "it is time for Millie and me to be off to her parents' home. Will I survive meeting them? I understand they are French Catholics about to withstand an English Protestant assailing their fortress."

They all giggled, and Carol just shook her head at me, as Edward took my arm, guiding me to the door.

"Millie, you'd best sign out," Carol called after me.

"Of course," I said, stopping at the desk and signing with a flourish. Thank goodness Miss Jackson was not on duty. I was spared that onslaught.

As we reached the door, Edward turned and said, "Oh, ladies, you might consider joining the USO. There are many more airmen, you know." I just laughed at his arrogance, hoping his conceited charm might win over the three French hens awaiting him in Ecorse.

"Where do we sign?" asked Carol. She had changed her tune. She shrugged her shoulders at me in a sign of surrender and laughed.

The ride home on the bus was uneventful except for the stares of the other passengers. I held onto Edward's arm firmly, as if to say, "He's mine." I did most of the talking as Edward wanted to hear all about my family. So I described each of them, avoiding their first reactions to him. He was going to be a surprise to them. With no warning, we would invade the hen house.

"And your father is a doctor?" Edward asked as if taking mental notes.

"Yes, a respected one. He is Chief of Staff of Wyandotte General Hospital. My brother will undoubtedly follow in his footsteps and become a doctor." I was proud of my dad and his stature at the hospital. Everybody loved him—the staff, his colleagues, and his patients. No henpecking there. His portrait hung in the lobby in a row with past chiefs.

"And your choice to be a nurse?" Edward asked, finally getting around to me.

"As close as I can get to being a doctor as a woman these days." I felt jealous that my brother would easily step into this role forbidden to me because of my sex.

"In England we call nurses 'Sister'," Edward said, changing the subject and smiling down at me.

"Well, that would be confusing for you to call me that," I said, tightening my grip on his arm.

"It seems you have plans for us," Edward said, reaching into his pocket for a cigarette. The passenger in front of us, an older woman who must have listened in on our entire conversation, turned around and said, "Edward, stay the course. You'll win them over. My Tommy fought in the Great War, and my parents objected to him at first, but he won them over. Yes, indeed."

"I'm sure he did, ma'am." Edward oozed his charm across the bus seat.

"We've been married over twenty years now. With five babies born." She beamed with pride and turned back around as the next stop was announced.

I turned and looked out the frosty window, my hand still on his arm.

"Ecorse, High Street. Next stop," the driver called out.

I rose, walked down the aisle, and stepped ahead of him to climb down the stairs. I was proud of my airman.

"Cheerio," Edward said to the driver. "You may be seeing more of me."

I laughed as he caught up to me. Standing on the corner, waiting for traffic to clear, he leaned over and kissed me. A soft, dreamy first kiss.

"Sister Millie," he said. "I see what you mean. You shan't hear that name from me again."

We walked the short way up Bourassa Street, and I

turned up the walk to the front porch.

"Double doors?" Edward asked, stopping to look the house over.

"My dad's office to the left," I gestured, holding my hand out to him as we climbed the steps to the brick porch.

We had arrived, and the moment of truth was before us. I tried the door, and it opened.

"Deep breath," I said, stepping into the ,foyer, tugging Edward behind me. I took my coat off and hung it on the hall coat rack.

They were seated around the living room in their usual places. Aunt Lill, Gramma Stell, and Mother commanded the sofa. They were all dressed alike in wool crepe dresses in muted tones of maroons and grays. Their coifs were perfect with tiny gray curls. Yesterday had been their weekly visit to Miss Georgette at the Hudson's Beauty Salon where they always sat patiently waiting, reading movie magazines with the latest Hollywood gossip as each one in her turn occupied Georgette's chair for a shampoo and set. Then it was lunch, a Maurice salad or chicken pot pie, both specialties of the house at the Hudson's restaurant.

Dad sat in his favorite chair near the fireplace, his pipe stand close by. He wore his suit from his day at the hospital, his pinstriped suit which he called his race track wear although he never went near a track. Pipe in his mouth, puffing, he saw Edward first and rose, walking slowly to us. Gary was nowhere in sight. Where was he? I had hoped he'd be my ally here.

"Well, who is this?" my father asked, extending his pipe-free hand.

"Edward, sir," my pilot said firmly, his first shot

over the bow.

"Flight Sergeant Edward," I added, my arm on his. I could feel his spine stiffen, pushing him to his full height.

"Come in. Come in," my father said, backing up into the living room. At least he was smiling. The three on the couch stared, their mouths set in matching grimaces.

"Sit, please." I gestured to the chair on the other side of the fireplace, Gary's usual perch.

"Not until I meet the ladies," Edward said, walking to the sofa with his hand outstretched.

They were stunned I could tell. Stunned and silent. For once.

"Let me see. Millie has described you all to me with such detail." Pointing to Aunt Lill, he said, "You must be Aunt Lill, who bakes scrumptious chicken with lashings of gravy and dressing." He reached his hand out to her and then pulled it back. "No, not enough. I should think a kiss on the cheek would be better." With that he leaned in and planted a soft kiss on her left cheek. Expecting her to recoil as if a snake had hissed at her, it was my turn to be stunned when she blushed and smiled. Number two. "You must be Gramma Stell, who loves western cowboy novels and taught Millie to read." Again he leaned in for a kiss, and it was Stell's turn to blush and flat-out grin. He had won her over, obviously. But here was his last challenge. "And you must be Millie's mother. A beauty like her, and I understand very protective of your daughter. I promise I shall never hurt her, Mama, or Mum as we say in England." Mama was a goner, too, jutting her chin out, expecting and reveling in her kiss on the cheek. I

34

looked over at my dad, and he rolled his eyes, laughing through the puffs of smoke in the air. I noticed Gary standing in the alcove, an extra dining room chair in his hand.

"Holy smokes," Gary said, "what have you brought into our happy home? Three in one blow. Smooth moves, Edward."

"Gary." Edward crossed the room in a second. "Put down that chair and give me a hug. We British are not all cold fish. And tell me about your studies. Millie says it's your last year."

And so the evening began. The ice not just broken, but smashed like the floes on the Detroit River. Edward was a hit.

****

It was still hours before the train would leave. Our mugs were empty, the pie gobbled down, when James announced he was going to get his kip. A nap. Good for him. As he collapsed on the sofa, I returned to my past. No longer trying to be anything but rude.

****

"We were just about to turn on the radio for the Lux Radio Theater," Gary said. "Edward, please sit in the comfy chair. I can sit on this dining room chair."

"Do you mind if I use your loo first? It's been a long hitchhike from the base to Detroit and then the bus ride."

"Of course, just up the stairs and to the right," my mother said, blushing. *Yes, Mother, even RAF officers need to relieve themselves.* I was impressed she was allowing Edward to use the family bathroom instead of the one in the office. I let him head up the stairs by himself, mentally picturing what he would see. I think I

35

had made my bed. Yesterday had been the maid's day to clean. Had I closed the closet door? Maybe it would do him good to see my gowns hung in an array of colors and soft, beautiful materials. He needed to know I did dance with other men often, my dance card full.

"Perhaps you should follow him," Aunt Lill said, wrinkling up her nose as if she had smelled a rotten cheese.

"There's no silverware to steal up there, Auntie," said Gary, laughing. "At least give him a few minutes to do his business." Gary had pulled the dining room chair into the living room, next to the piano and across from the ladies on the couch.

"Gary, really," my mother chided, "mind your manners." She stood and moved over to the fireplace mantel, rearranging knick-knacks and then crossing the room to the piano. She opened the bench and pulled out two pieces of sheet music, one "The Coronation Waltz," the other the Charleston hit from years ago, "I've Danced with a Man Who's Danced with a Girl Who's Danced with the Prince of Wales." She began humming the second one as she gave both pieces pride of place on the piano. Pleased with her choices, she returned to the couch, still humming.

"I can hear you down there," Edward called. "I promise I haven't pinched a thing."

My turn to blush, I hurried across the room and took the steps two at a time up to the second floor. Edward was standing, grinning, by the hall table, leafing through magazines. He held up the latest issue of *Life* with the Nazis Goebbels and Goering on its cover. "Not my chums," he said. Picking up *Time*, he smiled and said, "Ah, Gertie Lawrence, one of my favorite actresses. Much better." Last was an old copy of *Photoplay,* my mother's favorite Hollywood magazine. Clark Gable flashed a toothy smile at us.

"I saw him once," I stuttered, "at a traffic stop in Hollywood."

"Really?" he replied, crossing to the first bedroom. "Who sleeps here?"

"Me." My heart sped up as I followed him into my room.

"I should know that by the photos on the wall," he said, gazing from frame to frame of movie stars and posters for *Rebecca* and *Gone with the Wind.* He stopped in front of a framed issue of *Time.* Wallis Simpson, the Duchess of Windsor stared at us. "Not her," he almost moaned. "Of all the royalty, you put her in a frame?"

"She was just named Best Dressed Woman of the Year," I countered, head down, embarrassed, but then looking back at him.

He just shook his head and said, "I see you Americans need a little education. I ought to know, I am named after her besotted husband, Edward the Eighth. He gave it all up for her."

"You are named after him?" What did this mean? I realized I knew nothing about this man standing in my bedroom. "You know," I tried, "Meg knows a lot about Mac. He's from the Isle of Wight, lives with his widowed mother." He did not take the bait, remaining silent.

"Millie?" my dad shouted up the stairs, "It's time for the play to start."

"Come on, Edward." I grabbed his hand. "You can tell me more later." I could imagine the three ladies on the couch hissing and spitting at my dad to get us back downstairs.

I headed down the stairs, Edward behind me, but he stopped halfway down, shaking loose my hand. He stood, looking up to the ceiling, his hands folded in prayer. Out of the blue, he sang, "Hark, the herald angels sing, Mrs. Simpson pinched our king." He belted out the words and then started down the stairs again, this time pulling me behind. I could hear the uncertain laughter from the living room before we entered. Gary stood in the French doors applauding, his grin spread ear to ear. Edward bowed and sang again the first lines of the edited Christmas carol. "Our tribute to Wallis Simpson." He laughed. "She had our king by the short and curlies and bolted off to France with him." He walked over to the piano and eyed the sheet music, choosing not to comment.

Not knowing what to say, the three French hens sat on the couch, not even exchanging furtive glances. Lill stared at her rather large feet while Stell concentrated on Gary. Mother Dear gestured for Pa to turn the radio on. This radio was a family treasure, a beautiful piece of furniture in itself, of oaken wood. Below the speaker and knobs was a carved frieze of the nine Greek muses, all clustered about in languid poses in their flowing misty robes. My grandmother Mimi had taught me all their names when I was just a tiny girl when Pa had first brought the radio home to us and placed it in the corner of this room. It stood alone now, ready to bring us tonight's feature.

"The muses watch over us whenever we listen to the radio," I said to Edward, pointing to the frieze.

He walked over and knelt down before the radio,

tracing the sculpted ladies with his fingers. "O for a muse of fire," he recited. "Shakespeare, Act I, Prologue of *Henry V.*"

"My favorite was always Terpsichore, the muse of dance," I said. "I loved the feel of that name on my teeth and tongue."

Edward stood and gave me one of those looks that reached down and grabbed my heart and wrung it out, his blue eyes the icing on this valentine cake. "I quite fancy that minx Erato and her love poetry."

I heard a gasp from behind us and knew without a doubt that Lill was having her own heart palpitation. I bet she was dying to hear a verse from Erato if she'd only admit it.

"You better sit yourselves down before we need a hose for the couch," Gary said.

"Gary," Stell warned, pulling her wire rims off and rubbing them clean with her kerchief.

"All fogged up, Grandma?" he said.

Gary and my dad took their chairs on either side of the piano. The hens roosted on the couch, and we settled in, Edward in his comfy chair and I, avoiding the triple wide-eyed stares at my boldness, nestled at his feet. We loved the Lux Theater and tuned in every week. Tonight they were presenting a new version of *Rebecca* starring Ida Lupino, Ronald Colman, and Judith Anderson.

"Have you seen the movie?" Gary asked Edward, wondering if Edward was dreading this play.

"I don't get to the pictures often," he answered. "Do you mind if I smoke?" he addressed the room.

"Oh, of course not," my dad said, gesturing to the ashtray on the table next to us. "Just don't blow smoke rings in Millie's hair or Miss Jackson will get a whiff and expel her for smoking back at the dorm."

Bartholomew, my scruffy gray cat, chose that moment to make his dramatic entrance. His yellow eyes widened, sensing new blood as he luxuriously stretched and then sprinted over to perch on my lap. Rising up, he pushed a tentative paw toward Edward, his tail wagging a mile a minute.

"And who is this?" Edward asked, reaching to pet him.

"This is old Mew, short for Bartholomew," Gary answered for me. "Watch out. He can be a nasty old goat."

As if on cue, Mew hissed at Edward's offered hand, jumped off my lap, and ran from the room. "He's choosy in his pals," I said.

"Yes, I can see that. I'll win him over," Edward said, smiling. His mind was on something else. He'd already dismissed the silly cat. "Millie," he said, leaning over, "Let's read each other's favorite books. I can guess what yours is. I have mine back at the base."

I'm going to die of happiness. "Why, what a good idea," I said, looking up at him, my heartbeat accelerating as his smile widened.

Mr. Cecil B. DeMille broke in from the radio speaker, introducing the evening's production. Ida Lupino began the famous introduction describing her dream visit back to Manderley, a Manderley in ruins. We were all silent, so quiet that I could hear Edward and my dad's puffings on cigarette and pipe. The play went on with her meeting with Maxim de Winter, the widower in Monte Carlo. Her mousy awkwardness contrasted to his first wife Rebecca's beauty and grace.

Her sneaking out for drives with Maxim while her employer Mrs. Van Hopper languishes ill in bed. When she tells him she once saw a picture postcard of his Cornish estate, Manderley, Edward leaned down to me and whispered, "I'll show you a photo of our estate, too."

I was so engrossed in the play that this remark didn't even make a dent in my romantic reverie for a few seconds. "What? You have an estate?" I turned and asked, reaching my hand up to his knee. These bombs were landing in rapid succession in my heart.

"Shhh! Later." He patted my hand, leaning back, very aware of Lill's staring at my hand on his knee. If she could, she would have moved over and plopped herself on the floor between us. Thank goodness, she was too arthritic to become a human divider.

The first act ended with applause as the commercial ad came on. It was for Lux Flakes, of course. And what a bargain the announcer touted. For just fifteen cents, I could receive a beautiful *Gone with the Wind* brooch as originally worn by Melanie in the movie, a pin with four simulated pearls and a turquoise stone, encircled in a scalloped gold frame. If I sent a flap from the soap box with my money to New York, I would receive pictures of matching jewelry. Why yes, a ring, pendant, and matching earrings I could also purchase.

"What was that address?" Aunt Lill asked, reaching for a pen and pad on the pipe stand.

"Lux Flakes, Box 1, New York City," Gary replied, "That's a rather incomplete address for that big of a city."

"You know that ring will turn your finger green,

right?" laughed my dad, always looking at the medical side of things. No doubt he was seeing my finger removed because of a gangrene infection.

"Crikey." Edward laughed. "That'll be attractive."

"Who's for a drink?" Gary asked, heading to the kitchen. The three ladies on the couch were very quiet, straining their ears to translate Edward's accent as he spoke.

I leaned back and asked Edward what he had meant by an estate.

"We have one in Cornwall with a cove like Manderley. But we have peacocks."

"Peacocks?" said Lill. "Filthy creatures." Again her nose wrinkled at this new prospect that was even worse than rotted cheese.

"Colas?" Gary asked, returning from the kitchen with a tray of glasses fizzing with cola, leaning in between us with the glasses. Stunned, I took my drink and sipped. *Peacocks?*

Cecil B. DeMille invited us back to Act Two which ended with Manderley in flames. Next came another Lux Flakes ad, this time asking what item of feminine apparel worn last year could stretch twenty-five times around the world? Why silk stockings, of course. And what better soap to use to wash them out but Lux Flakes? After all, a little goes so very far.

Edward noted for us that silk stockings were a rare commodity in England now, and we all commiserated with the stories we'd heard of ladies having to draw black lines down their legs to mimic stocking seams. This was going well.

Then Cecil B. reminded us that the Lux Theater had been voted the best radio program for the past seven years and that next week we could look forward to a production of *Reap the Wild Wind* starring Carole Lombard and Jimmy Stewart.

I half-listened, for I was in Cornwall, dodging peacocks as I walked down to the cove. Edward's cove. Our cove. Our boat was moored there, The Nightingale.

****

That night I dreamed I was out on the sea alone, sailing in brilliant winds, brisk yet not threatening. The Nightingale skimmed the water, and I was at peace. As the afternoon wore on, I became a bit chilled. I went below for my sweater and a basket of sandwiches and biscuits Mrs. Danvers had packed for me. She always made tiny sandwiches the way the British love them. No crusts. Not much filling. These were watercress and cheese. Her scones with clotted cream and jam were luscious, but they would be for tea later.

Back on deck I checked the boat was on course as I tucked in, the food spread out before me on a kerchief on my lap. She had included a flask of sweet red wine so I sipped it with my sandwiches. Not too much. Just enough to relax and enjoy the sail.

I do so love the sea air and the breezes rushing across my body, lifting my hair and tossing it in all directions. Edward and I had shared such rare and beautiful moments on this very boat.

Pushing the remnants of my snack back into the basket, I checked course again and settled back, with a book Edward had given me to read, Before the Fact. *It was a troubling book about a woman who suspected her husband might be trying to kill her. Johnny, her husband, was a charmer and a liar. His wife kept catching him in his lies, only to forgive him again and again. He was a liar, she knew that. He gambled. She knew that. He owed everyone money. She knew that. And she thought he had killed before. Yet she stayed with him. There was to be a movie called* Suspicion *Edward told me, based on the book.*

I put the book down and lay back, gazing at the sky. Why did Edward want me to read this book? My throat began to close. I began to cough. The pain moved down my chest. I bent over, gasping. The wine? The wine?

Chapter 4

The next morning, back at the dorm, I slept in, troubled by last night's dream that had started out so well, yet become a nightmare. I had read the murder novel, *Before the Fact* at my mother's suggestion several years ago, one of the first thrillers I'd read, in fact. The film, *Suspicion,* based on it would come out this year on its tenth anniversary. Doubtless, our family would take it in as we went to the movies every week, sometimes twice in a week. *Photoplay* reported that Cary Grant would star with Joan Fontaine, who had made such a sensation in her first major film, *Rebecca.* But why this book in this dream? Was my subconscious warning me?

Last night I had just made it back to the dorm for the eleven o'clock curfew. Couples had set up positions outside in the cold, stealing goodnight kisses, locked in embraces while Miss Jackson played sentry just inside the door, the lobby clock set to chime the hour. My dad had driven me back while Gary had chauffeured Edward back to the base after an awkward farewell in front of the entire family. Edward had promised to give me his favorite book to read the next time he saw me, leaving its title a mystery as well as our next date.

"Wait," I had said, crossing the few feet to the spinet desk in the foyer. A full-length mirror stood near the desk, and I could see the group reflected, watching me in silence. I reached for the novel on the desk and turned back. "Here," I said, handing the book over to Edward. "Enjoy."

"Are you sure?" he asked. "It's well-worn and seems a treasure." He grasped the book in one hand and me in the other, wrapping his arm around my waist.

"I trust you. *Rebecca* will be safe with you." I had bent my head back for his kiss, ignoring the triple heart attacks from the sofa.

Those words in light of my dream now haunted me. Would I be safe with Edward?

The doors pushed opened and a crush of women hurried through, signing in at 10:59 on the dot, their cheeks red from the cold and some chafed by beards. Jack had been waiting for me in the lobby along with the ever-vigilant Miss Jackson. Jack was the only man in our nursing class. He had a slight limp that had kept him out of the army, although he had tried to enlist. No luck, so he had decided to help his country by becoming a nurse. He said he knew he'd never make it through medical school so he had settled for nursing. Being the only man, you'd think he'd have an elegant suite to himself. Think again. Our first year he had invited Carol and me down to see his room. In the basement. Totally isolated. He had a chair, and a twin bed, and a dresser. No windows. Nothing. Just institutional pea green walls. Not even a desk. He didn't have to wear pink, at least. He wore the same white scrub suits as the doctors. And no cap adorned his short haircut. We had become good friends, as Jack loved to dish the dirt. He was waiting now for details of Edward. We hunkered down by the fireplace on the settee, and over cups of cocoa, I gave him a blow by blow of the evening and my family reactions. But Jack was most interested in the curious bombshells of my pilot being an Edward the Eighth namesake, and his mind-blowing Cornish estate, complete with a cove and strutting peacocks.

"Oh, girl, you better get the details before you get in any deeper," Jack warned. "Who knows, Edward could have wives galore all over the world, from Detroit to Berlin. Another Henry the Eighth, and we all know what happened to his six wives." He drew his fingers across his throat to emphasize his warnings.

"Jack, please. You're being very dramatic and sounding a bit like Aunt Lill." The fire warmed the lobby, crackling and sending red sparks up the chimney.

"Not the dreaded Aunt Lill." He laughed. "The one you caught reading your letters from Guy. By the way, what's happened to Guy? And are you still a virgin?" Jack was bringing up ancient history on purpose, I knew, to make his point.

"Jack! Stop, please." I stood up and walked over to the fireplace, kneeling and taking up the poker to revive the dying embers. Shake them up a bit.

"Just curious. If you only knew what goes through my mind while I lie on my bed in my dungeon chamber. I worry about you. You naïve Catholic girl." I chuckled at the image of poor Jack, tossing sleepless in his lonely single bed. I was sure he had more to think about than my life. He never dated, as far as I knew.

"Guy and I are over, Jack. We just kind of drifted apart." I came back over to the couch and sat on the floor, my knees flexed.

"Besides he doesn't have an estate, or cove, or

regal ostrich." He laughed, cracking himself up, slapping me on the shoulder.

"Peacock, stupid." I laughed back, taking his arm off my shoulder, pretending to be repulsed by its presence. "Watch it," I warned. "I'm a virgin, or hadn't you heard?"

"Hussy," he hissed, ruffling my hair. "I'd love to stay and chat, but I need some sleep. Miss You-Know-Who just poked her head out of her cage. Down to the dungeon I go. Sleep tight." With that farewell, Jack vanished into the night, leaving me alone with the fire.

Yawning, I rose and moved, hoping to be invisible to avoid Miss Jackson. No use.

"Oh, Millie." *Damn.*

"Did you have a good evening with that young serviceman?" she said, rising from her desk, her uniform wrinkled after a long day. Even she was not perfect.

"Oh, yes. We went to my parents' and listened to The Lux Radio Theater." No details.

"Oh, I did, too. Excellent production. Don't order that ring, though. It will turn your finger green and lead to amputation. No one wants a one-handed nurse." She laughed, knowingly. "And where is your young man from in England?"

"A huge estate," I said, edging toward the stairway. "With peacocks. Got to go starch my cap," I said.

"Peacocks, you say? Filthy creatures," she said, echoing Lill. "Be off then. Stay pure."

I charged up the stairs and passed the kitchenette, and then turned back. There were already about four caps laid flat, soaked in starch, and then slapped onto the refrigerator door. They would dry by morning.

Pouring myself a glass of water, I leaned against the sink. I had so much to mull over. Carol walked into the kitchen with two caps dripping starch in her hands.

"Did one for you, too," she said, handing me one wet mess while she pushed hers onto the cold door.

"Thanks, I'll treat you to ice cream in return," I said, slapping my flat cap next to hers.

"No, we'll both get ice cream out of this fridge, and then you will give me all the details of your night with Edward. What a dreamboat."

****

James was snoring loudly from the sofa as I headed for the loo, my bladder bursting. As I passed by the kitchen, I saw little Maisie on the stone floor, playing with Nellie, the inn kitty. Wrapped in a hand-knit lilac sweater, undoubtedly Bette's handiwork, she looked so content for once that I just let her cuddle her new pet. She so deserved this peace at last. I would miss her. Maybe some day after the war I would find her back in London and tell her my story.

****

Two days at the hospital passed. Two days of more ladies in labor. More babies being born. I was on the labor ward. No more private executive wives giving birth with their lipstick and polished red nails. Those rich wives who were more concerned with the shade and endurance of their lipstick than the baby who would, of course, be reared by nannies. Mothers would stay in the hospital for five or so days after each birth. Doctors were aware of the size of the families, how many children were already at home. They sought quietly to give the harried, exhausted mother a few days in the hospital before she took up the duties of her brood again. No nannies for these families. For some reason, maybe because novels were on my mind, I thought of the Sue Barton books I had read as a young girl. Sue was the perky redhead nurse in a series that I had loved. I had defied my mother and read late into the night, intrigued by Sue's adventures as a student and senior nurse at the New England hospital where she met her future husband, Dr. Bill. She had refused his proposal of marriage at graduation, determined to pursue her career, when he moved to a country practice. The popular series of books had continued chronicling her life as a visiting nurse, a head nurse, and finally, a wife and mother. Even though my dad was a doctor, it was Sue Barton who had first filled my heart with the wish to be a nurse. And oh, how I still wanted that dark blue wool cape Sue wore over her uniform, its trim a bright red, hinting at the satin lining that swished and peeked out a bit when she walked, her nursing pin firmly in place over her heart. When I had received the black velvet stripe for my cap as a senior, I knew I was one step closer to the final pink graduate stripe and that stylish cape. Just a few months away now.

The cold blustery weather continued, a typical Michigan February that froze my toes in my sturdy white hose and bulky shoes as I dashed home from another dayshift of newborns. I was tired and hoped for a nap before another starchy hospital dinner of mac & cheese and mystery meat. I was on a full student scholarship, but still resented that someone was paying for this food.

Pushing open the heavy door, I crossed the lobby to sign in at the desk.

"Millie?"

"Yes?" I replied, looking to see who was on duty. It was Miss Ames.

"There's a package here for you. Feels like a book." She held it out to me, and I expected her to pull it back like a kid joking.

"Thank you, Miss Ames," I said, grabbing the package, wishing for some semblance of privacy while still trying to be polite. Miss Jackson's threat of an Alexandrine toss still rang in my ears. Miss Ames was another middle-aged sentry, seemingly devoid of her own life, here to make us follow the straight and narrow. They must all have their own Miss Georgette somewhere who pulled their graying hair in a tight bun that rode low on their necks some days and high on their heads other days. And they must all buy their wire rims at a discount store somewhere else. And their white uniforms at a different store. Or perhaps they shopped by mail, never leaving this fortress. What a curious way to spend one's life. Bullying and weaning out young girls as they aspired to be nurses, certainly a vocation that deserved a supportive hand, not a three-year rough voyage of rigor and expected perfection. Enough. What was in this package?

Hurrying up to my room where I was alone for once, I examined my mysterious mail. The return address was "E.S.C.O." What? I sat down on my bed, the starchy uniform crunching and cracking. I pulled my cap off my head and tossed it beside me, a few brown curls snagged painfully. I retrieved my nursing scissors from my pink pocket and cut away the twine from the brown paper. Ripping the paper, I saw a green well-thumbed book. Turning it sideways, I read aloud *The Collected Poems of A. E. Housman*. A note fell from the pages, and I read on blue stationery:

In exchange for your Rebecca, *I offer you the words of a British poet who could change words into verse that move me, especially now as I am far from my homeland. I look forward to spring when this frigid winter ends. "To see the cherry hung with snow." I hope to read some of these poems to you soon. They are even more beautiful when read aloud.*

I have procured tickets to hear Evelyn and her Magic Violins at the Michigan Theater this Friday night. I will pick you up at the dorm at seven.

Yours,
Edward Sebastian Christian Owen

I fell back on the bed, clutching the old book of poems. *So that's your name, your full name, Edward Sebastian Christian Owen.* How veddy British.

Down to business now. What would I wear for Evelyn? It was Wednesday. I might have to persuade Gary to make a mercy trip to the dorm with one of my formals, perhaps the green velvet. And maybe Mother could see herself clear to lend me her fur cape? Green was my color, and the dark fur so set off my eyes. Maybe the rhinestone clips in my hair. And would Miss Georgette be able to squeeze me in for a shampoo and set at Hudson's?

Chapter 5

I waited in the lobby after another day of babies and just one day after Edward's invitation. I could feel Miss Jackson's eagle eyes preying on me from her perch at the desk. My nose was buried in the book of poetry Edward had sent to me. Beautiful poetry. I so hoped I would see England, Edward's home, soon. He had said nothing of his family. I had no one to imagine on the beach at the cove.

"Oh, Millie?" She called from her desk, rising as if I were having trouble seeing her.

Hoping to vanish into the velvet couch, I read on or pretended to anyway. It was no good.

"Millie, are you intentionally ignoring me?" This time she flew to the wide lobby doorway, her wire rims in her hand.

"I'm sorry, Miss Jackson. I was just so engrossed with this book of poetry." I sank deeper into the couch to no avail. She was on to me like a vulture circling.

"Poetry? So that was the book in your mystery package from yesterday? The one with the strange initials in the upper left corner? Let's see if I can recall. Yes, I believe E.S.C.O. was printed very neatly. Am I correct?" She waited there in the doorway, expecting a response to quench her lousy nosiness.

The steam rose in my cheeks, burning red. How dare she? I could just see her shaking the package, turning it over and over, puzzling over the initials. I said nothing. Better to remain silent than explode. I bet she and Miss Ames had plotted opening it and rewrapping it. Maybe they had, for all I knew.

Exasperated, she marched over to me. I was trapped. Planting her sturdy shoes in the carpet before me and with hands on her hips, her glasses back on her nose, she glared down at me. "Wasn't your young man's name, Edward? That would account for the E."

"Yes, his name is Edward," I said, spitting out each word slowly and deliberately.

She turned as she heard the front door open. Looking past her, I saw my brother, Gary, weighed down with the clothes I'd asked him to bring for me. He was a walking pile of green velvets and furs.

"Gary," I called, "I'm over here." *Please rescue me from this old bat.*

Miss Jackson walked back over to him and said, "Put your things down here while you sign in. Will you be staying for dinner with us?"

"Sure. I'd never turn down a gourmet meal of hospital food," he laughed, plunking down my things in my lap, burying me.

"Where do I sign?" he asked as he crossed back across the room to the desk with Miss Jackson.

"Right here, young man," Miss Jackson replied. She always seemed to show more respect to men, and she positively worshipped my dad, as he was a doctor. Her oily simpering was enough to make me sick.

Gary signed with a flourish and added, "Always good to see you, Miss Jackson. I assume you are doing your duty and keeping these mad girls under control?"

"I do my best," she replied, blushing and hovering.

"And will you be serving your country when you graduate this spring?" she asked, peering into his dark eyes.

"I hope to go to medical school, and if the Army will pay my way, then I'm theirs, Miss Jackson," he answered, nodding to her as he entered the lobby.

"Gary," I called, my voice muffled from the clothes threatening to suffocate me.

"Oh, come on, old girl, if you're going to wear a fur cape, wear it on your back, not smothering your face. Not a good look for you at all. Edward will not approve." With that, he pulled the clothes off me. "Lead the way, sis."

We made a break for my room, and I gave a shout, "Man on the floor" as we hurried along the corridor. Carol opened the door for us, and Gary dumped the clothes on the nearest bed.

"A mink cape and you just toss it on the bed?" Carol chided, grabbing it up and wrapping it around her own shoulders. She twirled around the room, rubbing up against Gary. She always flirted with him.

"Carol." I laughed. "You're too old for my baby brother. He's not even out of high school yet."

"Almost. I'm a senior," he said, crossing to the mirror over the dresser. "I think I'm quite debonair. Just as handsome as a pilot, don't you think?" He pulled his comb from his jacket pocket and smoothed it through his dark hair. "There. Can we go eat? I'm starving."

"You must be if you're willing to eat this food," I said, grabbing the cape back from Carol and hanging the dress and it in the closet.

"Wait a minute. There's more." Gary said, pulling a small velvet satchel with jewelry from his coat pocket and tossing it over to me.

"These I will guard with my life," I said, popping the box into my uniform pocket. I didn't have to open it to know Stell had sent me her cameo and earrings to wear. Bless her.

Down the stairs and into the cafeteria, we made a splash as we got in line. The girls were always happy to see a man on board. Gary was his usual funny self, entertaining the troops. Mystery meat, potatoes, and overcooked green beans was tonight's hospital fare. Gary ladled gravy over everything, saying it was better to cover it all and just stab blindly with his fork at the full plate. He joked with the cook who had come out at the word of a man in her dining room as we chose a table. Taking his jacket off, he put it over the chair next to him.

"So, Mumu," Gary said, calling me by the name he had made up for me when he was unable to pronounce Millie as a little guy. "About this British pilot."

Here it comes.

"He was quite chatty on the way back to the base. Called it having an old chin wag. So I just may know more about him than you. He did wag his chin an awful lot."

"And?" I really didn't know what to expect and was more than a little envious of what Gary knew and I didn't.

"Do you know, for instance he is rather wealthy? Loaded, actually. Oh, almost forgot. He said to give you this." He reached over to his coat and pulled a picture postcard from the pocket.

I held it in my hand and saw an estate, situated above a cove, with a large lawn where a couple of peacocks strutted. Turning the card over, I saw the caption, "Sand Castles Hall, Cornwall, England." Next to the postage stamp was a family crest with a peacock, sword, and miniature castle on a ribbon beneath it.

"Holy shit. A picture postcard, just like the one of Manderley," Carol said, peering over my shoulder. "Weird. Very weird."

"Such language, Carol, you know that old bat above must have spies lurking about. And please, *Rebecca* again?" Gary continued, turning to me. "You are so obsessed. It was all I could do to sit through that play Monday on the radio. You owe me for that one. I suppose you ordered your jewelry? The Lux Flakes special?" He squeaked the last words out in a high pitched falsetto, rolling his eyes. "It'll turn your finger green."

"Oh, shut up, Gary," I said. He could be very irritating as all little brothers are. I looked down again at the postcard. A chill came over me, and I put it in my pocket, not sure what to say.

"So you're going to see good old Evelyn and her magic fiddles?" Gary wisely changed the subject.

"Yeah, at the Michigan," I replied, relieved to somewhat change the subject, although Edward still loomed.

"Should be a good show. We've been listening to her girls for years on the radio on The Hour of Charm," Gary said to Carol. He loved music and played drums and guitar. "And the Michigan should impress His Highness, Edward. All that French Renaissance art."

"It is beyond the human dreams of loveliness..." we both chanted together, laughing.

"What?" Carol shook her head at us, chewing on

the mystery meat, a tough chore for anyone.

"Just a *Detroit Free Press* review our Aunt Lill repeats to us every time we go there," I said, nodding to Gary to continue.

"...rising in mountainous splendor!" Gary finished in his irritating falsetto, conducting an invisible orchestra with his knife and fork.

Carol broke in. "Let me see that postcard again." I reached back into my pocket and handed it over to her. Head down, she seemed to be memorizing the black and white photo.

"Oh, another thing," Gary added. "He says they have a ghost at Sand Castles." Putting down his knife and fork, he now pulled his jacket from the chair and swooped it over his head. A low, eerie moan emerged from beneath it. "I am the ghost of Sand Castles Hall. Beware."

"A ghost?" I asked, amazed at this new twist.

"Holy ghost," Carol said, laughing. Soon everyone around us at nearby tables took up the laughter. Gary never failed to entertain.

"I am Cecil, the ghost, and I murdered two peacocks, a chicken or two, and then poisoned the lover of my wife, a cutthroat pirate, Manly Mustache, who roamed the seas on his ship, *The Dreamboat.*" Carol laughed hysterically, and the rest of the table took up the wave of guffaws, breaking out in applause for my brother.

Gary removed the coat and dropped it back on the chair, standing to take a bow. Then suddenly sobered, he sat back down and said, "Just be careful, sis. Keep your wits about you, as Aunt Lill would warn you. Besides, I think he touches up his mustache with mascara. Beware of his kiss."

"Boo!" Carol hissed at me, and I jumped out of my skin.

****

Of course, I dreamed again that night. It was not of Manderley or even of Sand Castles. Gary and I were children. We were riding on an old, creaking carousel. The animals were tattered, their paint peeling. Some had ears missing; one zebra had shed its tail. We were on Boblo Island, the amusement park, having come by boat down the Detroit River to this Canadian island. The calliope played an eerie song, one I did not recognize. Round and round we went. I knew I was charged with watching out for my little brother, but he kept switching animals, hiding from me. He was on a spotted brown horse, then a mottled giraffe, then a giant blue pig. I climbed down from my shabby pink unicorn, missing half its horn, and looked and looked for Gary, crying and tripping along the animal trail as the music played even louder and the carousel sped up. I clung to each animal as I passed by, determined to find my missing brother.

As the carousel circled past the benches where the adults sat, I heard my mother shout, "Where is Gary? Find him now. How can you be so careless?"

I started to sob, but then stopped as I saw Gary sitting with Lill on the next bench, licking a huge double-dip chocolate and vanilla ice cream cone and laughing at me, waving. Ice cream dripped from his chin down onto his corduroy trousers. The ride stopped, and I stepped down, relieved and angry at the same time.

We walked to the next ride, Gary hiking up his

59

pants, lagging behind. The Caterpillar. It looked harmless enough, so Gary and I climbed into a car. The caterpillar would ride in a large circle at a slant against the hill. The ride began its slow climb upward and around. We had completed the first full circle when everything went dark. We had not been prepared for the musty midnight tarp that dropped on us, and we both screamed and screamed. And clung to each other, terrified. A canopy had descended on us. We were terrified. I was in the dark.

Chapter 6

I was so nervous. Carol laughed at me when I came back from Hudson's, my hair freshly shampooed and pulled back with the sparkling clips.

"You look divine," she said. She was lying on her bed, all comfy in her robe, curled up with a book.

"That's my book," I said, realizing she was reading Edward's poetry book. "Give it back."

She tossed it back at me, and I ducked. All I needed was a black eye. But she had no right to read my special book. After three years in this dorm I was so tired and angry that we had no privacy at all.

I was wearing the soft velvet dress over my taffeta slip, panties, hose, and garter belt. Checking in the mirror, I kept moving the cameo pin around on the dress. It was a hand-carved piece in ebony of a pale figure of Camille Monet, the impressionist artist's first wife. She held a parasol in her hand, and her skirt was a whisper in the wind as she peered out on the hilltop. The brooch had been an engagement gift from Paris for an aunt back a few generations. It had certainly not been purchased with Lux Flakes box tabs. The pearl earrings were on my lobes.

"Oh, for goodness' sake," Carol hissed, jumping up from the bed and heading to the mirror. "Here, put it here." She took the pin and secured it right at the bottom of the slight v-neck. "There." She stood beside me, peering in the mirror. "Emphasizes the cleavage. Edward must love that full bosom, as your Aunt Lill would call it. Don't like that lipstick, though. Much too pale."

She reached into the top dresser drawer and searched around, pulling out another tube of bright red lipstick. "Here, let me," she said. "Pucker up." Leaning in, she dabbed the bright color onto my lips. Then she picked up a hankie, pushed it toward my mouth and said, "Blot."

"Oh," I said softly, pressing my lips against the cloth and stepping back to assess the full package, scrutinizing myself in the mirror. "Will I do?" I was so used to seeing my mousy brown hair and green eyes attempting to be pretty that I smiled at this new look.

"You are the cat's pajamas. The bee's knees. Beautiful enough for a king." She was looking at me with different eyes. New respect?

I started across the room to the door when I heard Carol yell, "Stop!"

"What?" I jumped at the harsh sound of her voice. "Shoes, you ninny. Shoes!"

"I forgot to have Gary bring my sandals," I cried, pulling my dress up to reveal my stockinged toes. "I'm dead."

"Wait a sec," Carol said, as she went to the closet and rummaged around in the shoes on the floor. I stood, watching and hoping, fighting back tears. What could she come up with?

"Ah, these will do. Practically new." She handed me a pair of black suede open-toed pumps. Indeed they must do.

"But your feet are bigger than mine," I pled,

picturing myself stumbling around in the slushy snow, then tripping and bruising Edward's feet.

"Beggars can't be choosers. Just try them on. Better too big than too small," she said, proud of her find.

She held my hand as I pushed my feet into her pumps. I suddenly felt like Cinderella going to the ball. Breathing deeply, I knew these too-large shoes would have to do.

The hall phone rang. "That's him. Oh, no," I whispered, panic rising in my throat.

"Come on," Carol tugged at my arm. "Deep breaths. Deep breaths. I'll see you off, but get your cape first and your pocketbook."

We headed down the stairs, the cape slung over my arm casually. I was walking at a very slow pace, careful not to trip. And there he was, so utterly handsome in his dress blues, chatting up Miss Jackson. She was at her giddy best, laughing, almost giggling.

Then he turned and saw me. I swear a nightingale sang as he crossed the lobby, smiled down at me, and reached for the cape to put around my shoulders. I don't know what happened to Carol or even to Miss Jackson. Mink around my shoulders and an RAF blue arm in mine, I breezed out the door with my man, not just any man, just as the bus screeched its brakes in front of the hospital. It was magic. Even the shoes seemed to fit.

The Michigan was on Bagley, not a long drive. We did get some stares from the other passengers. After all we were a bit overdressed for a bus ride, but it was wartime and they all showed Edward respect, nodding and smiling and whispering to each other. When we pulled up in front of the theater, Edward let out a slow whistle at the sight of the huge lit sign, beaming "Michigan" to the city. It was ten stories high. We were early as we entered the grand lobby, not yet populated for the evening. "Look up," I said, "my father always says to look up."

I watched Edward as he indeed looked up to see four sparkling chandeliers lighting the night and reflecting off the checkered marble floor.

"Magnificent," Edward said. "Good show."

A man in a theater uniform came across the long lobby and approached us. "I'm George McCann, Chief of Service for the Michigan Theater. He held out his hand to Edward, saying, "You must be part of the RAF advance team for the Grosse Ile base."

"Yes, we've just arrived last week, and this young lady has very kindly befriended me," Edward replied, tightening his arm around me as he shook hands with Mr. McCann.

"As you're early and Evelyn and her ladies are just now setting up, could I offer you a tour of our fantastic theater?" he asked.

"Lead on," Edward said, winking at me. "Show me everything."

"You are standing in the grand lobby, which is five stories high and a city block long. Follow me up the stairs for more."

"Right behind you," I said, so proud of Edward, for he so deserved this special tour after his struggles in England.

At the top of the stairs, with their brass rails and thick scarlet carpets, we entered the Corridor of Artifacts. It was a breathtaking collection of precious art objects and paintings on the walls and tucked into alcoves. Luxurious drapes and tapestries complemented the art. Busts of European kings and dignitaries sat on most unusual pedestals. There were oil paintings on loan from the National Gallery and an Empire Suite of furniture. A sculptured chariot with two alabaster horses seemed to race down the corridor at us.

Edward crossed the gallery to stand before a massive portrait of a nobleman on a majestic steed. "Hello, old chap," he said, addressing the portrait as if they were old pals. Gesturing me over, he said, "Millie, I'd like you to meet a friend of mine. Even though he's French, he's a cracker. Millie, may I present the Duke of Orleans."

"How do you do?" I asked, gazing directly into the piercing eyes of the man on the horse. He was majestic in his red uniform, saber at his side, helmet gleaming. I faked a little bow as I greeted the warrior.

Edward continued, "We have a Great Hall lined with my British ancestors at Sand Castles. The portraits terrified me with their size and severity when I was a lad. Even the ladies never smile."

This will never last, I told myself. What can this man possibly see in me?

"Exquisite," Edward said, gazing around him at it all. "Almost too much to take in at once."

"Oh, yes," I agreed. "We must come back."

"Are you big band fans?" asked Mr. McCann, pointing us back down the stairs. "We've got Glenn Miller and Jimmy Dorsey booked."

"Yes. Yes, please," Edward said, taking my arm.

With that Mr. McCann disappeared, and we made our way back down the stairs, which were crowded now as the concert would begin soon. At the center door for the orchestra seats, Edward pulled the tickets from his pocket and handed them to the usher. The usher gave me the program and helped us to our seats in Row D. It was a long walk down the aisle, and I was very aware that Edward and I were turning heads. I blushed as I thought of another possible aisle walk in the future. "Nothing but the best seats for our servicemen," our usher said. "I'll be joining up soon, myself."

"Good on you," Edward said, standing back to let me sit down first.

"Thank you," I said to the usher. "Good luck in the service." I sat down, leaving my cape around my shoulders, smoothing out the soft velvet of my dress. Edward sat on the aisle next to me.

"You call these orchestra seats?" he asked.

"Yes, why?"

"They're the stalls, for us," he said, "and we have to pay for a program."

"Let's see what Evelyn is playing tonight," I said, opening the program.

"Just all women on violins?" Edward asked.

"Oh, no," I answered. I was an expert on Evelyn after five years of listening to The Hour of Charm on the radio. My dad, the violinist, loved her. "Besides the demure Evelyn and other violinists, there is a bass, a guitar, a piano, a trombone, a harp, and two vocalists, the beautiful Maxine, and the sparkling Vivien. They've even made paper dolls for little girls of the three ladies."

Edward chuckled and opened his program. "Hmmm, magic. Let's see what's on the program for tonight. 'Rhapsody in Blue.' I so love that one. Gershwin at his best. 'The Last Rose of Summer.' That should bring a tear to my eye, thinking of English roses. 'Songs My Mother Taught Me.' I'm afraid my mum is not the singing type. A grand program."

The lady seated in the row ahead of us turned around and said, "Sorry, I can't help but hear your accent. So charming." She stared at Edward, her heart undoubtedly beating at a good clip under her blue chiffon gown. A bit annoyed, I watched as she boldly flirted with my Edward.

"Thank you. I find Americans love British accents. For some reason they assume I am intelligent just by my speech," Edward said, leaning forward toward the flattery.

"You know," she said, "Evelyn's ladies sign two-year contracts. They cannot marry nor weigh more than one hundred-twenty-two pounds."

"Is that so?" Edward asked.

She went on, "They have to style their hair in long bobs. They cannot wear spectacles. No dating. And they must memorize all the music. No music stands allowed."

"They may as well be nuns in a convent," Edward said.

A hush came over the crowd of taffeta gowns, tuxedos, and uniforms. As the heavy velvet curtain opened to applause, Evelyn stepped forward, her magic violin in hand. Edward leaned over to me and put his arm around me. My heart flipped as I anticipated a kiss, a blush already crawling up my cheeks. Edward nuzzled up against my ear and whispered, "Don't wear that bright red lipstick again. It makes you look like a tart."

Chapter 7

"He said what?" Meg asked me. We were on the bus from Ecorse as it made the trip once more to Grosse Ile. I shouldn't have told her after the fit Carol had pitched. She'd been angry, as it had been her lipstick that had given me the tart appearance. I sat back and waited for another barrage. And it came.

"How very rude of him to call you that," Meg launched at me. "What did you say back to him? I'd have hauled off and smacked him a good one."

"Honestly, Meg, you would have done no such thing. You'd have done the same thing I did. Just wiggle out from under his arm and try to enjoy the concert." I looked out the bus window, hoping the tirade would stop.

"And what happened at intermission?" Meg continued, leaning over closer to my turned head.

"Oh, he told me in London they call intermissions, intervals. Just small talk, and then he excused himself to have a cigarette." Maybe that would be enough to calm her.

"What did Gary say?" Meg asked. "He'd punch him for you." I turned back around, just in time to see her land a punch in the air.

I gazed back out the window, blowing a cloud onto the pane and drawing a heart with my finger in the icy blur. I sighed and said, "The lady who'd flirted with him turned around to me and asked if I'd like to borrow her handkerchief." I looked back again, hoping she'd stop.

"You mean she had heard him, too?" Meg's eyes grew wider, and her red lips puckered into a tsk-tsk. "How embarrassing."

"Apparently, but I was not going to smudge my lips and end up blotched, so I just turned around and pretended to search for him. Enough?"

"What did he say when he got back to his seat?" Her interrogation continued. She was relentless.

"Oh, he said in England they pass tea right down the rows, or ice creams," I replied. "Just more small talk. So the violins began again, and the music was beautiful. He put his arm around me again, and by the end of the show, I'd completely forgotten his remark."

"Liar," Meg hissed into my ear, the same one that Edward had murmured into. "If you'd forgotten what he said, why are you telling us now?"

"Well, he was a bit abrupt after the concert. We walked out into the lobby into the crush of finely dressed couples, Edward's arm around me. He pulled me behind one of the brass side railings, and I turned toward him. He is so handsome, Meg. My heart was beating hard, and people were rushing by in a blur of colors. He kissed me, really our first true kiss, and my knees buckled. He was holding me up by one hand on my back; his other cupped my face as he smiled down at me. He began to laugh softly. 'What have I found here in America?'"

"*What* has he found? Like you're an object? A piece of meat?" Meg shattered my reverie, and I sat back against the cold leather seat, vowing not to tell her another word. "If he's there tonight at the base, I'll…"

"You'll do or say nothing, Meg. Promise me." We were driving over the bridge and would arrive at the base in minutes. I yanked her arm and repeated, "Meg, promise me."

"I promise nothing. He'd better treat you right. What would Father Champion say? And I bet your sofa full of women at home don't know what he said either."

I stared out the window again, silent, retracing the heart with my finger. She reached over and drew a big X right across it. She kept talking, now about Mac and how wonderful and thoughtful he was. How he was even moving his mother from her home on the Isle of Wight because it was so near Plymouth, and she was in danger of the Nazi bombs raining down on that city. Yes, he was moving her to the country away from the Blitz. She had diabetes, you know, and her eyesight was failing, so he'd found her a nursing home in Devon where she would be safe and well cared for until he could take care of her after the war.

I was never so happy for a bus ride to end.

The bus crawled to a very slow stop on the icy road at the base gate. Out the window I could see a line of blue in the twilight. The RAF was here to greet the USO girls waiting on the bus. The driver slid the door open and about six of us made our way up the aisle and down the steps.

"Fair ladies," one said, "follow us."

"Yes," another said, "the Olds house has officially opened as the USO headquarters."

Each airman stepped forward and took the arm of each girl, and we slid and stumbled along the road back toward the Detroit River where a magnificent old house, formerly the summer home of the wealthy Oldsmobile family, awaited us. Its lights burned in the February night as a light snow began to fall, welcoming us into a warm foyer. Beyond we could see a roaring fire in the marble fireplace. We could hear the gramophone playing an off-season version of Bing Crosby's "*White Christmas*." We could dream, couldn't we?

Mac was there and greeted Meg with a kiss. He was much taller than her and picked her up in his arms and twirled her into the building, sparing her dainty heels from the wet piled snow.

Once inside, I looked around and had decided to join a group of guys playing cards, but Father Champion walked across the room and beckoned for Marge and me to join him. He was holding a small camera and gestured for us to follow him. "Time to take your photos for your official USO identification cards," he said. "Over here in the good light."

Marge posed first, then I did. We didn't even take time to check our makeup or hair. I hated having my picture taken on a good day, let alone this hurried photo. Thank goodness the snood I wore was containing any errant curls. We just stood, proud as peacocks as Father snapped away. Thanking him, we returned to our card players for some raucous teasing about the photos.

My Edward was nowhere in sight that entire evening.

That night back at the dorm I avoided Carol, staying down in the lobby, offering to fill in at the desk for a green-at-the-gills Miss Jackson. February flu had leveled her. There was little traffic through the lobby so

71

I filled the hours with daydreams of my pilot. Finally tiptoeing into the room after curfew, I undressed in the dark and crawled under the starched sheets. I knew I would dream.

****

And I did. It was Christmas, and I was on the bus down Woodward for a few days off with family. The bus kept hitting banks of snow and careening from curb to curb, throwing us forward and backwards in our seats. The driver tried to brake the bus for my stop across from my house, but the bus, with a will of its own, plummeted forward on and on, out of control until it, in spite of the driver pumping the brakes over and over in a panic, suddenly weary, surrendered and screeched to a halt on the Rouge Bridge very close to the railing. The frozen river beckoned below. The door opened and Bing Crosby himself climbed up the steps in his usually congenial mood. He was dressed as a priest.

You could hear the mumblings. People were saying that it'd be all right now that Bing was here. He walked up the aisle, stopping by each person, checking to see if they were injured or shaken up in any way. He was blessing passengers, making the sign of the cross with his hand, intoning, "May all your Christmases be white. May all your Christmases be white."

When he made his way toward me, he stopped, took a kerchief from his coat pocket, leaned in toward me and roughly scrubbed at my lips. "May all your lips be white, always white."

****

"Let's go for a walk," James said. "The rain has stopped, so if we mind the puddles, we should have a decent walk about." He had roused himself from the sofa.

Ian came over to the table. I tried to pay our tab, but he touched my hand gently and said, "Let this be on Bette and me. On such a day as this, you should not pay."

"Thank you so much, Ian. Promise me you'll watch out for Maisie from a distance until she can return home, please."

Pulling me to him in an enormous crushing hug, he replied, "Of course, of course, love." He turned away from me fast, but not fast enough to bar me from seeing the tears as they crawled down his weather-beaten face.

James helped me with my coat, and we walked out of the Punch & Peacock for the last time in my life.

Chapter 8

It was three days later that I returned to the dorm to see Edward once more freezing on the steps. I hurried up to him and stood silently, waiting.

"I read *Rebecca*," he said, shivering, his hands in his pockets. "I'm keeping the book warm inside my coat. Must keep the old girl warm. I've named her Tillie."

The second Mrs. de Winter never has a first name in the book. So Edward had done the honors.

"You did?" I asked, once more done in by this man and his gestures, forgetting any idea of asking where he'd been the night I'd been at the Olds house and he'd failed to appear. "Why Tillie?"

"She seems a bit of a git, don't you think?"

"A git?" I asked, puzzled. Sometimes he lost me with his British expressions.

"A ninny. An eejit."

Oh, I thought. Am I a ninny, too, in his eyes? And what was an eejit anyway? Irritated, I drew my coat tighter around my shaking body, stomping my feet in my sturdy white shoes to summon warmth. It didn't work. Cars drove by, kicking up a wave of slush at hapless pedestrians scurrying to and from the hospital.

"Is it mystery meat on the menu tonight?" he said, pulling one hand from his pocket and cupping my chin as if saying, "You can't get away from me even if you try." I didn't try.

"Come on in. Miss Jackson will be happy to see you."

He slid his arm through mine, and we ran up to the door, hellbent on the future.

Miss Jackson opened the door for us, gushing greetings at Edward. I deposited him in the lobby at her mercy, knowing fully he was perfectly capable of holding his own with the formidable matron.

I flew up the stairs, eager to rid myself of that ugly pink uniform and my clumsy shoes. Carol greeted me at the door, on her way to the lobby.

"Wait a sec," I said. Things had been a bit tense as she had pushed her campaign for me to back off Edward to extremes. She had no idea that whatever inroads she had made in my resolve had just been snarled in the traffic jam called Edward, currently fending off Miss Jackson in the lobby.

"What's up?" she asked, her lips pursed in a none-too-friendly way. "Did you want to borrow my lipstick again?"

I gripped the door for support as I pulled off my shoes and said, "No, but you need to know Edward is in the lobby being entertained by Miss Jackson while I change?" I ended that sentence as a tentative question, my head down, eyes averted.

"You're a ninny," she said, grabbing my wool-covered arm away from the door. "I suppose I should go rescue him." She pushed by me into the hall, leaving me bewildered at the change in attitude.

"Ninny, my ass," I called after her, pulling off my coat and heading to the dresser drawers for my green sweater. Plopping it on the bed, I turned around to the closet to hang up my coat and search for my gray wool trousers. Perfect for a casual evening of mystery meat and literary talk. No time for a shower. I tore off my uniform and deposited it in the laundry bag, excitement growing at the vision of the evening. Getting rid of the obnoxious garter belt and white hose, I pulled on the itchy trousers and then the sweater. Crossing to the mirror, I surveyed the ravages of a day of baby labor, not daring to apply a new coat of lipstick. The girl who gazed back at me was certainly not a ninny, maybe a somewhat naïve Catholic virgin, but no git. I grabbed his poetry book from the nightstand, and, laughing, dashed from the room.

Downstairs, there he was, seated by the fire on the loveseat, his coat guarded by Miss Jackson who perched next to him, giddy in her devotion. Carol sat in the armchair facing the fireplace, leaning toward him in earnest conversation as I approached the trio. Edward stood and crossed the lobby, holding his hand out to me. Miss Jackson stood, too, moving across to another chair, surprisingly leaving half of the loveseat for me. I could see that *Rebecca* lay on the table by Edward's side.

Taking his hand, I let him guide me back to the loveseat. There was silence as I sat down.

Miss Jackson began sputtering about how intriguing it was that two people would read each other's favorite books. "Why, I find that enchanting," she said, her eyes on Edward.

Enchanting? From the woman who had said she could throw me out on Alexandrine at any time?

"Yes," said Carol, rolling her eyes at me behind her hand to avoid being bounced out herself. "Positively enchanting."

Edward turned to me and said, "I did promise to read you these poems. Shall I?"

Miss Jackson jumped up from her chair, beside herself in expectation of this handsome airman reading in his British accent. "Oh, please do," she all but drooled.

"Please," I said quietly, accepting that we would have an audience tonight.

"Just one moment, please," Miss Jackson said as the bell rang at the desk. She sprinted across the lobby in record time, taking care of business and then making a muffled phone call. As she came back over, Jack, our male student clumped through the door, stomping his shoes on the mat. "It's gonna snow. I can feel it in my tired bones," he said to no one in particular.

"Jack," Carol called, "come warm your weary bones by the fire. We have a guest."

Miss Jackson sat her old bones down in the chair again as Jack crossed the lobby.

"Well, well," he said, pulling off his coat. "Edward, I presume?"

Edward rose again, and held out his hand. "Your hands are cold as poor old Willie."

"Willie?" Jack asked, "One of your pilots?"

Edward laughed and walked over to carry a chair back for Jack near the fireplace.

"Thank you, old chap," Jack laughed, mimicking a British accent. He took off his heavy coat, placed it on the back of the chair, and sat down. "And what are we doing?"

"Edward was about to read us one of his favorite poems," Carol offered, her animosity over the lipstick vanished into air.

"Oh," Jack said, "our very own Lawrence Olivier."

"Please," Miss Jackson almost begged.

"Very well," Edward said, rising to stand by the fireplace, facing us all. "This poem is from *A Shropshire Lad* by A. E. Housman."

He began:

"Loveliest of trees, the cherry now
Is hung with bloom along the bough,
And stands about the woodland ride
Wearing white for Eastertide.

Now, of my threescore years and ten,
Twenty will not come again,
And take from seventy springs a score,
It only leaves me fifty more.

And since to look at things in bloom
Fifty springs are little room,
About the woodlands I will go
To see the cherry hung with snow."

Edward closed the book and looked up at us, tears in his blue, blue eyes. "In Cornwall," he said, "at Sand Castles Hall, soon the daffodils will bloom. This snow..." His voice trailed off as he sat down next to me. I took his arm and squeezed his hand.

Miss Jackson broke the silence. "It must be so difficult to be away from your home, your country."

"Yes," Edward said, "but I am grateful for the chance to share my English memories with fine Americans like you."

We were interrupted by Mrs. Cole and her teacart. I

looked over at Miss Jackson, who was grinning at me. "I've ordered tea and cookies for us all to tide us over until dinner."

"Will you be Mother?" Edward asked Miss Jackson, fully aware of his effect on everyone in that lobby.

"What?" Jack asked. "I'm lost."

I spoke up, aware I had been uncharacteristically quiet. "That means to pour the tea."

"Why, yes, of course." Miss Jackson was now blushing from her gray curls to her sturdy toes.

I noticed the fine hospital china on the second shelf of the cart. She was pulling out all the stops indeed.

"Millie," Edward said, turning toward me and patting my leg, "why not read us the opening of *Rebecca*?"

Worrying about his hand on my leg, I grabbed it and raised it, only to realize that Miss Jackson was so intent on perfecting her Mother role that she had missed the gesture.

"Edward," she asked, looking up, "how do you take your tea?" Butter would have melted in her mouth.

"White, please," he said, quickly adding that meant with cream only.

Once our teas and cookies were handed all around on the Spode blue china, we sipped and munched in silence. By then a few more students had joined, seated around our group on the carpet. The word was out that a certain airman was reading poetry in the lobby.

"Please," Edward asked again, "Read to us, Millie."

"Oh, I'll try, but I can't compete with your accent," I said, giving in, but not without butterflies leaping about in my stomach, floating on a sea of tea. I stood and walked to the fireplace, not believing I was actually about to do this thing.

"But I love your accent," Edward cooed, locking eyes with mine.

"But we don't have accents." Carol corrected, "You do, Edward." Everybody laughed in a stiff, polite way as I waited by the fire.

I opened up the worn book and began:

"Last night I dreamt I went to Manderley again. It seemed to me I stood by the iron gate leading to the drive, and for a while I could not enter, for the door was barred to me. There was a padlock and a chain upon the gate. I called in my dream to the lodge-keeper, and had no answer, and peering closer through the rusted spokes of the gate I saw that the lodge was uninhabited.

No smoke came from the chimney and the little lattice windows gaped forlorn. Then, like all dreamers, I was possessed of a sudden with supernatural powers and passed like a spirit through the barrier before me."

Edward rose and came to stand beside me. I closed the book and gazed up at him—what had I done wrong?

"Millie," he said, grasping my free hand, "No doors will be barred to you at Sand Castles, I promise. No padlocks. No chains." With those reassuring and surprising words, he leaned down and kissed me on the cheek. I gasped and blushed as Edward possessed me like all dreamers. It may sound corny, but there was an audible collective sigh in the room. For the moment, they all were in love with this pilot, even Jack.

Everyone at first fell silent, then Jack burst out, "Bravo, Olivier." He applauded, nodding and encouraging everyone to join in. Miss Jackson rose, pushing the teacart away, clapping her hands together in glee.

Edward and I returned to the loveseat, now a perfect spot for us. I looked at Carol, who now too was standing, applauding a relationship she had once discouraged. I now noticed even more girls had come into the lobby, some kneeling around us, others dressed in coats, hanging about near the door.

"Another poem, Edward. Please," Miss Jackson asked, almost commanded.

"Very well, if you insist," Edward rose, and then knelt by the fire, stoking the flames. Rising, he took his position by the fireplace, opened the book, dramatically cleared his throat, and read:

"Oh, when I was in love with you,
Then I was clean and brave,
And miles around the wonder grew
How well did I behave.

And now the fancy passes by,
And nothing will remain,
And miles around they'll say that I
Am quite myself again."

This one left the room quiet again and puzzled. We looked at each other for answers.

"And Housman is saying?" Carol asked, breaking the silence, addressing her question to Edward.

"Oh, it's just a lark," Edward said, sitting down near me again. "Just a lark." Another Edwardian enigma.

The door opened and a couple made their way into

the lobby, shaking off snow and stamping their feet. "It's a blizzard out there," one called out.

"Perhaps you should skip dinner and make your way back to the base early," Miss Jackson suggested, crashing back down to earth. "I need to get back to my desk."

The magic died as everyone went back to their lives, leaving Edward and me alone. The show was over. We looked at each other, happy to be abandoned at last.

"Psst!!" I heard a summons from behind the kitchen door. I rose, just in time to see a hand reach out and grab me. It was Jack with a plan, more a plot.

"Listen, you can't send your pilot out in this storm, especially after his daffodil tears. I can sneak him down to the dungeon if he doesn't mind sleeping on the floor. Or maybe in the bathtub?"

"But if we get caught it'll be Alexandrine for us both," I replied, scared silly, my voice low.

"Trust me, I've gotten away with worse," Jack said, pushing me back out into the lobby.

"Spend some time on the couch with your sweetie, and then make a show of saying good night in the snow. Send him around to the back door, and I'll be there at eight to let you in." He was impatient to get down to his room, I could see.

"But what about dinner? He'll be starved," I worried, eyeing Edward on the loveseat.

"I'll grab you something edible from the dining room when I eat. Got it?" His patience gone, he disappeared, or so I thought.

"Got it. Thanks so much, Jack."

He was back, his voice barely audible. "Just

helping out young lovers. Even if he dumped you in that last poem, Millie. Now scat."

With that he was gone, and I returned to a puzzled Edward and very softly explained the plan. Once he got it and was complicit in our plot, I hugged him and said loudly, "Tell me more about Sand Castles. What an odd name for a great home."

"My dear," he began. "There is a beautiful sandy beach tucked within a spacious cove. The sea laps its shore, eroding its timeless edges, sometimes breaking in fierce storms, attacking. Then the peacocks disperse, seeking safety above the cove in the trees…"

****

Of course I dreamed again that night, restless knowing Edward was well-hidden in Jack's dungeon, half-expecting Miss Jackson to burst into my dorm room and eject me straight into the snowy boulevard. I hadn't even told Carol about the plan, not fully trusting her still.

When I did sleep, I dreamt I was at Sand Castles. It was spring, a glorious spring. All was in bloom around me. The scents given off by the lilacs, intoxicating. I lay back on an old towel in the sand and was so happy, so loved. Edward was not about, perhaps off fighting his war from the air, a very brave lad. But I knew from the Welsh gold ring on my finger that we were one, and nothing, no one, not a storm, not Adolf Hitler could come between us.

Suddenly a man dressed in nineteenth-century clothing and leaning on a cane made his way down the slope to the cove where I lay. He had a distinguished beard, tinged with gray, and spectacles perched on his nose. He wore an old straw floppy beach hat at odds with his tweedy suit.

"My lady," he bowed in an exaggerated way when he had reached my towel, "I am A. E. Housman, a dear friend of your husband." Straightening up, he pulled a paisley kerchief from his jacket pocket and wiped his brow, wet from the exertion of his descent into the cove.

"The poet?" I asked, jumping up, smoothing my spring cotton skirt, sand sprinkling about.

"Yes," he said, his eyes searching mine in vain as I wore sunglasses. "Please remove your glasses as Edward would want me to see into your eyes while I relate his message to you."

"What message?" I asked, my stomach churning. "No one can separate us," I said aloud to this poet, the lilacs, and the sea.

Housman began, his eyes locked in mine as he stepped forward toward me. "Edward quotes:

'And now the fancy passes by,
And nothing will remain,
And miles around they'll say that I
Am quite myself again.'

"That is all," the poet said, drawing a rough castle in the sand with his cane. "Good day."

Chapter 9

I was awake early, that nightmare still lurking in my head, a not-so-subtle premonition. Housman had walked away, the sand crunching under his feet, leaving me behind, baffled and sad. I pushed it back, way back in my mind, remembering Edward in the dungeon. He couldn't be happy about his sleeping conditions. And a night with chatty Jack must have worn on his nerves, too. Not wanting to disturb Carol's sleep, I pushed back the covers and gingerly lowered my feet to the cold dorm floor. How deep was the snow? Could Edward get a bus out of Detroit if the roads had been cleared? The hospital received first priority for snow clearance, so there was a good chance the bus route was open this morning. Rifling around in my dresser drawer in the dark, I found my underwear, and slipped into it, and pulled on my robe. Grabbing a washcloth, towel, and toothbrush, I headed down the hall to the communal bath. I had it all to myself at this early hour, but there was no time for a shower. The mirror reflected my lack of sleep. Too many wrinkles for one so young. "Ablutions," Edward called this washing-up routine, abbreviated today in my desire to shoo him back to the base. After brushing my teeth, I patted on a bit of pancake make-up. Nothing more was allowed for working on the wards. Back to the room, still in the dark, I now started the ritual of donning my uniform, so routine after three years that the dark didn't slow me down at all. First the white hose, then the pink stiff dress. Next the white cuffs attached to the sleeves by silver studs. I reached onto the chair for the white kerchief and spread it around my neck, fastening it with a silver pin. Last came the starched cap, which I perched far back on my head, securing it with a bobby pin. I was proud to wear the black velvet stripe on its brim, the sign of all the hard work it had taken to get to senior status, having survived two years of Miss Jackson's constant surveillance and threats. The cap was held together by the silver buttons that were engraved with the GH which stood for Grace Hospital. I left my room. There was no sign of having awoken Carol, who claimed she could sleep though the war if we ever entered it. One last stop to check out the clothes I'd thrown on in the dark in the bright bathroom mirror, and I was off down the stairs.

As it was too early for Miss Jackson to be on duty at her desk, I glided across the lobby to the kitchen undetected. I grabbed a jar of milk from the refrigerator and a few leftover cookies from the tea cart, wrapping them in a napkin, and then headed down the stairs. Stopping in front of Jack's door, I listened for sounds of life. Standing there, my ear to the door, I jumped and squealed as someone grabbed me around the waist from behind and began tickling me. "Up early, aren't we?" Edward nuzzled into my kerchief as I squirmed, trying to turn around, but he had me pinned to the door.

The door flew open, and I fell back against Edward as Jack appeared, groggy in his pajamas. Checking us out, huddled in a hug, Jack sighed, and then grumbled, "Whose idea was this anyway? I need coffee."

Laughing, Edward and I followed Jack back into his room, a very messy room. Clothes were stacked in a sloppy pile on the floor, the empty laundry bag lazing beside it. The dresser was littered with a heap of dirty ice cream bowls; tea cups, some cracked; pop bottles; and cookie wrappers. The rug on the floor was spotted with stains of various size and colors, its one corner curled forward, as if trying to trip unwanted guests. The bed was a glorious jumble of twisted sheets and blankets, fighting to get free of the dingy flat pillows tossed against the iron bed frame. The closet gaped open revealing another mountain of clothes on the floor. A lone wooly pea coat hung from the rod.

"Welcome to the dungeon," Jack said, his arm sweeping the room. "The maid is off today."

"Oh, Edward," I said. "Wherever did you sleep?"

"I told him he needed to tidy up the place, but I fear my request fell on deaf ears," Edward said, gesturing about. "Doesn't the dragon lady conduct military inspections of your rooms?"

"Seriously, where did you sleep?" I asked again, worried at this obvious lack of hospitality.

"In the bathtub down the hall," he replied, rubbing the back of his neck.

"Oh, no, really?" I said, frowning at Jack.

"Take those green eyes off of me," Jack said, wagging his finger in my face. "I checked on him once and he was curled up, sleeping like a baby."

"Jack was the perfect host, making sure I had a pillow, though cola-stained, and he gave me two blankets—one to lie on, the other to cover me. Thank you, sir!" He bowed with great panache, bending forward from the waist.

"You're so welcome, your pilot-lordship," Jack whispered, yawning and pilfering the dresser mess to find a half-eaten cookie. "Coffee, my kingdom for a coffee. That's Shakespeare, ducks!" No bow from Jack for Edward. Just sass.

"Almost," Edward replied. "Any RAF chap is fine as long as he has what we call the three S's. A shit. A shower. And a shave. Sorry, love." His blue eyes snapped at me like little imps getting away with bad behavior.

I blushed to my toes as Edward hugged me to him, and Jack began to laugh at us both. "I think you've embarrassed Millie, our Catholic kid."

"Please," I countered, breaking free of Edward. "I'm well-acquainted with every S you can think of, as a nurse."

"That's my girl," Edward said. "Now is there anything I could eat besides stale biscuit crumbs?"

"Oh, I forgot," I said, pulling the small jar of milk and a few cookies from my uniform pocket.

Jack made an apple appear from who-knows-where. It was bruised, but edible. He bowed before Edward and said, "An apple is all I can offer you."

Edward took it, looked it over, and bit into it, the questionable juice spotting his chin. "Delicious."

I pulled off the paper cap from the little glass jar of milk, and handed it over. Apple in one hand, milk in the other, he smiled as he filled his empty stomach. Then I gave him the cookies in the crumpled napkin. "Ah, afters," he said, handing me back the milk.

"Afters?" Jack asked, grabbing the milk and sipping from the bottle.

"What you call dessert, I believe," Edward said,

munching.

"I heard a bus go by when I was in the lobby, so looks like the roads are cleared, and you'll be able to get out of here," I said, reaching to brush a crumb from Edward's mustache.

"Do you know what we call these?" Edward said, pointing to his mustache.

"Fur beneath your nose?" wisecracked Jack.

"No, as a matter of fact this bit of fur is called a cookie duster," Edward said, proudly showing off his fur piece.

"How appropriate," I said, brushing a few more crumbs from his mustache, and looking closely to see if there were any traces of mascara on it as Gary had suggested. "Now let's get you upstairs to the bus stop."

Taking one more gulp of milk from Jack's bottle, Edward straightened his jacket, ready to face the February snowdrifts.

"You'd better walk down to Woodward to catch the bus so Miss Jackson doesn't spot you at the hospital stop," Jack advised.

"Come on, Edward. Follow me," I urged, grabbing his hand.

Holding on, Edward followed behind me as I wove our way through a labyrinth of tunnels to come out by a side entrance.

"Wait," Edward whispered as I pushed on the door, "say goodbye properly, please."

I turned around to be crushed into his arms in a passionate kiss, followed by several more before we both came up for air.

He rubbed the back of his neck. "A bit sore from my bathtub bed," he complained. "Tonight," he said, "if you can get to the base, we have a showing of the British picture *Gaslight*. I saw it in England, and it's very good."

"In this snow?" I asked him, not sure the roads would be cleared downriver by then.

"You could catch the coach," he said, his eyes searching mine, hoping.

"Coach? Oh, the bus," I said, remembering his vocabulary lessons. "I'll try my best."

"Let's try our best at a knee-trembler," he coaxed, pushing me up against the cold concrete wall, his mouth on mine.

"A knee-trembler?" I whispered into his mouth.

"You'll see," he answered, bending and reaching his hand up my long skirt.

I gasped as his hand traced its way, tickling my white-stockinged leg up to the line of my hose.

"That's my little USO girl," he teased, his fingers moving up and sliding under my garter elastic. Snap! He pulled on the taut elastic, several times. "Like strumming a finely-tuned fiddle." He laughed. "What would Evelyn think?" His head had slid down to my cloth-covered breasts as his fingers wandered higher to my panties. "Damned starch," he complained. My arms held tight to his back, my legs becoming less and less reliable. One hand still below, he reached with the other to unbutton my uniform. His hand slipped inside the pink, and I felt for the first time his fingers seeking my breast in its silk bra. "Too many layers," he said, pushing under the bra and finally touching flesh.

I couldn't help the groan that rose from my throat as my knees began to shake and his other hand found its target between my legs in a long, slow stroke. My nipple erect, he squeezed.

Looking into my eyes, both hands moving at once, he said, "This is a knee-trembler, my darling Millie."

Arching back, I breathed hard, welcoming, yet fearing this gush of new feelings. I might have fourteen formals hanging in my closet, but none of those dates had touched me in this way. Not this Catholic.

"Don't fight it, Millie. Let go," Edward urged, his mouth again finding mine. His tongue penetrated my mouth, making the violation complete. Tremors shook me against that wall and my knees finally gave way. Pulling his hands free to catch me as I began to fall, he said, his face close to mine, "That's the way good Catholic girls do it." He laughed. "Father Champion would approve that you're still intact, love."

Recovering my senses, and pushing him away, I stooped to re-arrange my uniform skirt, knowing I would risk a demerit for the wrinkles Edward's hand had made. I could feel the wetness in my panties. Buttoning my top, I looked down for damage there. Passable. Maybe.

"I'm sure you'll pass muster," he said, stepping farther back to check me out. "Your loved-up look will fade. And when you feel that wet you'll think of me all day."

"Oh, Edward," I said, lost for words.

"She speaks," he mused, his arms around me again. "We need to buy you some sexy smalls," he added.

"Smalls?" Even not knowing the word, I felt a blush moving up my face.

"Underthings," he said, "yours look like you borrowed them from Aunt Lill."

"I'm sorry," I said, flustered and embarrassed.

"They seemed to do the trick anyway."

"Much more than the wool trousers last night. I hate women in trousers. You may as well be a mechanic working on our planes. Don't wear them again. Why hide these legs?" he asked, reaching down and grabbing me. More wrinkles.

"See you tonight at the base," he commanded and with one last, lingering kiss, he was out the door and down the alleyway. And me? I did a slow collapse to the floor, shaking all over again.

****

James and I walked along, the slush splashing up on our shoes. It was a quiet walk, and we were still both a bit tipsy. I was sad to be leaving the people who I'd come to love and rely on. Most of all, little Maisie, who Edward and I had met in the train station that day. Her life had been so altered by that chance meeting. I would miss her. I knew it would be a long war for her, I could only hope it would be a good war in the end for her and that she would return to her parents in London, happy.

"I'm still pissed," said James, clutching my arm.

I started to ask him what he was mad about when I remembered that "pissed" was British for being drunk. I chuckled, thinking back over my last year's education from piddling vocabulary to the dark side of love.

"Pissed enough to take that train with you to wherever you're going," James said, slurring his words a little and grabbing my arm harder. "Yes, I shall be your escort, love. The RAF will demand it. Let's hope the train is not too crammed with buggers like me," James said, picking up the pace so we could board early. I so longed for the time to think back over the past months. Surely Mr. Hitchcock could make a hell of a movie with my life.

****

That day at the hospital things did not go well. A lady in labor I was with most of the day hemorrhaged right after delivering a baby boy and died. It was a shock to everyone. The charge nurse, Miss Browning, hurried me away to another patient while she and the doctor consoled the angry father. I could hear his shouts and sobbing down the hall. "What am I going to do with a baby by myself? You killed my wife. She was perfectly healthy before you got hold of her." I peeked out the door of my new patient's room to see more people arriving. A hospital administrator, Mr. Bourassa and a man I recognized as a lawyer who had lectured us once on hospital legal issues, Mr. Adams. Next an older woman arrived and threw her arms around the distraught husband. I longed to go help him because after all I'd been talking to him all day as he had waited in the lounge, updating him on his wife's labor. But I knew to stay away. I'd been worried about a wrinkled pink dress, but this far outweighed my minor problem in gravity.

"What's going on?" my patient, Mrs. Newman, asked. She had checked in early that morning in the very early stages of labor. Her doctor predicted an afternoon delivery when she would be knocked out with twilight sleep and the baby delivered with forceps. That was standard practice, but rarely, very rarely, standard became tragic and the mother or baby was lost.

"Oh, just an upset father down the hall," I said. "Can I get you anything? Would you like a backrub?" I tried not to let my voice reveal my sadness at the loss.

What would that husband do with a baby on his

own? "Remain objective," Miss Jackson always warned. "Without that ability to distance yourself from the patient, this nursing profession is not for you."

"Oh, yes, please. A backrub would be wonderful," she said, too worried about her own labor pains to pursue an explanation of the shouting man any further.

The day wore on. The sobbing faded. And by the end of my shift, I walked into the lounge and told Mr. Newman that he had a baby girl to join the other three children at home.

I slushed my way back to the dorm, eager for a shower to cleanse away the remnants of both passion and grief. How much death had Edward seen in the war which had ravaged England for two years now? And would America ever enter the conflict? And would Gary be safe?

Chapter 10

Gary ended up being my ride to Grosse Ile that night. The buses were running at irregular times, pushing through the snow, still drifted across the roads in some areas. He had called me, saying Edward had invited him to the base on the condition he picked me up at the dorm. Clever boy! I would sign out for the night, not sure if I might end up sleeping in a bathtub somewhere, but eager for romance and shocking adventures with my handsome pilot.

Naked in the shower, I let the hot water stream down my body, lingering at my breasts, then coursing down my abdomen to my legs. I touched areas I had never sought out before, the nuns having admonished us never to look at our bodies as we bathed as they solemnly advised cutting our bathing to as few minutes as possible. Just in and out the tub, if you please, young Catholics. I put my fingers to my lips, tasting as the water soaked my head and hair. Turning the tap off, I stepped out and viewed myself in the mirror over the sink. What would Edward see when he looked at my body free of starch, kerchief, and nurse's cap? I laughed and, still shy, made a mental note to look into a set of silky smalls. Thank goodness there was no rationing in our country.

Toweling my hair, I walked back across the hall.

"You're naked," Carol shrieked. "What's gotten

into you?"

Not embarrassed at all, I grabbed my robe off the chair. "Forgot my robe," I said, smiling. Not wanting to admit Edward had indeed gotten into me.

Avoiding the trousers hanging in my closet, I chose a blue sweater and skirt to show off my legs for Edward. It was all for him now. Rifling in a drawer, I pushed aside all the Aunt Lill panties and found a flimsier pair of Carol's somehow mixed in with mine. What luck. Pulling them on under the robe so she couldn't see them and demand them back, I gathered up my clothes and went back across the hall to the bathroom to dress.

"You're being mysterious," she shouted, groggy from a nap, but awake enough after my naked romp to hope for an update on Edward. "Any new poetry?"

"Sorry, been very busy. We had a new mother die today. The father was in an awful state, and they had to send for an administrator and a lawyer. The charge nurse shuffled me away to another patient, of course," I called back from across the hall.

Clothes on, I surveyed my face and hair in the mirror. No time for a Hudson's appointment with Miss Georgette. Edward would have to see my hair au natural with its curls. I clipped it back, still damp, and then gave my face the once-over. A dusting of pancake and a hint of Tangee pale coral lipstick just might "pass muster" with my pilot. Smacking my lips on a piece of toilet tissue, I crossed back over to Carol.

"Where tonight?" Carol asked, sitting up on the bed, putting her shoes back on for dinner.

"To the base with Gary for a picture. *Gaslight.* A British thriller."

"At least let me do your nails," Carol offered. "You must have time for that."

I looked down at my hands, dried and wrinkly from the hospital solutions they soaked up all day long.

"Okay, if you hurry," I said, sitting down at the desk.

"Color?"

"Something very pale," I said, remembering the fate of the red lipstick.

Carol pulled the extra chair up to the desk and sorted out a file and polish. Opening the bottle, she pulled the tiny brush out, scraped the excess polish off it, and attacked my left hand first. I had brushed the file away as taking too much time.

She carried on, both of us quiet and earnest to get the job done in record time. With both hands finished, I held them up, and she blew on one while I blasted the other.

"There. Let's hope this shade has more luck with your pilot. Have fun," Carol said.

"Let's walk down together," I said, grabbing my purse and coat with one last glance at my nails.

"Don't put on your gloves right away," she cautioned.

In the lobby I signed out, and Carol moved on to dinner. I spotted Jack sitting in the lounge. "Jack," I called, crossing to the loveseat. I sat down and lowered my voice. "Thank you again for last night. I owe you."

"The day will come, my dear. The day will come," he said, rolling his eyes. He lowered his voice even more to a whisper. "I saw you two by the door to the alley. I had gone to see if Edward got the bus okay, and well, there you were. Shameless."

"I have to tell you this, Jack. Edward calls that, you know, what you saw, a knee-trembler."

"Well, I didn't see much. I knew I had to get out of there fast, but a knee-trembler, huh? Very funny. Too bad I'm a monk here in my dungeon with my bum leg. No dashing uniform for me. Just these white scrub suits." He poked at the starched white, wishing it were army khaki.

"Just be glad they're not a starchy pink," I said, laughing and rising as I glimpsed Gary coming through the main door. Standing, too, Jack helped me on with my coat.

"Thanks, Jack. We're off to the base for a picture screening of a British movie."

"Have fun, and say cheerio to his lordship," Jack called with a quick farewell bow as he headed down the hall to dinner while Gary and I walked out into another snowy evening.

Gary had Dad's Cadillac, so we set off in style down Alexandrine and over to Fort Street. The Detroit roads were cleared, but still slippery, but downriver I knew the conditions would worsen.

"Hey, Mumu," he kidded, "do you remember the time when I was about twelve when I took Dad's car for a little joyride?"

"How could I forget that? What a brat!" I said, chuckling as I recalled him skillfully reversing the car down the driveway, his head barely above the steering wheel.

"I got to the end of the driveway and had to decide which way to go, left or right."

"And Mom had a fit."

"Remember her on the back porch, waving a

kitchen towel and shouting, 'Gareth, Gareth! Come back!' "

"And that didn't stop you. Then Lill and Stell rushed out onto their front porch and shouted at you to stop."

"Dad was up in his radio room on the air with his buddies so he had no clue what I was doing," Gary said, "but the three French hens were in a state, flapping and clucking."

"Shouldn't have left the keys in his car. Never did again," I said, rubbing a spot to look out on the side pane.

"So off I went, straining to see out the windshield and turning right to side streets, avoiding Jefferson traffic," Gary said, sitting up straight as if he were a kid again, peering over the steering wheel.

"Very wise, since you could hardly see."

"Lill, bless her heart, tried to chase me down the block, while Mom kept waving her towel and now screeching for my dad, 'Lawrence! Lawrence!' " Gary was laughing hard now, proud of his escapade.

"Where did you go?" I asked, looking out the frosted car window, feeling safe with my brother's skillful maneuvering through snowy streets. "You never did confess where."

"Right over to my buddy Andy's house. Just drove by waving, shocking the hell out of Madame Mourguet, who was out on the porch enjoying the sunset and embroidering."

"Oh, yes. Andy's mom. She was soon on the telephone, alerting our parents."

"I had just turned the corner and headed back home in triumph, only to see you, Lill, Stell, Mom and Dad, even Bartholomew, the little scamp, waiting on the sidewalk. Lill, who could always turn you to stone with one of her glares, stepped forward as I pulled the car up the driveway and shut it off. Mission accomplished. Aunt Lill moaned that I could have been killed. And then you were all washed over me like a jumbled wave of family, crying and hugging me, even Dad."

"Amazing. You got away with it. You'd think you would have been swatted with the dish towel at least," I marveled, shaking my head. We dropped into a sibling silence then, watching the roads, content to be together for the evening.

Soon we approached the bridge for the island, and my heart sped up to a dangerous beat. Crossing over the bridge, I peered down into the ice floes. This was a very serious winter, the worst in years. Poor Edward coping with awful weather and a terrible war. Maybe I would be his reward for it all. My cheeks flamed as I thought back to our knee-trembler. I was certainly his willing pupil. Wouldn't Aunt Lill give me a vicious swat with that kitchen towel if she knew.

As we neared the gate, a guard stepped out with a clipboard. "Names, please."

Gary rolled down the window. "Gary and Millie Beaubien," he said.

"Guests of?"

"What's his name?" Gary asked again. My brother was not known for his unfailing memory. He barely remembered his own name.

"Edward Owen," I replied, a bit exasperated, my newly polished fingers tapping on the door handle.

"Go ahead," the guard replied. "Head to the Olds mansion near the river."

"Thank you," I called across the front seats.

"Be careful. Mind the ice."

And we were off across the slick rough road, headed toward the lights of the old house ahead. I was aware that night lights must seem welcoming to Edward after years of blackouts in England. As we pulled up at the grand porch, I spotted him waiting at the door. Standing next to him was a woman in civilian dress. I felt the first pang of jealousy shoot through me. Who was that woman standing so close to my Edward? Gary parked the car, and we slid our way up the icy wooden steps.

"Gary, Millie," Edward stepped forward, shaking Gary's hand and reaching to hug me.

"Edward, thanks for the invitation. I've delivered Millie safely to you," Gary answered, eyeing the lady next to Edward.

"And you are?" I questioned her, trying to drain the envy from my voice.

Edward laughed at my reaction. "Down, girl. At ease. The lady claims she knows you."

She stepped forward, offering me her hand, saying, "I'm Sue Taylor. Do you remember me from the bus that day? You told me all about the USO?"

Shaking her hand, I blushed pink for my stupidity. "Of course, Sue. Taylor from Taylor. I'm so happy you have joined up."

"Let's go inside. The picture will begin soon," Edward said, taking my hand and whispering, "Charming to see you green with envy, my dear. I thought Sue could keep your brother occupied and away from us for at least part of the evening."

Taking my coat and handing it over to a volunteer,

Edward took my hand, kissed it, and said, "I hate nail varnish. Don't wear it again."

Defeated again and shaking my head, I walked arm in arm with him into the screening room. He could build me up like a big balloon and then just stick a pin in me and watch me collapse. His criticisms confused me. But I soldiered on. The good outweighed the bad.

A projector was set up and the first picture reel seemed ready to go. Gary was nowhere in sight as we looked about the room. It wasn't too crowded, maybe about ten servicemen and twenty or so USO girls. Great odds for the guys. Edward surveyed the room and picked out a rather secluded loveseat for us, tucked into an alcove yet still within viewing distance. The movie screen was set up on one side of the room with a few rows of chairs in front of it.

"Over there," he said.

"But Gary," I said.

"Gary will take care of himself," he answered, ushering me to the loveseat. "They promise tea and sandwiches during the interval."

"Perhaps I should go help," I said, feeling guilty that I had not lent a hand in preparing the sandwiches.

"Don't you dare," Edward hissed, sitting down and then pulling me after him. "You are doing your duty by cheering up this poor lonely airman far away from home and hearth. Now kiss me."

Smashing his mouth against mine, bumping my teeth, he left no doubt where my place would be for the evening.

I pushed him back just in time to see Gary and Sue come into the room, looking for seats and probably me. Sue spotted us first and hurried over, Gary behind her.

"This house is so beautiful," Sue said, "and the view onto the river just spectacular."

"It's swell," Gary said, looking down at us. "But when you're a rich auto baron, the sky's the limit. Old Man Olds probably paid for the stars up in the Detroit sky out there, too. We're going over there," Gary said, pointing to the front row seats.

"There's a poster for *Gaslight* over by the food," Gary said.

"Yeah, sounds really good. I love a scary picture," Sue added, holding up a small flyer for the film. She read, "An insane criminal tries to drive his wife crazy in order to find hidden jewels in her Victorian mansion."

Gary interrupted, asking, "Would this qualify as a Victorian mansion?"

Edward laughed and said, "I saw this picture last year in London. If you fancy being scared, it's for you. And you'll never quite trust your mate again, trust me or don't."

I said nothing, but Edward's words went to my heart, dredging up all my nightmares.

"If it's that good, Edward, I may just have to sit up front. I do love my pictures," I warned.

Gary backed me up, saying, "Oh, yes, my sis will have her ear to the radio next week when the Motion Picture Academy Awards will air. *Rebecca* is nominated for so many awards; she wouldn't miss that for the world."

"And Dad has radio buddies who can relay the news fast," I said, cheering up. The truth is I would never know the truth about Edward on this side of the Atlantic. My mind had split the movie conversation and my love life into two separate topics. Perhaps I was avoiding what I could not know for sure.

"Come on, Gary." Sue tugged at his arm. "Looks like they're about to get going."

They crossed over to the front row just as the lights dimmed and the projector started to spin the reel round.

My heart beats fast as the picture opens with an old Victorian lady, sitting and doing needlepoint. I am there with her. We are alone together in my mind. Old chums. But then without warning, she is brutally strangled from behind. Shocked at the suddenness of the assault, I reach for Edward's hand, and he obliges me by tucking my shaking body inside his arm, patting my hand, and saying, "It'll be all right, I promise. I'll protect you from the wicked villain."

The movie continues, introducing us to Bella and her new husband as they arrive at their new home which has stood vacant for a long time. The mood grows darker and darker as Bella begins to doubt her sanity as she misplaces items, as pictures disappear from the walls, as the gaslights flicker. Her husband insists she is lying to him. That all is well, save her mind. "You're losing your wits," he says, always hovering, always accusing. Her valuable brooch goes missing. Where can it be? She eavesdrops as her husband flirts with Nancy, her maid.

I want to shout out to Bella, telling her to leave that house, that her husband is up to no good. Instead, I cower, hiding against Edward's chest.

With an evening piano concert before them, her husband, Paul urges Bella to wear her brooch. She can't find it, but covers up by saying it doesn't match her gown. He says he can't find his pocket watch as they leave for the party. Reaching into her purse, she finds the watch and breaks down in tears, doubting her own sanity, causing an embarrassing scene. Making excuses, Paul hurries her to the cab. Bella confronts him, begging, "Hit me. Hurt me. For heaven's sake, speak to me. Paul, how can you torture me like this?"

I feel tears stream down my face. How can I trust anyone when this evil exists in the world? When devils like Hitler seek to control the world?

"I once knew a girl who died in an asylum. It's the eyes how you first know," Paul hisses at her as she sobs.

I am crying now, and I have to get closer. "I need to move closer to Bella," I say to Edward, drawn and hypnotized by the flickering gaslight. I stand and creep in the dim light to one empty seat beside Sue, leaving Edward behind, alone, speechless.

Sue looks up and pulls me down next to her. "This is creepy," she says.

At last, Paul is trapped in his own snare; the rubies and brooch betray him. Bella asks to speak to him alone. Captured, he is tied to a chair as she approaches. She threatens him with a letter opener, but has no real intention of harming him. "You tried to kill my mind," she says.

With that, the credits roll. The lights come up. I look over to Edward, but he is gone.

Gary leans over to me across Sue. "You okay, Mumu?"

"Yes," I say softly, "I...I never realized how easy it could be to control someone."

"But this was a sinister man," Sue said, seeing I was upset. "Not your average husband."

I looked down at my nail polish; my fingers went

to my lips, tracing them, feeling the pale coral lipstick. I was aware of Sue's wool trousers rubbing my thigh. Control could be easy. The gaslights could be made to flicker. The brooches could be hidden. I was aware of blue wool legs in front of me, hands holding out a cup of tea toward me. Trembling, hoping I wouldn't spill, I took the cup and sipped, not ready to meet Edward's eyes. I didn't want to betray the fear I felt. Gary and Sue stood and headed out for the sandwiches. Edward sat down beside me, sipping his own tea.

"All right?" he asked, frustrated that I wouldn't look at him. "Didn't know what to think when you bolted."

I nodded, my eyes down, just wanting to get away. Silence, until I finally straightened and forced myself to look him in the eye, smiling, as my trembling lips betrayed me.

"Oh, love, did Paul scare you?" He laughed. "You can be such a ninny."

He put his cup down, taking mine, too, placing them both on the empty chair next to him. "I have a surprise for you, darling," he said, pulling a small green velvet pouch from his jacket pocket. I looked away in fear, not wanting to know what he had in store, afraid he'd lure me back from the edge of sanity I was approaching. The realization that my life was hurtling too fast toward a man I did not know.

"Please," he begged, pulling my face toward his. "Please." He took my hand and placed the dark satchel in it. I was aware of the soft velvet against my skin as he caressed my palm with it. "Go on, open it. I know you will love it."

Music started playing in the room next door on the

gramophone. The first notes of "A Nightingale Sang in Berkeley Square" spilled over into this room. *Courage, you ninny.* I picked up the satchel and tugged the tiny green cords open. Turning it upside down, I shook it until a brooch fell into my hand. *Not a brooch. What terrible timing.*

Edward smiled at me and took the brooch in his hand. "Look, it's the Lux Flakes *Gone with the Wind* brooch. I knew you fancied it, so I got the tab from the washing up soap from Aunt Lill, swore her to secrecy, and sent to New York for it. I knew you'd be chuffed."

Laughing through my tears, I said, "Please help me put it on, Edward. It's not rubies, only a turquoise stone with pearls encircling it, but I do love it. I do love it."

He leaned forward and fastened the pin to my blue sweater. A perfect match.

"Do you want to dance with me?" he asked, mimicking our very first conversation.

"I have been dancing," I continued the reverie.

"But not with me," he smiled, touching the brooch, proud of his purchase.

Edward took my hand, and glancing again at the brooch, his gift, he walked me into the ballroom, and we danced the night away once more.

****

I knew of course I would dream that night. Once back home in Ecorse for the night, I had shown off my new brooch, not even mentioning the scare and the doubts I'd had over seeing Gaslight. I had first chided, and then thanked Aunt Lill for her little conspiracy with Edward. Gary had dropped me off and then taken Sue home.

So I drifted off, the brooch on my nightstand. I

soon found myself in the old mansion in the movie, but it was somehow moved to Cornwall from Pimlico Square in London. I was walking alone along the beach in the cove and clouds loomed on the horizon. The sky was a mixture of gray and yellowish clouds tinged with red. Red skies in the morning, sailors take warning *ran through my head. If movies were in black and white, my dreams were vivid with color.*

Edward appeared with a peacock trailing behind him. "The nasty bugger tried to bite me," he shouted above the rushing waves curling against the rocks and sand.

I laughed and ran the few steps between us, happy he was again home on leave. He seldom talked about his war. He told me I was his respite, and he preferred my not knowing.

"How long this time?" I asked, taking his hand and shooing the peacock away, kicking sand at it.

"A fortnight," he replied, stopping and raising my hand to kiss it in an elaborate gesture. "I thought I might not return. Just hide here with you forever."

"You're joking, of course," I said. "You are my brave pilot, hero of the air."

"I would not joke about desertion," he said, his eyes deadly serious. "Do you know the phrase, 'LMF?'" he quizzed me, head down, continuing to walk beside me.

"No, help me out," I said, his seriousness setting off an alarm in my heart and head.

"Lacking in Moral Fiber," he said in a hushed voice, just loud enough to be heard in the cove. "They shoot you for that."

Chapter 11

I awoke with a jolt in the early dawn, disoriented by someone yelling for help. I sat up, reaching for the lamp pull. I heard a commotion in the hallway and then realized where I was. I was at home in my bedroom, the room at the front of the house. The speaker for my dad's office was in this room. A patient with an emergency must be on the steps of his office. Rising, I grabbed my chenille robe off the chair and my slippers from under the bed. The door opened a bit as I reached for the knob. My dad poked his head in and asked, "Millie, I may need you. Are you up?"

"Coming, Dad," I answered, almost bumping into him. He had pulled on slacks and a shirt, already covered with a white coat. Together we headed down the stairs, the others left sleeping. Crossing into the home office, I turned on the lights and surveyed the room for instruments we might need. All looked in order and ready to go. Dad had gone into the small waiting room to see who was at the door. I followed behind, and as he opened the door, we both saw two men, one propping the other up.

"Doctor Bo," the man said, "Please can you help us? My buddy here is bleeding."

"Come in. Come in," Dad urged, reaching to help support the wounded man. Together they moved him into the office and lifted him onto the surgical table.

The man moaned and seemed to pass out, quiet. I moved quickly to set up a tray for suturing wounds and assisted my dad while he pulled on rubber gloves. I watched as he did a cursory examination to assess the damages.

"Looks like several wounds on the face and head," he said to me, reaching for sterile cloths I had ready. He began to swab away the blood. "What happened?" he asked.

"Well, we was in a bar across on Jefferson, minding our own business, when these guys in uniform started minding ours. They started talking real loud about cowards who wouldn't join up and pointing at us."

"So you thought you'd shut them up with your fists?" Dad asked. "Millie, we need a lot of stitches here. I don't think anything's broken though."

"Nothing broken but a coupla beer bottles," the man said, trying to see his buddy over my dad's stooped head and shoulders.

"Sir," I interrupted, "if you would wait in the outer room, it would help us."

"Exactly," said my dad. "Millie, alcohol, please. I don't think I need to numb the area because this man is out cold as it is."

"Please," I repeated to the stranger. He slouched across the room in an unsteady gait, and I heard him collapse in a chair.

My dad leaned over and began stitching the head wound first. "I wonder what the soldiers look like," he mused. The patient moaned again, but showed little reaction to the needle puncturing his skin with black thread.

The man in the waiting room shouted back, "They beat on us and ran. I say they was the cowards. If that's being a soldier, you can have it."

"Moving down to the wound on his face, Millie," my dad said. "I've got all the glass shards out."

Just then Gary, now awake and to the rescue, poked his head in the doorway. "Bet you don't get paid for those stitches," he said, taking in the bloody scene.

"Neither Joe or me has any money, Doc," shouted the voice from the waiting room. "If you want money now, better stop them stitches right now. Just let him bleed."

"Don't worry," I called back to the man. "We can bill Joe."

Gary rolled his eyes, intent on watching the medical procedure for future reference. "Right, that'll happen," he said. "Dad's been charging nothing or accepting payments in chickens and eggs for years. These two obviously drank all their money."

"Nothing wrong with a good omelet, Gary, or Lill's baked chicken." Dad laughed, standing up, finished with his work.

"Millie, write out a bill for five dollars and put it in this man's pants pocket, please. Gary, sit with him until he's ready to walk. I'm going to make coffee," Dad said, giving up on more sleep. In a few hours it would be time for church.

"I already have the coffee brewing," called Aunt Lill from the kitchen. She, of course would be up, having seen the lights go on from her porch next door and not wanting to miss a minute of potential gossip for the monthly bridge club ladies. My mother slept on as usual.

I scribbled out a bill and deposited it in the grimy pocket, knowing full well that this particular five-dollar bill would never come back to this address, not even in a chicken's beak. I cleaned up the mess from the suturing and waited. The man in the waiting room had been quiet for a few minutes, possibly passed out, too.

"He's coming round," Gary said as Joe squirmed on the table, struggling to sit up.

"Let me up," he mumbled. "Where are those guys? I'll kill them."

"Easy," Gary urged. "You've been in a fight, and the doctor's sewn your head and face up." He backed up, fearing Joe might swing at him.

"How'd I get here? Where's Bob?" He swung his legs over the table edge and made a feeble attempt to stand. Staggering and almost falling, he leaned back against the table.

"Bob," he called out. "Are you there?"

Bob came stumbling into the room, lurching to the table. Gary stepped back, standing by me, and we watched as the two men grabbed each other in a drunken, messy hug.

"Owww," Joe yelled. "My head. Get me the hell out a here."

"Let's go," Bob said. "Lean on me, Joe. I won't let these assholes touch you again."

Gary couldn't get to the waiting room door fast enough to let them out. The "assholes" would have coffee and then be off to mass to pray for the likes of Joe and Bob soon.

We all met in the kitchen, and Aunt Lill poured us cups of strong coffee. We sat down around the Formica table, our coffee now accompanied with stale cookies from the bread box.

I sipped coffee, dunking my cookie in it. My dream came back to me. LMF. I turned those letters over in my mind. Where had I heard them before? I couldn't have made them up.

"Dad," I broached the subject, "have you heard of soldiers being labeled LMF?" He had been a surgeon in the Great War. He had never spoken of his year in France other than to say he had completed a course in orthopedic surgery back then. What horrors he must have seen as the wounded soldiers arrived at his field hospital. The amputations, the mustard gas, the infection.

"Lacking in Moral Fiber. That's a British term used to label servicemen we referred to as in shell shock in the last war or suffering from battle fatigue in this war. I saw many soldiers who were mentally incapable of further fighting. The top brass had no use for this weakness and called them cowards."

"Let's change the topic," Lill said, uneasy. "Did you manage to get the tickets for the *Fantasia* premiere at the Wilson Theater?"

"Yes," Dad said, "It's one of fourteen theaters across the country premiering that new Disney picture with Fantasound. It's the first time stereophonic sound is being used for motion pictures." He sipped his coffee as we all fell silent. Subject successfully changed.

"Dad, can I bring Sue?" Gary interrupted, dunking his stale cookie to make it edible.

"Sue?" said Aunt Lill, her ears pricking up for gossip as she leaned forward for more.

"A girl I met on the bus and talked into joining the USO," I said, throwing her some red meat for the bridge ladies.

"She's got her own car," Gary said, dunking another cookie. A car was a star quality for any woman in his eyes.

"She must be older," Aunt Lill mused, holding back on tsk-tsking at the thought of an age gap. Her eyes sent the repressed message though. "Who are her people?" she asked, meaning what ethnicity was her family.

"No idea," Gary said. "But can I bring her?" He leaned back in his chair, balancing it on two legs. He knew Aunt Lill hated this perch. She'd yelled at him for leaning back like that since he had first graduated from his high chair. Here he was almost a graduate of high school, still leaning back precariously. And I knew that yes, Sue was several years older than Gary, but I kept his secrets just as he kept mine. A most important conspiracy of silence of late.

"Sure, bring her," Dad agreed. "And you ask Edward, Millie. We'll make a night of it. There's supposed to be some good classical music in the movie. I've reserved a box for us."

"How elegant," Gary said to me. "You'll have to wear your new brooch."

"Brooch?" Aunt Lill asked, "What brooch?" Even she was dunking her cookie now.

"Oh," I said, "You know, the one you conspired with Edward over."

"Hope it doesn't turn your ball gown green," Gary said, rising from the table. "I can get a few more hours of shuteye," he continued as he walked over to the stairs.

"We'll get you up for church, Gary," Lill reminded

him, standing and picking up cups and plates.

Fantasia. We'd make a night of it. LMF would be forgotten for another magical night, a gift from Mr. Walt Disney.

****

The train pulled into the station, and James, having retrieved my luggage from storage, walked along the slowing train while I stood with the luggage.

The train, at a stop finally, puffed its last clouds of steam as we waited for the passengers to leave the cars. They bustled out, in various sizes and ages, half asleep from their long journey, some rubbing the cinders from their eyes, others yawning in the early evening sunset. Children with red eyes, clutching stuffed teddies to their chests, stumbling down the steps by themselves or dangled from an adult hand, just like Winnie-the-Poohs, were eventually lifted into arms so as not to be trampled by the impatient adults. At last came the troops, soldiers of varying services and ranks, spilling out onto the platform. They smiled as they spotted James, a mate in uniform, offering him the compartment they were vacating. "Privacy," one in blue winked, "for you and the lady."

"Millie," James said, "climb aboard, and I'll load your bags."

I hurried onto the train, and James followed, blocking further passengers by placing my bags on the seat next to me. He piled the other bags next to him across from me. "If anyone asks, we're newlyweds," he said adamantly. "Sergeant Owen and his Mrs."

"James." I shook my head at his choice of surname. Settling back into the leather seat, waiting the fifteen minutes we had before the train pulled out, I peered out

115

the window, saying a silent farewell to Cornwall and the family estate I had loved.

"So, my lovely wife, you will excuse me if I get my kip, righto?"

He was asleep in seconds. And I returned to my life story.

****

At 8:30 in the morning on the dot, we arrived at St. Francis Xavier Church for mass. As predicted, Stell reminded us that it was our family which had long ago donated the land for this Catholic church. Set along the river, it was a peaceful place on Sunday morning when no buses ran or cars bustled to work. All the shops along the road were closed as people walked to several churches of different denominations. This Sunday morning ritual always calmed my nerves. Today I would kneel and pray for all the men who were now in service of their countries around the world. I had graduated from the church high school three years ago in good stead and won a full scholarship to nursing school. I would include the hospital in my prayers, but not Miss Jackson. She didn't deserve prayers.

We walked solemnly down the aisle to our usual front row seats. The pew was always left open for us in deference to our ceding of the land to the church decades ago. My mother and father nodded to parishioners they had known for years as we neared our pew. My dad and Gary tipped their hats to some of the oldest old biddies in the congregation. We filed in, Aunt Lill and Stell first. Then Gary and me. And last Mom and Dad. We ladies all wore fashionable hats with veils and fur-trimmed boots, knowing the other parishioners always watched our wardrobes, especially the bridge club members.

Now the mass could begin. It was a mass conducted entirely in Latin with lots of incense and candles. The priest's back was to us as he, surrounded by altar boys, celebrated the service. After the opening rites, Father Champion moved to the lectern for his sermon. He was usually only semi-boring, so I semi-looked forward to hearing his message for today. At least it was in English.

"My fellow Catholic servants of God," he began.

Gary whispered, "Here it comes. Good thing I have mastered sleeping with my eyes open." I shushed him as he cowered from Aunt Lill's glare.

"Today," Father continued, "I want to thank and salute the women of this parish who have chosen to serve the country and its servicemen and women by joining the new organization established just this month by President Roosevelt. It is called the USO for short, which stands for United Service Organizations. Mary Ingraham has been charged with bringing our president's vision to life. Six organizations have combined in their efforts to fulfill FDR's mission of offering 'a home away from home' for servicemen. These organizations are the Salvation Army, the YMCA, the YWCA, the National Catholic Community Service, the National Travelers Aid Association, and the National Jewish Welfare Board. The USO will provide morale and recreation services to uniformed military personnel.

"As you may know, we currently have a squadron of RAF pilots at the Grosse Ile Naval Base. They are here under the direction of their squadron leader to oversee the construction going on there and to prepare for the arrival of RAF cadets this August for flight training. They have undertaken the supervision of the building of a new runway and barracks. The USO has been given the beautiful Olds summer home on the island, its mission to keep servicemen connected to family, home, and country. And so we thank you, young ladies, and welcome any other women who might join this very worthy organization. I have been over to the island and seen the lively dances and movies and tasted the food. The men thank me profusely for the hospitality. I tell them if it were our American servicemen over in the European Theater of Operations, I could only hope there would be someone who might lessen the loneliness and homesickness with a dance, a card game, or a cup of tea. One more thing. Ladies who have volunteered, I have your new USO identification cards. Please pick them up after mass."

He seemed to look straight at me as he turned and walked back to the altar, intoning Latin prayer. Aunt Lill leaned over past Stell and Gary, half rising from the pew, to pat me on the arm. Finally, she just stood up, turning to the parish and pointing at me, and mouthed the letters, "USO."

"Sit down," I hissed. "Just please sit down."

That afternoon we observed another family tradition, the Sunday roast dinner. I bustled in the kitchen with the ladies, all wearing aprons over our Sunday best. Gary and my dad sat in the sunroom reading the *Sunday Free Press*. My dad puffed on his Sunday cigar. The radio played a classical piece broadcast from New York on NBC. This peace was broken by the phone ringing in the hallway on the spinet desk.

"I'll get it," I called as I picked the receiver up. "Hello?"

"Edward, here. Is that you, Millie?"

"Why, yes," I replied somewhat startled as this was the first time he had called. "Are you all right?" I asked, sitting down at the desk.

"Righto," he said. "I'm at the beer store around the corner from you. I managed to hitchhike a ride from the base."

"Oh, you are. We're just preparing a roast dinner."

"I could murder a roast and a proper cup of tea," he said, sounding most desperate.

"Wait," I said, almost whispering. Putting my hand over the phone, I swiveled around in the chair and called to the ladies in the kitchen, "It's Edward. He's around the corner at the beer store. He says he'd give his eyeteeth for a roast dinner. Can I invite him?" Mumble. Mumble.

"Yes, you may invite him," Stell called, ever the grammarian.

"Thank you. Edward?" I asked, uncovering the phone in my hand.

"Right here," he answered.

"Come over," I said, "I can't wait to see you."

"Roger," he said and hung up.

Standing up from the desk, I turned and checked myself out in the mirror on the closet door. I'd have to do because he was already ringing the doorbell. I looked good for him, as good as the photo on my USO card. I was so proud of that card. I had showed it off to everyone after church with the same smile that shone back at me now from the mirror.

"For goodness' sake," Mother said, running to

open the door, tossing her apron at me, "he must have run all the way over."

Soon Edward was standing in the foyer, and my heart was in my mouth.

"Millie," my mother called to me, "come take care of your pilot." She hurried past me, grabbing up her apron I'd left on the desk. I crossed her path and greeted Edward with a big hug and quick kiss, always aware of Lill's possibly peering eyes.

"I know your family loves ice cream, so I brought some from the beer store," Edward said, handing me a paper sack.

Touched at his gesture, I took the small bag in one hand and his large hand in the other. "Follow me. Let's go see the aunt pile in the kitchen. I read that's what the Duke of Windsor calls Kensington Palace in London. The aunt pile."

He laughed and said, "I have to explain our connection to you eventually. Lead on, Millie, love."

Pushing the kitchen door open, we saw the three ladies in their Sunday best, scooping potatoes and stuffing into bowls, tossing salads, their hair curled by the oven heat, the windows fogged over. Two large chickens, baked to a crispy perfection, roosted on the table. I hoped the delicious aroma was sending Edward back to happy days at his estate.

"May I slice the capons for you?" Edward asked, picking up the carving knife and scraping it back and forth along the knife sharpener with the panache of a swashbuckler.

"You may," Stell said as all three ladies stepped back, giving wide berth to this stranger brandishing a now very sharp blade. "My husband usually does the deed, as he is a seasoned surgeon." Mom laughed, half-expecting a massacre ahead.

But no, Edward attacked the birds with skill and grace, and as a result we had a serving plate full of thin chicken slices with legs left intact edging the platter.

"Let me carry it to the table," I said, nodding for Edward to go ahead toward the other kitchen door. He swung it open, holding it for me as I walked the few steps to the large oak table, now covered with a French lace tablecloth. The best silver surrounded each place setting of Limoges china, hand painted in a delicate pattern of blue forget-me-nots. Fine crystal wine and water glasses stood sentry by each plate next to delicate cups and saucers. In the center of the table sat a set of silver candlesticks, their thin blue tapirs already lit. I set the platter of chicken at one end of the table.

"Gary, Dad," I called. They had not budged from the sunroom, too engrossed by the radio and newspapers. "Edward has joined us for dinner." I pointed Edward toward a seat next to mine on the side of the table in front of the glass French doors that led to the living room.

"Edward," Gary crossed the room and shook his hand, "good to see you again."

"Likewise, my son," echoed my dad, grabbing his hand. "We didn't hear you come in."

The three ladies formed a parade into the room from the kitchen, each carrying another dish. Their aprons were left behind, and they had obviously crammed together in front of the hall mirror, tucking errant wisps of hair behind their ears and freshening lipstick and repowdering noses.

Sitting down in our usual places, Grace having

been said, the dishes began to circle the table and soon our plates were full and glasses gave off the essence of a fine Bordeaux.

"I'm right chuffed to be here," Edward said, spooning potatoes and gravy into his mouth.

The meal progressed in a formal manner, each person attempting polite conversation.

"I saw the book *Mrs. Miniver* on the sideboard," Edward said, chewing his food, waiting for a response, eyeing the ladies.

"Yes," Stell, the librarian and book critic of the family, replied. "We've all read it."

"And?" Edward asked.

"We loved it," Lill said, wiping her mouth with her linen napkin, leaving a smear of pink lipstick on it. "It was such a lovely glimpse of England, and she was such a remarkable lady, careening from one incident to another, but always on top at the end."

"She seemed obsessed with what word the windshield wipers repeated over and over," Dad said.

We all turned to look at him, and Gary voiced what we were all thinking, "You read it, too?"

"We hear Greer Garson will play her in a picture next year." I changed the subject, seeking Edward's eyes, worrying this meal was becoming a crashing bore to him.

"I miss that England before the bombs fell, before the blackouts, before the children were evacuated," Edward said softly, his eyes on mine. "Before I left my home."

Dad rescued us all as he changed the subject. "Edward, we have tickets for the premiere of the Disney movie *Fantasia* at the Wilson Theater. We have a box reserved for the family and would love for you to join us."

"I suppose it is another grand theater like the Michigan?" Edward asked.

Here comes the Detroit history lesson. Lill began the story. "This theater is named after Matilda Dodge Wilson. She was the third wife and, later, the widow of John Dodge, the auto magnate."

"It seems the automobile rules everything here," Edward replied, reaching for another roll.

"But that will be changing," Gary explained. "FDR says we're to become the arsenal of democracy. No pleasure cars will be built, just planes and tanks."

Stell took up the tale. "She and her sister-in-law, married to Horace Dodge, were among the wealthiest women in America when they were both widowed within a year and sold the Dodge auto company. Matilda remarried and set out to build a performance theater to rival the theaters of Europe."

Jumping in, I added, "Wait'll you see this place. It's the bee's knees. So elegant and furnished with wood paneling and lit torchieres on the walls. Silk drapes and luxurious carpets that make you want to throw off your silver slippers and run your toes through the nap."

"That's all fine and good, but Edward, you might be more interested in the new Fantasound speakers," Gary said, pointing his fork at Edward to emphasize his musical knowledge.

"What's that?" Edward asked between the candles and across the table to Gary.

"It's been dubbed that especially for the movie, *Fantasia*, but it's a way of separating the sound so it comes at you from both sides."

"They'll also have a little show selling war bonds before the movie," Dad added.

"Thank you for that. We need your help," Edward said, his voice dropping. "Are you for America entering the war?"

"Not if it means Gary has to serve," my mother snapped, then grew quiet.

"That may happen without us entering the war, old girl," Gary teased. "Best way to get through med school would be to let the Army pay for it."

"Your father served in the Great War. That's enough for one family," Lill said emphatically. "Anyone for more wine?"

"Please pass it this way," Edward asked. "I lost a cousin in that war, the so-called 'war to end all wars.' "

"So sorry to hear that," I said, once again feeling the tug of sorrow bringing us down. I reached for Edward's hand and he looked over at me, his eyes welling up.

"Perhaps you've read his poetry. Wilfred Owen?" he said, recovering a bit.

Everyone around the table said no.

"He was a great officer and very fine poet. Killed days before the Armistice by a sniper in France. A tragic loss for English literature."

"And your family." I consoled Edward as best I could, surrounded as we were by prying eyes.

"I'll check at the library tomorrow," Stell offered.

"I suppose you've heard of President Roosevelt's fireside chats?" my dad asked.

"Yes," Edward replied, "You have Roosevelt; we have Churchill."

"His last chat, end of December, made it clear we would build ships, planes, munitions. Anything England needs. He named us the arsenal of democracy, as Gary said," Dad continued.

"But you won't send American forces," Edward interrupted, and silence ended the meal.

Dinner demolished to a platter of bones and empty bowls, I was surprised to hear my dad say, "I'm going up to the radio room. Edward and Millie, come on upstairs with me if you like."

Stell stood and started clearing the table. "We'll do the dishes and serve dessert later in the living room."

"Tea?" I asked.

"Please, later, with afters," Edward said, smiling at me.

Gary headed back into the sunroom and the papers. And we followed Dad through the French doors across the living room and up the stairs from the foyer. Dad, Edward, and then I arrived on the upstairs landing and stood awkwardly until Dad spoke up. "You two looked like you could use some time alone without your Aunt Lill. You know her parents lost five babies and just Lill and Stell survived. Stell is fine, but Lill? Why she survived I'll never know. Just pure stubbornness, I guess. Now go ahead into your bedroom, Millie. Have some private time with your pilot."

Edward laughed and shook Dad's hand. "Thank you, sir."

"Go on," he said, turning me around and pushing me toward my bedroom door. "And close the door behind you."

Edward didn't need a second invitation. Taking my hand, we entered the room and closed the door behind us. On the other side of the door, we heard my dad say loudly, "So, follow me, Edward, and I'll show you a state-of-the-art radio set-up. I can talk to hundreds of people all around the world."

"What a marvelous father you have," Edward said, plunking himself face down on the bed, his long legs dangling off the end.

Hesitating and embarrassed by my dad's generosity, I walked over to my desk and pretended to shuffle my vase full of pencils and stack the papers. I gazed out the window down to the sidewalk, empty on a Sunday afternoon. Then I was aware of Edward's arms around my waist. Reaching around, he took my hands, freeing them of their fake task. "Come lie down with me," he whispered in my ear. "Please."

Still holding my hands he sat on the edge of the bed, his eyes searching mine. He pulled me onto his lap and I panicked, trying to get away.

"Shh," he whispered, holding me down. "Trust me."

"Not in my bedroom. Not in my parents' house," I begged.

"Not even a snog?" he asked, nuzzling my neck as I turned back to him.

"A snog?"

"This," he murmured, crushing my lips with his, his tongue separating them, searching.

A groan rose up my throat to meet his tongue, and his hand moved to my breast. "Lie down beside me," he urged, lying back and moving me with him, then adjusting our bodies together on the bed. "You need a bigger bed," he laughed. "This is a child's bed."

"And I am a child?"

"Let's say inexperienced," he said, pulling himself up against the headstand, almost sitting. He moved my head against his chest and began to stroke my hair.

"Talk to me," I said, my voice muffled against his chest.

"About what?" he asked, with a little irritation in his voice. I knew a "chin wag" was the last thing on his mind this Sunday afternoon.

"Your war. You never talk about what you've done in the war. Where you've flown. What planes? If you've been in combat." I looked up to see storm clouds cross his face and darken his eyes.

"You expect me to lie here with a beautiful lady beside me and whinge about the war?" he grumbled.

"No, I'm asking you to share your life with me," I asked, not daring to look up at him.

He sat up, pushing me aside, almost roughly, and said, "I need to use the loo."

I lay back on the bed and pointed him to the door. "You know where it is." He closed the door behind him, leaving me a mess. What was he hiding?

I was tempted to lock the door and hide. What was I doing with this stranger? I shivered as the *Gaslight* images—the brooch, the watch, the old lamps—swamped my brain, carrying with them that walk in the cove in that other dream and the letters LMF. I heard voices through the door. He must be talking to my dad. Maybe they could talk to each other honestly, two war veterans of different generations. My dad never talked of his service either.

Lying back, I held my tears. I would not let him see me cry. Nor would I make love to a man who wouldn't talk to me. I'd had enough of British vocabulary lessons and foxtrots. The door opened then, and a sheepish Edward asked quietly, "May I join you?"

"Of course," I answered, scooting over toward the wall.

"Not too far away, please," he said, pulling me back toward him, tucking his arm around my shoulders. "I'm sorry," he said, turning me toward him. I felt like a doll manipulated this way and that. He lifted my chin and I expected a kiss, but no, he seemed dead serious. "I shall tell you three things about my war. Three things only."

"Thank you," I offered, not sure of what to say.

"My darling," he said, staring straight into my eyes. We were so close together yet so far apart, the war between us. "Number one, I was at Dunkirk. You know Dunkirk?"

"Of course, we followed it in the papers, on the radio. Such bravery when all those private boats set sail to rescue thousands of stranded troops in France."

"Number two, I flew and fought in the Battle of Britain. You must know that one, too. The war bit when Churchill thanked the 'few who were owed so much.' I'm one of the few."

His eyes darkened even more as he continued. Would I regret making him confess his war like this? He tightened his arm around me as if holding on for courage. I had removed the offending nail polish, not that he seemed to notice.

"Number three, I promise myself," he said, "that I shall never make friends again among the pilots for the remainder of this bloody war. I have lost so many. I have seen so many drown at Dunkirk. I have seen so many planes crash into the sea, downed by the enemy.

Today I learned a good mate of mine flew his plane into a mountain in Wales in the fog. His wife is pregnant with their first child. I have written to her and shall visit her when I return to England. But no more friends. No more mates. I had to get away from the base today when I heard he was dead, so I came here." He was crying softly now, the tears wetting my face, too, mixing with my own. I lay there, not knowing what to say or do. I turned away from him, lying on my own, but he pulled me against him, his arm reaching across my chest. We lay there together and fell asleep.

****

I dreamed, of course, exhausted by his three hushed confessions, and from the night's duty in my dad's office. I again walked the beach at the cove, again alone. Edward, gone to war again. Who knew where? My bare toes squished in the sand, waiting for the tide to curl round them, then drown them. It was a hot summer's day. The bees buzzed in the garden above, the roses in glorious blooms of brilliant rubies and oranges. I must pick a basketful for luncheon. I watched the sea as I paced the cove; a sailboat bobbed not far out, anchored while vacationers swam, cooling off in the bay. I sat down in a lawn chair, tossing my straw hat on the sand, baring my shoulders to the sun as I dropped my towel.

I noticed something in the water ahead and sat up straight. Puzzled, I stood up, walking to the edge of the lapping waves. Was I seeing things? Was someone there? Someone in distress? Drowning? Tossing my sunglasses on the sand, I ran into the water and swam in long, sure strokes toward whatever was out there. About twenty-five feet out from shore, I extended my arm for another stroke, but hit something in the water. Treading with one hand, I surveyed the water around me, splashing the surface with the other hand, hoping to make contact. I jerked back, as my hand touched the soggy, yet firm object. It was the torso of a body, face down. I screamed as I recognized the RAF blue of a uniform jacket. In a panic, I tried to turn the torso face up so I could see if it was Edward. Struggling in the deep water, I finally wrenched the body over and stared into what was left of its face. It was not Edward.

There was no time for relief though, as a baby's cry rose above the waves, slapping in my ears. Letting the body go, I swam toward the raucous screams. There, swaddled in a parachute, lay a sweet little baby boy, naked, its face contorted in cries.

"Hush, little one," I soothed, pulling the tiny boy from the tangled silk. I left the torso behind, turning on my back and doing a gentle backstroke back to shore, the baby resting on my chest. As we approached the shore, I lay back, floating, allowing the waves to gently take us home.

****

I came awake, gradually aware that Edward was leaning over me, shaking my shoulder. "Your dad just said your mum had pie and tea ready downstairs," he said, brushing an errant curl from my forehead, then kissing my brow.

"Did he come in?" I asked, worried, sitting up against the headboard.

"No, just talked through the door," he said, swinging his legs over the bed to the floor.

"I could murder a cuppa," he sighed.

Somehow I knew we would never talk about "his

war" again. How ridiculous that people talked about having a good or bad war as if it were a hobby. What could be good about any war? For anyone? The quiet whispers were talk of shell shock or battle fatigue, and now LMF. And here sat this man on my bed in such pain for "his war." My dream had sparked an idea. My mother's weekly bridge club could take up the cause of Edward's friend's widow. I would provide a layette of baby clothes. They could spend this meeting, and then the next week at their homes embroidering the bibs and blankets, "bits and bobs" as Edward would say, for the baby. It could be in England within weeks.

"You're quiet," Edward said, as I sat up. He put his arm around me and cupped my chin. "Have I scared you? I didn't mean to pull a wobbly."

I laughed at his British slang. It felt good to laugh. I was his morale at this point. This I knew. Father Champion would urge me to show compassion for my pilot.

"Come on, old chap," I said standing up, feeling under the bed for my shoes. "Time to murder a cuppa and tuck into apple pie. With ice cream, of course."

Reaching for my hand, he said, "Ah, you've removed the varnish. Thank you."

****

Back at the hospital the next morning, I started my last rotation before graduation, on the cardiac unit. Carol had already finished this three-month duty. So she sent me off with this advice: "Bring something to read or take up knitting. It's the most boring three months at the hospital." Boring, because the beds were chocked full of patients who had mostly just had heart attacks. The remedy was two weeks of bed rest. No surgery. No physical therapy. Just long naps.

With this advice in mind, I arrived on the ward with a book and knitting needles. That little babe in England would soon have a yellow cardigan with darling little duckies on its collar and green pearl buttons trailing down to welcome a British spring. "Jumpers," Edward said they called these sweaters over there.

And the day progressed as predicted. I had little to do but change bedding, offer beverages and snacks, serve lunch trays, and knit. And look forward to the *Fantasia* premiere the next Friday.

****

I had been reliving my story as the train chugged its way toward my liberation from England, mostly looking out the streaked window, almost numb with punch, fish pie, sponge cake, and tea. I turned back to James, another stranger sent from who-knows-where to get me to my next port of call.

My story was interrupted by a rap on the carriage door. James rose, ready to fend off passengers with our marriage fib. Instead a lady dressed in a Salvation Army uniform appeared as he opened the wooden door. She held a tray in her hands with tea cups and biscuits. "Complimentary, for all the servicemen," she said, offering us the tray.

"My wife is American, a member of the USO," James half-lied, taking the tray from the lady.

"Yes," I abetted his crime, "I've served many a cup of tea." I blushed from chin to brow, holding out my hand to her.

"We all must do our bit." She laughed, backing into the aisle. "God bless."

Chapter 12

We arrived at the premiere at the gorgeous Wilson Theater in style in my dad's Cadillac. Aunt Lill and Stell followed behind us in Gary's less-than-luxurious Ford sedan. My dad always parked very near the theater entrance as he told the attendants he was a doctor and needed easy access for emergencies. Gary, not so fortunate, dropped off the pile of aunts and his date, the elderly Sue, at the curb, and then went off to find the nearest parking spot. It was an extravagance to be driving in the first place and not riding on our usual bus or streetcar transport. Edward, of course, was accustomed to the "tube" as he called it, the underground that stretched far across London. Now, many of the stations had been hijacked as bomb shelters during the Blitz, the relentless German bombing of London night after night. Edward as a teen, he had told me, had started out "his war" with his older brother, Gerald, in the fire service, a valiant effort to stanch the fires and rescue victims of the German bombs in Plymouth. His teenage years were in stark contrast to my brother Gary's years, larking about with his pals, driving the aunts to bridge clubs, helping in his dad's office with medical emergencies. Emergencies that included brawls with beer bottles, not wounds from bombs.

The Detroit skies were lit up that night, not by

German bombs but by huge searchlights, their long beams sweeping through the night. We walked along the sidewalk, Mom and Dad ahead of us. We were two couples of two different wars, seeking respite from the conflict. We joined the line waiting to be allowed into the theater. Neon lights blurted out "Wilson Theater" above us. Elegant ladies in their gowns and gentlemen in their dress suits stood around us, laughing in anticipation of a Disney animated picture.

Edward turned to me and pulled off my glove. "Let's see. No nail varnish." His finger traced my lips. "Pale lippy."

"Do I pass inspection?" I asked, laughing at his control.

"Yes, ma'am," he replied, snapping to attention. "And I?"

"Devastatingly handsome," I rated him. "Who doesn't love a man in a uniform?"

The doors opened and in we went, Gary, Sue and the aunts now aboard. We were all decked out in our finest. I had chosen a rose wool crepe dress, with an empress-style bodice, that stretched to the floor. As a tip of the hat to Edward, I had pinned his brooch to my shoulder. I wore my velvet cape as tonight there could be no borrowing my mother's fur, as she wore it across her shoulders. The aunts had insisted on wearing hats. Aunt Lill did love a hat, as she had been a milliner in her youth, working for J. L. Hudson's. "Hats make the outfit," she was always saying. Tonight Lill and Stell's dresses in blue and peach were crowned with matching look-alike velvet concoctions with veils half-covering their eyes. The hats, trimmed with black beading, were stunning creations. "After all," Lill had said this afternoon, "Edward is used to London high society, and we must not let him down with our appearance."

I had laughed at that, thinking back to the man crying on my shoulder the weekend before. He was just trying to survive his war. That's all.

We entered the crowded lobby, oohing and aahing at the European décor; the wood paneling, silk drapes, and fancy torchieres glowing from the walls. "To the left, sir." The usher pointed when Dad showed him our tickets. Up the marble stairs we traipsed like ducks in a row in a glittering parade. Crossing the floor, we approached a row of gilded doors leading to separate boxes. Ours was in the center. Edward did the honors, holding the door as we all filed in two by two. The box was also beautifully appointed, gold paint laid against the paneling. Velvet Victorian chairs in two rows faced the stage. Lill again took charge of the seating. "Edward and Millie in the front row with your parents," she directed at me. "The rest of us, second row," she added.

"Yes, ma'am," Edward agreed, taking her gloved hand and bowing with a kiss.

I giggled at Lill's deep blush as she fell for this pilot all over again. Recovering, she clucked at us all to sit down. And so we did, marveling at the scene around and below us as we watched all the others streaming in for this important night.

Edward helped me take off my cape and place it on the back of my chair. I turned toward him and he laughed, his fingers touching my *Gone with the Wind* brooch lovingly purchased with a Lux Flake box tab for me.

Lill leaned over from the back row, having spotted

the pin, too. "I helped with that, you know." She reached to touch it. "Not too gauche for the price. A finely made chapeau would set it off perfectly."

I just shook my head, thankful Edward was willing to put up with my family's antics. "Sit down, old girl," Gary said, pulling her down next to him. "The show's about to start."

On the stage, men in uniform were gathering. The red velvet curtains opened as the huge organ ascended from the orchestra pit. Each theater in Detroit prided itself on its own classically trained organist. The Wilson was no exception, and tonight it showed off the organist's musical skills by having him play a rousing chorus of Irving Berlin's "God Bless America," a song made famous by Kate Smith. As the organ rose to stage level, the audience stood as one, cheering. Edward took my hand, and I could see tears forming in his eyes. Once settled back in our seats, city officials joined the servicemen, and young boy scouts carried a large banner across the stage, urging us all to buy war bonds. Then the Color Guard marched down the center aisle to the stage to present the flags as the organist played. Once on the stage, they stood at attention, proudly bearing the flags of the United States, the state of Michigan, and Detroit. The audience rose and cheered. Edward and my dad saluted the flags. I stood, moved to my soul, fighting back tears.

Mayor Jeffries of Detroit stepped forward, urging us to sit. Waiting for order to return, he stood quietly. I felt Edward trembling against me as we sat back down. Leaning against him, I sent courage to him with a nod and smile. The chattering stopped, and the mayor spoke. "Tonight we urge you to buy war bonds.

England has fought bravely for two years now. She needs our help. As some of you know, we have recently welcomed a squadron of Royal Air Force airmen to the Grosse Ile Naval Base. They are here as an advance troop to oversee construction on the base before hundreds of RAF cadets will arrive starting in August to begin flight training far away from the curse of Nazi bombs." Peering out into the audience, his hand shielding his eyes, he asked, "Are we so fortunate as to have any of those airmen with us tonight?"

"Edward," I whispered, squeezing his hand.

"Up here," Gary shouted, standing to point out Edward.

"And over here," another voice came from the main floor to the right.

"Please stand, so we can properly salute you," the mayor asked.

"Edward, stand," Lill hissed, her hand on his shoulder. Mom and Dad clapped. We all stood with him as he rose, saluting. The servicemen on stage rose, too, returning his salute, then turning to their left and saluting the other RAF pilot. I was never so proud of anyone or anything in my life. I knew then I would follow Edward anywhere.

Fantasia was rather anti-climactic after that, but we loved it with its prancing elephants and confounded Mickey Mouse as the sorcerer. It was a brilliant triumph, blending animation and classical music. Edward was enthusiastic, loving it all as he conducted the music quietly, his long hands in the air before him. He had told me how his chums at his last base often produced their own sound and light shows. Playing classical records on the gramophones and linking them to loudspeakers, they accompanied the music with floodlight beams streaking across the sky. His mum, as he called her, had made sure he had a sound education in classical music at an early age. He played the piano, but not well, he told me, too frustrated that his small hands could not attack the great classics. I smiled, imagining the airmen, lying on the grass at an airfield watching the skies as the lights flashed, crisscrossing overhead in accompaniment of the chords of Beethoven and Bach.

Afterwards we made our way back down the stairs to the lobby only to be engulfed by a tidal wave of people, all wanting to shake hands with Edward, to welcome him to the country and wish him and England well. My dad and Gary guarded Edward on either side as we ladies stepped back, taking it all in. I had no doubt at that point that America would eventually join this war and Gary would join the fight. Edward looked at me, and I could read panic in his eyes; perspiration beads were forming on his forehead. He needed to escape. I turned and saw an usher coming toward us. "Please," I called to him, "can you help us clear the way to leave?"

"Ladies and gentleman, please clear the way for the airman to leave with his family." The usher pushed into the melee and forged a path for Edward, my dad on one arm, Gary on his other side. We passed by the war bond booth where a long line waited to give money.

"Look at the queue," Edward said, nodding to his left. "You do care about the old sod."

"We'll pay by mail," Dad said, waving one of the brochures he'd picked up from a table in the second floor lounge. "Just get to the cars," he urged.

Once home and out of the confusion, we sat in the living room and reviewed the evening. Gary had dropped Sue off at her house, trying to kiss her goodnight under Lill's surveillance. He reported back to us, cracking us up with his imitation of Aunt Lill. "I could see her from the porch, desperately scraping the window and finally risking rolling the window down to get a good look. Stell wiggled her face into the window, too, almost knocking off her chapeau."

"Oh, Gareth, that's just not true," Lill argued, her stern glare telling Gary to hush.

"Now Edward was certainly the man of the hour tonight," Stell said, taking the spotlight off Gary as he went to the kitchen in search of a cola.

Edward, embarrassed by the continued attention, looking down at his feet, said quietly, "I can only hope they made a big profit in aid of the war effort tonight. If it meant being crushed by the crowd, it's worth it."

"It was a beautiful evening," Lill said, alone on the couch as Mom and Stell prepared tea and pie in the kitchen.

"The music was wonderful," Dad began the critique.

"The animation of *The Nutcracker* was so funny," Gary said. "Any chance I can get a cola instead of tea?" he yelled out to the kitchen. "Sorry, old chap," he nodded at Edward. "I much prefer a pop to your tea. The Boston Tea Party still sticks in my craw."

"Don't drink tea on my account," Edward replied. He was seated in the comfy armchair, and I sat at his feet. "You trounced us, and we lost the colonies forever."

"What parts did you like best?" I asked Edward,

looking up at him, changing the subject.

He absentmindedly stroked my brooch with his fingers, looking around him, and added, "I quite fancied *The Rites of Spring*. I have come to love Stokowski's music of late."

"Good choice," Dad agreed, "but I couldn't get over that dumb Mickey Mouse in his wizardry robe trying to stop the brooms in *The Sorcerer's Apprentice*."

Mom and Stell entered the room. Stell carrying the tea pot, Lill with custody of the pie, cherry this time.

"Let me help," Edward said, jumping up and helping them set the trays, cups, and pie on the small table in front of the couch.

"Gary, your cola," Lill said, holding the bottle out to him.

The ladies bustled around the table, cutting pie and pouring cups of tea. Edward delivered the snack to all of us, one by one, and then sat back down in his chair behind me.

"Dad," I asked, "could you play the last song in the movie for us, *Ave Maria*?"

"Please do," Edward seconded my request.

"Yes," he agreed, "and perhaps a bit of Beethoven's *Pastoral Symphony*."

Edward nodded his head. "They did an excellent job of that, too. I'd like to see that picture again."

Dad stood, finished his tea in one gulp, and put his half-finished pie on the table. Reaching into the small cupboard under the piano, he pulled out his violin, stood, and tucked it under his chin. Leaning over the piano keyboard, he played one note, and then plucked the same note on his violin. "In tune," he smiled, turning around to us.

"Now don't cry, Aunt Lill," Gary said, chuckling. "And please, no singing 'Jerusalem,' if you please. I just can't handle you hitting those high notes tonight."

"Hush," Mom chided Gary, her eyes on Dad as he slowly drew his bow across his instrument, playing the first notes of Shubert's beautiful hymn to the Blessed Virgin Mary. My father had played it at my grandfather Albert's funeral. I was only a toddler then, but I would never forget hearing him play that day while tears slid down his cheeks.

I settled back against Edward's legs, my eyes closed as I soaked in the beauty of this evening. Who knew what was to come? But just for this night we were all here in this room, the fire warming us, the pie and tea filling our stomachs, Dad's music touching our hearts. Looking up at Edward, I saw the tears brim over and stream down his face as he mouthed the words, "I love you" to me, cupping my chin in his large hands.

****

The next morning everyone was up early as it was Bridge Club Saturday. Edward had ended up spending the night, sleeping on the living room couch. This morning Lill had washed out his shirt, socks, and unmentionables and ironed his shirt to military perfection while he luxuriated in the bath. I was banished to the kitchen lest I steal a look at him, charged with making a Waldorf salad for the ladies. Gary's task was to set up the four card tables in the living room while Dad went over to the Blossom Restaurant on Jefferson to pick up the chicken pot pies for the luncheon. Lill was mixing a punch at the sideboard, having hung up Edward's pristine shirt in the office. Bartholomew was hiding under the dining room table, aware that his peaceful Saturday was about to be assaulted by the chit-chat of a dozen of Ecorse's crème de la crème.

"Aunt Lill," Gary asked, sniffing the punch, "what can I do now?"

"You can take Edward's clothes up to him in the bath."

"Of course," he replied. "God forbid Millie gets a load of his ass as he rises from the bubbles."

"Gary, enough," Stell called from the kitchen, noticing the blush burning my face as I earnestly stirred the mayonnaise into the grapes and apples and then sprinkled the walnuts on top. "That boy knows no shame," she whispered as she rinsed off the good silverware in the sink.

The doorbell rang as Gary disappeared up the stairs with Edward's clothes. "That must be Mrs. Snopes," Mom said, "always early." She opened the front door to an indeed early Mrs. Snopes.

"I hope I'm not too early," she said, almost knocking Mom over as she entered the living room, avoiding the tables and chairs to claim the couch. She was wearing a purple tweed suit and around her neck a mink wrap of fine quality. "I'll just sit here until the others arrive. How many are we today?"

"I think twelve or so," Mom said, excusing herself to run upstairs and check her own make-up now that the bathroom was free.

"Lillian," Mrs. Snopes called, spotting her through the French doors, tending to the punch, "is Millie still keeping company with that handsome pilot you told me all about?"

In the kitchen I mouthed an exaggerated *Good God* to Stell and pointed to the back door as an escape route.

Then I heard Edward's British charm assail Mrs. Snopes with "Would that be me? I am a pilot, after all."

I hurried out to the living room to see him shaking hands with Mrs. Snopes. "And what a lovely chapeau," he continued. "You know we are rationed in England. No new hats or frocks for our ladies."

She patted her hat and adjusted her mink, which had begun a slow slide down her left shoulder. "So pleased to meet you."

"Your pet seems to be escaping from around your neck. Otherwise you look smashing, quite charming."

With that, flustered, she stood and made a beeline for the punchbowl and Lill in the dining room, pulling her mink back around her neck.

Edward and I just watched her flight, shaking with laughter. This was going to be a most memorable bridge club. Gary joined us, having heard the exchange. "This will be the duel of the minks," he warned. "Beady black eyes at dawn. Snopes has got booze on her breath."

The ladies arrived in twos and threes until the living room was indeed filled with minks and hats and veils. Mrs. Labadie. Mrs. Bourassa. Mrs. Maybauer. Mrs. Mourguet. Mrs. Meurisse. Twelve in all. The ladies were a fashion parade, oblivious to the war in Europe for the most part. Just here to play cards and gossip. Their hair coifed and nails manicured at J. L. Hudson's. Their clothes purchased at Kerns or Crowley's and tailored by neighborhood French seamstresses. Theirs a world free of rationing. They wore their silk stockings and leather pumps and carried their bags to restaurants, theaters, and nightclubs. No blackout curtains. No evacuees. No rationing coupons. Their sons were leaving home for the university, not war.

And so it was up to me to break the illusion that protected them. After they were all there and had eaten their pot pies and Waldorf salad, sipping their punch and gossiping, I presented my Edward to them. He had been hiding out with Gary in the office, waiting for his cue. Mrs. Snopes nodded in her best I-told-you-so look to the ladies at her table as I began, "Ladies, we have a special guest today. May I introduce you to Flight Sergeant Edward Owen, who is stationed on Grosse Ile as part of an advance group for the RAF cadets who will arrive in August?"

"Ladies," Edward spoke up, gesturing for the excited jabber to tone down. "I am pleased to meet you all. I quite fancy your hats. Not for myself, of course."

I bravely waded in. "As you might know, I have been working with the USO, the new service organization started in Ecorse by Father Champion. Our headquarters is in the Olds summer house on the island. That's where I first met Edward."

My dad stepped forward at that point, making a trio with Edward and myself in the foyer just abutting the living room. "We would like to ask your help today for a very special cause," Dad said.

"A good friend of Edward's was killed in combat a few weeks back," I said, reaching over to the desk for a box. Edward took hold of it as I continued, "He leaves behind a wife who is expecting their first child."

Mom stood up at her table and added, "I went to Hudson's this week and bought a lovely layette for the little one."

Stell stood and finished the request. "Today instead of our usual bridge, we would like to ask you to form a little sewing bee and embroider the clothing for the wee one."

"I have knitted this tiny yellow cardigan." I took the sweater from the box and held it up to mumbles of "how cute" and "how adorable."

Edward said, "Please, my friend would be so honored..." I reached for his hand as his words petered out.

Gary came though the French doors with several baskets of threads and needles and placed one at each table.

"And will Dr. Beaubien be sewing, too?" asked Mrs. Meurisse, one of our French tailors. "I hear he has a beautiful stitch."

And so the afternoon passed with good talk and good will and Edward taking turns sitting at each table having a good chin wag, as he said, with the fine ladies of Ecorse. On Monday the lovingly embroidered layette made its way across the ocean. Perhaps, we hoped, this gesture would bring a smile to a young widow.

Chapter 13

Edward said he had a surprise for me. He told me only to wear my prettiest gown and be ready at the dorm at seven-thirty. The girls—and Jack, of course—all cluttered my room as I tried to gather my wits about me. Jack was under wraps as he was not allowed above the ground floor, but he was not about to miss this. Gary was once again enlisted to drive his old Ford up to the dorm and deposit in the lobby an armful of clothes. Mom had volunteered a shopping trip to the department store of my choice to select a new gown, but I refused in a gesture to wartime frugality. The more I talked to Edward, the more I felt our entry into the war was inevitable no matter what the pacifists said. So Gary brought my black satin gown, with the v-cut bodice and off-the-shoulder lace straps and very full skirt. Pearl drop earrings would be my only jewelry. My hair would be pulled back and curled around one of those fashionable but horribly named rats. Pale lippy and no varnish, of course.

"What if he asks you to marry him?" Jack said, sitting on my bed, spooning ice cream from a bowl.

"We've only known each other a month," I said. "For God's sake." But I half-hoped this was Edward's mission for the special evening.

"Jack," Carol said, "go wait in the hall while she gets her clothes on."

"But what if someone sees me?" he asked, fearing a resounding thud on Alexandrine Boulevard as Miss Jackson hurled him out of the dorm.

"Go next door to my room," Allison said, pointing to the left. "Quickly." She pushed him out the door.

I don't know how I managed in the crowded room, but I somehow got dressed, and Jack was invited back. The chattering stopped as everyone surrounded me.

"Wow," he said, looking me up and down. "I'd propose."

The hall phone rang. Everyone giggled and jumped around like frogs hopping from lily pad to lily pad, everyone knowing what that ringing phone meant. HE was in the lobby.

Deep breath and down the stairs we went, spilling through the door into the lobby, then we all were quiet, trying to reach for some decorum. Jack had taken a different route to arrive on the other side of the lobby, pretending he had just risen from the dungeon.

Miss Jackson hushed us. "Girls. Girls. Edward is in the lounge."

I had put my velvet cape on upstairs so she wouldn't see my décolletage and faint. "He's called for a taxi."

"A taxi?" Jack asked, crossing the lobby to us. "I told you."

We walked, or rather I walked, followed by a gaggle of giggling girls, into the lobby. Edward stood, and his smile welcomed me before his words as he crossed over to us. "Ladies," he said, "how kind of you to escort Millie. I'm sure she's safer than a warship on the high seas."

The girls ate that compliment up, blushing and

laughing.

"Get your own man," I chided them, taking Edward's arm.

"Don't wait up," Edward said. "Everything will be tickety-boo."

His slang sent them over the moon, and we heard their voices all the way out to the taxi at the curb. The taxi driver was waiting beside the car, and he opened the door for me. Edward helped me bundle my dress into the back seat and then hopped in beside me. When the driver slid in behind the wheel, Edward leaned over and said, "Vanity Ballroom, please."

"Oh, Edward, who's playing there tonight?" I asked, so excited at the night ahead.

"I just dropped another couple off there," the driver said. "Tommy Dorsey's there with Frank Sinatra."

"Excited?" Edward asked. "Nothing but the best for my girl from the USO," he said, pulling me close to him in the cool February night.

My anticipation grew on the trip down Jefferson to Newport Street. I'd never been to the ballroom, but I had heard of its marvelous décor. I oohed when I caught sight of the huge neon sign on the side of the building that glowed "Vanity Ballroom, Dancing."

Edward hugged me closer and stole a quick kiss as the driver gave us a history of the ballroom, explaining its art deco design and huge Aztec sculpture. "You can't beat all that for thirty-five cents each." He ended his mental tour as we drove up to the curb. "You're on the second floor," he said. "I bet there are a thousand people there tonight."

Out of the car and across the sidewalk to the front doors and then up the stairs. What a sight. What a night.

Edward took my cape and checked it while I waited by the grand doors, fascinated by the colors of the swirling gowns as the couples danced by. I couldn't see the orchestra from here, but the music throbbed to the greens and blues and reds of the dresses. As Edward took my arm and we entered the ballroom, Frank Sinatra, backed by the Pied Pipers, sang the first notes of his hit, "I'll Never Smile Again."

"Dance with me?"

"But…" I started our routine.

"You haven't danced with me," he interrupted. "Just shut up and dance."

It was like jump roping to get into the swirl of dancers, but we did it, and with my head on his shoulder, we crossed the floor in a smooth foxtrot, my black shirt billowing behind. Edward sang in my ear, "I'll never smile again. What good would it do?" Heaven lay ahead, and the Pied Pipers were leading us there.

We danced several times and then broke away to be alone, as alone as you can be while surrounded by a cast of hundreds of couples. Making our way to the large bar, Edward ordered two colas for us. They did not serve liquor, only soft drinks.

"Over there." Edward pointed, carrying our drinks. "Follow me." He had spotted two empty chairs by a window. As the orchestra was on a break, we could actually hear each other talk above the couples. It was as if everyone had decided to speak low.

"This is all so beautiful, Edward. I will always remember this night."

He sipped his drink and turned to me. "I quite fancy ballrooms and orchestras and lovely ladies."

"In England?" I asked, excited to hear more details of my mysterious Edward's life.

"My brother Gerald and I grew up attending dancing lessons and then graduating to formal dances. I was a chubby, awkward toddler, bowing and tripping on my own feet, not knowing quite what to make of my shy little dancing partners at first. Then the old charm took over, and I became one's perfect partner."

"At Sand Castles?"

"Yes. Look you may as well know. I have a confession to make."

My heart sank as I waited, anticipating the worst. Edward turned toward me and looked straight into my eyes with the truth.

"I am called Edward after the Duke of Windsor. He is my godfather."

My eyes must have popped wide, because Edward laughed and tipped my cola against his in a toast. "Yes, Edward Albert Christian George Andrew Patrick David, mostly known as David before becoming Edward the Eighth, King and Emperor, is my godfather."

"I don't know what to say. Lill is my godmother. She can make a most lovely chapeau." I was stunned by this revelation, awestruck by the royal connection. And wondering what Edward could possibly see in this Ecorse-bred nursing student.

He laughed. "The duke is a blighter as far as I'm concerned. Abdicating, and now sitting the war out in the Bahamas. He's doing everything he can to keep your country out of the war. My dear godfather and Wallis, his American duchess, are apparently great chums with Hitler."

I could see he was upset; his contempt so bitter it again revealed a dark hopelessness in my pilot. This would not do. Putting my drink down on a small marble table, I said, "Frank's back from his break. Let's dance." I took his trembling hand, and this time it was I who led us to the dance floor.

****

The train had stopped, and we were fidgeting, waiting for the trip to begin again. "I need more tea. Where is that trolley lady when one needs her?"

"If this train doesn't move soon, I'll miss my boat."

"That would be a ship, I presume," James corrected me.

The train jerked and then threw me forward. James reached out and caught me before I could tumble into the aisle between us. Outside the window, steam puffed down the sides of the car while a whistle blew in sharp blasts up ahead. We were off, as I took the first steps on the first leg of my journey home.

****

Back at the dorm and stripped of my finery, I fended off a battery of questions from the girls. We were all curled up together, legs and arms spilling over from the two single beds in our dorm room. Having raided the kitchen for bowls of ice cream, we relaxed and I played coy, fending off their most intimate inquiries. I did, however tell them that Edward had confided the name of his regal godfather, the Duke of Windsor. Jack was not a part of this late night gossip. He'd have to be caught up in the morning at breakfast. If we made it to breakfast, that is.

Finally alone with just Carol, I waited for the onslaught. And yes, she did attack.

"How can you fall for that garbage? The Duke of Windsor his godfather? Oh, did I mention that King George is my uncle? Don't be such a twit." She pulled the sheet back and crawled into her bed.

"Carol, not tonight. Please, I've had a wonderful evening, and I don't want it ruined." I sat at the desk and ran a comb through my hair, my finery exchanged for cotton pajamas.

"Fine, but no need to close your eyes to sleep. They're already shut tight." With that last cutting remark, I crossed to my bed and, tucking myself in, faced the wall and away from any further criticism.

****

Yes, I dreamed. I dreamed we were in the Bahamas at a grand ball. The Duke and Duchess led the way to the dance floor. A string trio played a familiar tune, but I could not put my finger on its title. After a few spins around the floor, the Duke gestured for us to join them. Edward and I waltzed beside them, our feet barely touching the ground at this honor. ˈ

A tap on my shoulder, and I was looking into the blue eyes of the Duke as he cut in on Edward.

"I say," the Duke said in his clipped accent, "our Edward has chosen a frightfully beautiful lady for his love. We are honored to dance with her."

I remained silent, afraid of breaching protocol. How does one speak to a king, Edward the Abdicator so to speak? I looked behind him, hoping Edward would rescue me, but he was nowhere to be seen.

"Looking for Edward?" the Duke asked. "You shan't find him. He has asked the Duchess and oneself to care for you, and we shall." As if on cue, the Duchess came from out of nowhere, grasped my hand

with her spindly fingers, and we were a trio in an awkward dance.

The music continued, and I recognized it as the manic waltz from the movie Gaslight. We spun in circles, and dizzy, I struggled to keep my balance as nausea gripped me. I was in their control. They were holding me up, my only support, as the music pulsed through my body and mind. I stared into the Duke's face as it melted, cracks flaying his pale skin. His blond hair parted and flaked from his head, sprinkling like Lux flakes on his shoulders. A dark carpet of short hair now lay in a bad cut above his ears. His eyes grew black, and as his fair skin oozed away, a ruddy complexion took over, and a mustache took up duty under his nose. The Duchess threw back her head and roared at this new husband, her thin face contorted in raucous laughter. I knew this new face. Edward had abandoned me to Adolf Hitler. The trio struck up the first notes of "I'll Never Smile Again" as the musicians rose to their feet, leading us behind them out into the courtyard like pipers in the field. The music slowed to a dirge as we heard the bombers fly overhead. "Our song, please," the Duchess requested of the trio. The mood lifted as the pipers broke into a spirited version of an old hit tune, and she sang along, the Duke joining in as they left me and danced a wild Charleston. Together they sang, "I've danced with a man, who's danced with a girl who's danced with the Prince of Wales." I knew that sheet music was in our piano bench in Ecorse. Collapsing in a heap on the porch settee, they sang again at the top of their lungs, "Glory, Glory Alleluia! I'm the luckiest of females. For I've danced with a man, who's danced with a girl…"

Chapter 14

I assumed my position at the nursing station on the cardiac unit. The charge nurse was making rounds with the specialist. I busied myself with charts, not daring to pull out my knitting before the doctor left the unit. I was working on a scarf, a blue one. Meg had arranged a group of girls as a knitting circle to fashion scarves for the airmen. This would be my first offering. I hadn't seen much of Meg lately. She had found herself an airman, Mac. As I said, he was tall, dark, and handsome, of course, and also from a fine family like my Edward. We didn't see much of Mac and Meg though, as apparently Edward and Mac did not get along. Edward gave me no reasons for the rift, dismissing Mac as an upper-class twit, lacking a chin, as a result of years of inbreeding. Rather harsh, I thought. I gave myself a mental note to have lunch with Meg. Maybe we two could sort out this feud between our men.

Doctor Baker walked by the desk, nodded at me, and left the unit. Doctors had very little to do with students. How Sue Barton, my fictional heroine, had ever had a chance with her Dr. Bill was beyond me. Those worn books, riveting tales of the redheaded nurse, were still on my bookshelf at home. I reached into my tote bag and pulled out my needles and yarn. Another day of knitting lay ahead, only interrupted by lunch trays and sponge baths. The quiet of needed rest descended around me. Knit one. Purl two. After last night's drama, I hoped I would not fall asleep, my head slumping into my lap, my needles poking my thighs.

The day crawled by as my RAF blue scarf grew, contrasting with the pink of my uniform skirt as it inched its way toward the tile floor. Some fortunate airman would never feel the Michigan cold again. Four o'clock and I was out the door and across the boulevard and into the lobby. No Edward on the steps today. Time for a nap before dinner maybe, I thought as Miss Jackson stood at her desk, flagging me down.

"Millie!" She waved, something in her hand. "I just took a message from your pilot. 'Meet me at Cliff's Bells at seven.' She read her note aloud so everyone in the lobby could hear. "Rather curt, don't you think? And commanding?"

Exasperated at her nosiness, I grabbed the paper from her hand and, silent, walked away, hoping she'd get my message.

"Millie," she called after me, "no need for you to be rude, too."

Once in my room, I stripped off my uniform, tossing it toward the laundry bag. Carol was on afternoons on the maternity unit, so I didn't have to worry about tangling with her again. Checking my watch, I gauged I had time for a nap and shower before dinner here in the dorm. I needed a chin wag with Jack to cheer me up. I hated to agree with Miss Jackson, but Edward's terse invitation was bothering me, too. What was up? Down to only my underwear, I crawled under the covers and soon drifted off to a dreamless sleep.

Dinner was sausage and beans, not one of the

hospital's best gourmet meals. I passed it by, making myself a salad and pouring a cup of coffee. I had begun to drink both my coffee and tea "white" as Edward called it. Carrying my tray, I saw Jack over a few tables. He was alone, so we could talk. He really had become my best friend here at the hospital. My only confidant.

"Sit down, girl," he said as I pulled the chair out across from him. "Another exhausting day with the cardiacs?"

"You bet." I laughed. "That scarf gets longer and longer. I'll finish it tomorrow."

"I see you wisely eschewed the beans and sausage. Good choice." Jack was munching on a sausage as we squared off opposite each other.

"Jack," I started with my latest worry, "when I got back to the dorm, Miss Jackson was waiting with a message from Edward to meet him at Cliff's Bells tonight."

"You mean the Duke of Windsor's godson, don't you?"

I sighed. "You heard."

"Girl from the USO, it's the talk of the hospital."

I could imagine, cleaners squeezing dirty water from their mops, stopping for a good "Did you hear?" with the aides delivering trays. I could just see students, their eyes wide, their starch chafing, pursing their lips in imitation of the Duke and Duchess. And Miss Jackson and the other instructors... And the doctors...

"Not you, too, Jack. Please." I pinched my arm as I was feeling faint, my heart too fast at the thought of the gossip machine pumping its news through the corridors.

"So what do you think he wants?" Jack said,

pushing his sausage around his plate, eyes down.

"I have no idea," I said, wishing Jack would look at me. He was being evasive when I needed advice.

"My advice," he said, looking directly at me. "Take a taxi and be careful. You've only known him a month. One month, Millie. That's four weeks. That's thirty days. Not even that in February."

With that, he abruptly picked up his tray, food half-eaten, and walked away, turning his back on me.

Tears came to my eyes at this rebuff by a friend. I pecked at my salad, alone, and finishing, stowed my tray. Stiffening my back and resolve, I walked over to the desk phone and dialed for a taxi.

Fifteen minutes later I was on my way to Cliff's Bells. The same chatty driver who had taken us to the Vanity Ball ferried the taxi again.

"Where's your pilot?" he asked, opening the door for me.

"Waiting for me at Cliff's Bells on Park Street," I said, hopping into the back seat. "I'll get that," I said, reaching for the door as he walked back around the cab to the front seat.

"I love Cliff's Bells," he said enthusiastically. "Best jazz club in Detroit. I heard the Duke there."

"The Duke?" I asked, sinking into the leather seat, cold against my legs.

"You know, Duke Ellington. No cooler cat than him."

Of course, that Duke. Not Edward's Duke of Windsor.

I shivered at the mention of a duke, any duke. We drove the short drive in silence. He kept looking back at me in the mirror. He must have been thinking that this lady in his taxi was not the same woman he'd driven to the ballroom with her airman a night ago. This one was solemn, preoccupied.

The sun had set in the winter sky as the taxi pulled up to the curb. I could just make out Edward waiting for me just inside the entryway. He hurried out to the taxi, opening the back door for me.

Rolling down his window, the driver said, "Take care of your lady. She seems a little down. Maybe the jazz will pick up her spirits."

Edward slipped the driver a few dollars as I stepped out of the car.

"What's your name, mate?" Edward asked the driver in a gesture of friendship.

"Jim," he answered, offering his hand through the window.

"Thank you, Jim, for ferrying my lady safely across the city," Edward said, handing him more money. "Could you pick her up later, about ten? This should cover it."

"You can count on me," he promised, revving the engine and charging off into the night.

We walked into the club together. Edward had saved a booth for us away from the stage where a sexy lady was singing a cool jazz tune. "Over here." He pointed, reaching to help me out of my coat.

We sat near each other in the booth. Edward signaled to a waiter, and I ordered my usual, a Tom Collins. Edward ordered whiskey, neat. There was a basket of nibbles on the table.

I reached for it and dug into it, nervous. I had no idea why we were here in this secluded booth. It must be something big. And it was. Our drinks arrived;

Edward lit a cigarette, and leaned forward, seemingly engaged in the jazz. I knew otherwise. I sipped my drink and waited.

The singer finished, and the lights came up a bit, revealing the Aztec deco.

"This city loves Aztec art deco," Edward mused, tipping the last of his whiskey down his throat. "When a good friend of mine was killed in a bombing raid, a gunner in the rear of the plane, and the plane returned to the base, the squadron had to hose what was left of him out of the plane." He was blurring his sentences together in a fog of painful memories. "All I could do after was go into town to the local pub and drink this," he said, lifting his glass and gesturing for another to the waiter. "Whiskey makes me forget. I'm sorry; did you want another Tom Collins? Whatever that is?"

"No, I'm fine for now." Waiting, I was still waiting for the truth of the evening. His mood was dire. Hopeless.

The waiter brought the second drink to the table, and Edward told him to keep them coming. "I suppose you're wondering what this emergency meeting is in aid of," Edward said, turning toward me. The coldness in his eyes chilled me. This was another new Edward.

"I am curious," I said tentatively, meeting his eyes straight on.

"Have your friends at the dorm all warned you off me?"

"I won't lie. Yes, they have."

"And well they should. After all, what do you really know about me? I'm just a bugger in blue who wants to get in your pants. That must be what they say."

"Oh, Edward, no one has been that crude," I said,

tears welling up and overflowing down my cheeks.

"That's why I love the very bones of you, Millie. You believe in me. God knows why."

He gulped the whiskey down and swiveled toward me, his arm reaching round my shoulders. Pulling a kerchief from his pocket, he dabbed at my soggy face. "My squadron is moving on to Pensacola, Florida where we will oversee the restoration of the base there. The plan is that RAF cadets will train a month at Grosse Ile, and if they survive that, they will move on to advanced training in Florida. Everything cock-a-hoop."

"Oh, no." That was all I could manage. Our month was over. Our four weeks. Our twenty-eight days.

"Come with me to Florida." He spoke in a rush, the alcohol emboldening his tongue, his gaze locked in mine.

Stunned at the request, I took a drink, concentrating on the cool liquor as it anesthetized my brain, numbing my senses.

"Please." He cupped my chin, his plea touching my heart, but also confusing me.

"And do what?" I mumbled, against the hand gripping my face.

"I'm asking you to marry me, you little fool." He released me, leaning back, picking up his drink again. Waiting.

I had to laugh at his cleverness, invoking Max de Winter's proposal in *Rebecca*. He must have practiced. He smiled at my recognition of his ploy.

I would play along. "I love you most dreadfully," I quoted, carrying the fictional proposal on.

"Is that a yes?" he asked, swigging his drink down

and now gripping both my arms.

As if on cue, the lady, back from her break began to sing, "I got it bad…" Edward kissed me, crushed me against him, and on fire with our "dreadful love," we both were oblivious to the warning in the next line in the song, "and that ain't good."

****

Jim, as promised, returned me to the dorm before curfew. He chatted away on the ride. I paid no attention, lost in thought, reviewing the plans Edward had laid out. Jim was to play a part in our escape. Edward had boarded a bus on Woodward to get back to the base. There would be no more time off before the squadron left for Florida by plane.

Back at the dorm, I found Jack in the lounge, not so subtly waiting. He was seated at the grand piano, casually plunking out a few feeble chords. I signed in and walked over to him. "Taking up a concert career?" I asked.

"Not with these paws," he said, holding up his dry hands. All students had dry hands, victims of the constant scrubbing to keep them sterile. "So?"

"Let's sit down over here," I said, knowing I had to confide in Jack, for he would play an important part in the plan Edward had laid out over several whiskeys, neat.

"You were one night off in your prediction of a proposal," I said, smiling bravely at Jack.

"I knew it," Jack almost shouted.

"Shh!" I begged. "You'll wake the sleeping giant."

"That old battleaxe," Jack hissed, lowering his voice. "Spill it, girl. All the gory details."

I told Jack everything, even about our new friend

and co-conspirator-to-be, Jim. Edward was flying with his squadron at the end of the week. I was to follow by train, leaving from the Detroit depot. Edward had bought my ticket, so that was all set. He had booked a room for me at a boarding house in Pensacola where I would stay. It was near a Catholic church where we could be married. When he was sent back to England, I would follow by ship.

"That boy has thought of everything." Jack sighed. "And even before he proposed."

"Pretty sure of himself," I said, hugging Jack. I was so glad he was not giving me a hard time over these hurried plans.

The problem would be breaking the news to my parents and Miss Jackson. I knew they would be furious. Unhappy, to say the least, that I was walking away from my family, my education, and my country in a time of war. I could hear Lill screeching about submarines trolling the Atlantic with torpedoes now. The fact that I would one day be Her Ladyship Mildred, Mistress of Sand Castles Hall, would carry no weight at all.

Jack pulled away from my hug, stared me down, and said, "People are going to hate you for this decision, lady."

"I can't face them," I said. "Will you help me?"

"Don't expect me to tell anyone anything. Not my job," he stated emphatically, starting to rise.

"Sit back down," I said, tugging at his scrubs. "I wouldn't expect you to do that."

The lobby was empty now, lights dimmed, as I explained his role. "All you have to do is leave a letter from me on Miss Jackson's desk at exactly the time and day I tell you. I'm going to tell Gary what's happening and ask him to give a letter to my parents."

"That I can do," Jack said, relieved. "As long as no one sees me. I can wear surgical gloves so no one can dust for prints." He turned his eyes away, but not before I could see tears forming.

"You idiot," I said, hugging him again. "I'm going to miss you so."

"You'll be rich. After the war, you could send me a ticket for passage on a liner to visit you." He rolled his eyes at me, mocking my soon-to-be aristocratic status.

"That's a promise." I watched as Jack rose and crossed the lounge, his limp somehow more pronounced, as if this task I had assigned him weighed on his whole body as well as his mind.

The timing would be important. Miss Jackson could not open her letter before my parents read their letter or she would undoubtedly pick up the telephone and call my dad. I did not want them to learn that way. Tomorrow I would call Gary and arrange to meet him, maybe at Hudson's for a final chicken pot pie.

****

Monday evening I sat across from Gary in the restaurant at Hudson's. I had finished the blue scarf on duty today, tying up ends. A light February snow fell outside the department store as window dressers changed the mannequins from winter wools to spring dresses, the hems up this year to save cloth as a wartime measure. The Motion Picture Awards were on the radio tonight. Edward's purloined proposal seemed to me an omen that *Rebecca* would capture the statue for Best Picture.

"How's Edward?" Gary asked, slicing into his pot

pie. "Word is the squadron is pulling out soon. Destination unknown."

"Destination known to me," I repeated, savoring the rich chicken gravy.

"What do you mean?" Gary looked alarmed as though he expected bad news, his dark eyes searching mine.

"Our destinations are one and the same," I said, putting down my fork, ready to tell the truth. The restaurant buzzed with ladies in their hats, some with children, well-behaved in order to earn their ice cream clown desserts, another specialty of the house. "I'm going with Edward to Florida. Pensacola, to be exact."

"You can't. This will kill Mom and Dad." He put down his fork, too, his pie half-eaten, the gravy congealing on the Limoges china. He was ready for battle.

"You can't change my mind," I said, prepared to stand my ground.

He looked at me, tearing up. "Please, Mumu, don't throw it all away."

"I'm not throwing anything away. I'm just taking a new path." My voice had a certain desperation to it. I so needed Gary to understand and accept this decision.

"You've known this man for one month. Four weeks. Thirty days." He had begun his objections. I did not correct the thirty days to twenty-eight. That would not serve my cause. Why was everyone insistent on giving me a math lesson on months of the year?

"My mind is made up. Edward is flying with his squadron. He has bought me a ticket for the train to Pensacola from Detroit." I countered with my best argument.

"He thinks of everything, doesn't he? And what about marriage? I bet he hasn't thought about that." He was angry and protective now.

"Please, lower your voice," I urged. "You're wrong. He has proposed."

"What, no ring?" Gary asked, reaching for my left hand across the table. "I thought he'd go for the thirty-five-cent ring that matches your cheap brooch. The Lux Flake special."

"How can you be so cruel?" I said, tears beginning to slide down my cheeks. "I thought you liked him."

Chastened, he pulled his hand back from mine, reached into his jacket pocket, and took a handkerchief, and slowly stroked the tears away from my face.

"Don't cry, Mumu. Don't cry," he soothed me, his voice in a rhythmic lullaby. "How can I help? What can I do? Besides punch Edward in the face?"

"He hasn't had time to buy me a ring. Instead he's given me this," I said, reaching into my pocketbook. I opened a small satiny pouch and dumped a compact out onto the table between us.

Gary picked it up and said, "Not just any compact."

No, it wasn't. It was an RAF silver compact with its wings and logo on it. *Per ardua ad astra.* "Through adversity to the stars," I translated for Gary. "Edward and I will get there, but not without struggle."

Gary smiled a tentative smile, giving me some hope that we could reach the stars.

We finished our plans, but not our meals. Gary had calmed down and agreed to leave the letter for my parents early on the table in the radio room where my dad checked in with all his buddies on the air every morning. My dad would see it well before Jack left the letter on Miss Jackson's desk Saturday afternoon. I was not scheduled for hospital shifts that weekend, and they would hardly be pressed to replace me on the cardiac unit Monday as my scarf was finished. By the time the letters were read and the hysteria rampant, I would be well on my way to Pensacola.

Gary and I walked from the restaurant and waited by the row of elevators, knowing this would be the last time we'd see each other for maybe a long time.

"May I pick you up and drive you to the station Saturday, sis?"

"Thank you, but Edward has taken care of that, too."

"Edward again," he said, tearing up once more.

The elevator door opened, and a uniformed lady slid the gate open with her white-gloved hands. "Going down," she said. We stepped into the elevator with a push of customers, clinging together, backed against the wall. "Going down," she repeated, poking her head out the door, checking for more customers, and then repeating one last time, "Going down."

"I hope not," Gary said, his eyes on his feet. "I sure hope not."

We walked out onto Woodward together. A brisk wind blew up the sidewalk from the river, jostling shoppers and challenging hats. Gary had parked the sedan in a spot right in front of the department store. I hugged my coat around me and followed him to his car. This was going to be our last goodbye for a while. I knew this.

"Sis," he tried once more, his hands on my shoulders, "are you sure?"

"Yes," I said, my voice as firm as I could make it

with a quivering lip.

The crowds pushed by us, oblivious to the drama playing out by the old black Ford. Gary let go of me; head down, he began to kick at the front tire. "I'd better take care of this old jalopy," he said, "with plants making ships and planes, there'll be no more cars built for a long time."

"Gary," I said, taking his gloved hand in mine. "I'll be okay, I promise." One last hug and I turned away, the trolley stop my destination.

"Wait, sis," he called after me.

Turning back to him, I stiffened, waiting for his last plea. "What?"

"The letter for Mom and Dad. How will I get it?"

"Oh, I'm such a ninny. Almost forgot." I opened my pocketbook and pulled out the infamous letter. "Here."

"You're not a ninny," he said. "You're my brave Mumu."

"You'll make me cry again," I warned, taking his hand. "Goodbye for now."

Clutching my letter, he walked around the car and opened the door. "Don't miss your trolley," he shouted above the wind, and then disappeared into his jalopy.

****

The week passed in a slow dirge on the cardiac ward. We lost a patient whose heart was too far gone for the rest and relaxation cure. Other than that, I mostly knit all week. I was determined to knit a special farewell scarf for Jack as a thank you for his complicity with my elopement, as I had begun to think of it. My green knits and purls would brace Jack against the March winds while I lazed on a Pensacola beach with

167

Edward. The scandal would be reviewed by the bridge club in minute detail. Mrs. Snopes would be in her element, flapping her mink stole, patting her best hat, her lips prattling a mile a minute. My mother would be absent from that gathering, feigning illness, as the crème de la crème of Ecorse castigated her errant daughter. Lill and Stell would be shuttered in their house, ruing the day they invited that pilot into their home. My father would go about his work at the hospital and his office, refusing to engage in conversations about his AWOL daughter. Gary would disappear with Andy, having delivered my missive and then denying any knowledge of its contents. And Bartholomew would nap on my bed, a little gray furball able to stretch out at last, but unable to find my face to touch with his paws.

Friday night Jack and I sat in the lounge together for the last time. I made an elaborate presentation of the green scarf. As expected, he tried one more time to talk me out of tomorrow's train ride. I handed his letter over to him, reviewing the instructions one last time. Then I was off to pack, with a hug. Carol was working an afternoon shift, so I had time to pack and make the room look as normal as possible. I was leaving some items on my dresser to throw her off. My textbooks would remain on my desk. No need for them on the beach. I had planned it all very carefully. I had seen Jim's taxi out front of the dorm Wednesday and asked him to pick me up at six in the morning for the train station.

The next morning I fumbled around in the dark, showered, and dressed in the bathroom. Carol slept through it all. Heading down the stairs, I stopped at my mailbox one last time. A note was there from Gary. Four words: *Rebecca* Best Picture. Gary. I smiled, realizing I had completely forgotten the Motion Picture Awards. Tears welled in my eyes at this last gesture by my brother. I would miss them all. I stiffened my back and my resolve and tiptoed across the lobby to the big front door. I stopped and turned back for one last look around my school. My heart was breaking for the past, but bursting for my future. Opening the door, I could see Jim outside his taxi, already out of the door, running up the steps to grab my suitcase. I had packed light, assuming I could replenish my wardrobe once in Cornwall in the appropriate style for the wife of the heir to Sand Castles.

"Millie, let me take that," Jim said, keeping his voice low in the cold morning.

"Thank you, Jim," I said, handing over the case. My mind was wavering, but my heart was steady as Jim opened the door for me and I crawled in. Storing the case in the trunk, he closed it with a slam, and I looked around to see if anyone had heard.

"Okay, we're off," he said, pushing into his seat behind the wheel.

I didn't look back as we headed to Woodward Avenue. Jim made small talk, but I took very little of it in. I was already on that train, Florida-bound.

It was a short ride to the station in the early morning, not many people on the streets yet. Jim pulled the taxi up to the curb. I'd been here before, but the beauty of this station and the anticipation of my journey sent chills down my spine. Stepping out from the car, I looked up to the winter sky and said a quick prayer for a safe trip.

Jim collected my suitcase from the trunk and carried it over to me as I stood by the car door. "You all right?" he asked. "You look kinda pale."

"I'm fine. Here, Jim." I paid him the fare and added a generous tip in payment for his part in my elopement.

"Godspeed," he whispered, taking the money, pushing it into his pocket, and reaching out to hug me.

"Goodbye," I said softly and turned before the tears came as I entered the imposing building, leaving Detroit and the hospital far behind me. In my heart I knew what I was doing, the choices I had made. But Jack and Gary's warnings chipped away at my resolve. *Edward, I need you.*

Chapter 15

The station was not as crowded as I had seen it before, so I had a clear passage over to the huge departure board. Checking my ticket, I scanned the long list of trains and found mine. It was not far from where I stood, so I could take my time, weighed down by my suitcase. Platform 5. Platform 5. Platform 5 became my mantra as I walked along, making believe I was the bravest person in the world, at least in this station. Platform 5. There it was. Turning left, I walked along the platform. A conductor spotted me, and taking my suitcase, asked for my ticket.

"Let's see, not first class, so let's get you on the right car," he said, eyeing me. A woman traveling alone was not a common sight for him.

"Thank you," I said as he escorted me to a waiting car.

"Should be plenty of room. Let me help you on," he said, taking my hand and starting me up the steps. He followed behind, and I realized he would be helping me stow my suitcase.

"Here," I said, pointing to an empty seat nearby.

"Very well," he said, allowing me to sit as he lifted the suitcase to the rack above the seat. "Have a good trip."

"Thank you." Then he was gone. And I was alone. It would be a two-day trip. I was not in a sleeper car.

Edward's ticket had not been that generous. I had told no one that, fearing more rebuke and accusation. Why couldn't that rich aristocrat buy you a sleeper ticket? Would he have had to sell a peacock or pawn a family heirloom to let me have a peaceful night? I assured myself that I would be perfectly fine all night sitting by this window, watching for my new life, saying goodbye to my old.

The train pulled out of the station right on time. I wedged my handbag between the wall and myself as my dad had told me to do on my first train ride all the way to California five years ago. "In case you fall asleep," he had said, "it'll be safe." I watched out the window as Detroit faded away. No tears. I imagined my dad reading my letter. He would cry, I knew, but then brace himself to tell the old gals. Gary would urge them to let me go. There should be no heroic Florida chase to bring me home. It wouldn't work, he'd tell them. Miss Jackson would read her letter and explode like a zeppelin across the lobby.

****

As the train chugged south, I drifted off and dreamed. The train was pulling into the Frisco Station in Pensacola. I immediately fell in love with the mission style of the building that greeted us. Passengers on the car began to pat at their hair, arrange their hats, and smooth their wrinkled clothes. They stood, reaching above for their suitcases, slinging northern winter coats over their arms.

As I reached up for my suitcase, a gentleman across the aisle stepped over and said, "Let me help."

"Thank you," I said, standing in the aisle watching him retrieve my only belongings in the world.

"No problem," he said. "Are you a military bride?"

Blushing, I answered, "Almost a bride, my fiancé is an RAF pilot stationed here."

"Good luck," he said, moving forward to exit the train.

I followed behind him, knowing he would help me with my suitcase again. And he did.

I stood alone on the platform. The train was late arriving, but Edward would have gotten an update on the arrival time, I was sure. Walking along the platform, I saw a canteen set up by the Salvation Army and walked toward their smiling faces.

"I'm waiting for my fiancé to meet me," I said. "He's an RAF pilot stationed in Pensacola. Have you seen anyone like that?"

"Lots of servicemen have passed by us," a female member said, "He'll be by shortly, I'm sure."

"Have a donut and coffee while you wait," another lady said, pointing to the table of goodies.

I was hungry, so I took their offerings and was struggling toward a nearby bench when the lady stepped around the table and reached for my suitcase. "Let me get that for you."

"Thank you so much," I said, following behind her blue uniform.

Sitting down, I sipped my coffee and ate the donut, grateful for their hospitality. It was growing dark now. I sat, waiting and waiting. I watched the Florida world go by and realized I had no way of contacting Edward. When the Salvation Army closed up shop for the day, I was alone on the platform, as the last train had arrived for the day.

The hours passed. Chilly, I wrapped my coat around me. Edward, where were you? The night passed on and on as my joints stiffened, and my eyes reddened with tears. I watched as the Salvation Army canteen reopened for breakfast. More donuts and coffee.

"You're still here?" the lady asked, bending over me with coffee and a chocolate donut. "Do you have a way of contacting your young man?"

"Not really," I said, tears welling up in my eyes. "I must look a fright," I continued. "When he finally gets here, he won't even recognize me."

"You know, a lot of these airmen are just big kids. They break rules like smoking around the planes and then get put on restriction," the lady said, sitting down on the bench beside me.

"Yes, you're probably right," I agreed. "He's been a bad boy. That's all."

****

I jerked awake when the train stopped. We were at another station in another town, in another state further south, one of so many that I had lost count. They all blurred together. I could feel the temperature rising. No need for a coat now. The train left this station as I looked across the aisle at the man from my dream and shuddered. I felt like Bella as Paul gaslighted her. Panic rose in my throat. I felt trapped on this endless train ride. I let the slow rhythm of the train wheels turning and turning calm me. Deep breaths, eyes closed. I would be fine. I would be just fine. I summoned courage and opened my eyes to look out the train window at the blurring vista. On track once more, I reached into my handbag and pulled out the only book I had brought with me, Housman's poems, Edward's favorites, and began to read as the train chugged along. I remembered I had a roll of Life Savers in my purse and reached for it, knowing Edward would be there when the train pulled into Pensacola. My British life saver.

And indeed he was. I stepped off the train, and before I could get my suitcase hauled to the platform, Edward crushed me in a big hug. Releasing me reluctantly, he yanked my suitcase down the two steps and pulled me aside to let the other passengers disembark.

"Edward," I said, "I had a dream that you deserted me at this station. I waited all night. You never came."

"Ninny, I'm here in the flesh. Pinch me." I did. He yowled as I grabbed his arm and dug my nails into his jacket.

We walked together, almost skipping past the Salvation Army canteen to the end of the platform and into the station. I was giddy with sleepiness and hunger, but very much alive with love. I told him all about the long trip, saying that the night had not been too bad although my neck was stiff, and I had really slept very little. He promised to give me a backrub later.

"Now you know what it felt like to sleep in Jack's bathtub," he laughed, rubbing his arm. "I've been filling out the forms so we can get married," he said. "I have a jeep outside to take you to the boarding house."

I said nothing, just smiled up at Edward as we hurried along in the heat. I would not ask why he had the jeep or how. "Have you ever been placed on restriction?" I asked, remembering my dream.

"Of course," he said, "I have a nasty habit of smoking around the planes. It's been explained to me that I am putting everyone in peril by sneaking a fag around the 'Yellow Perils' we train on. Why do you ask?"

"That dream I had," I said, "when you deserted me."

Out in the sun, the palm trees swayed like feathers in the sea breezes. I felt like I had entered Eden with my Edward and told him so.

"But Eden didn't work out too well for Adam, did it? I prefer Florida." He laughed.

Over in the parking lot the jeep awaited us. Edward lifted my suitcase into the back, deposited me in the front seat, and revved the engine. The top was down, and we flew through the city down Garden Street passing by St. Stephen's Church.

"That's where we're getting married," Edward pointed.

I turned to get a better view, looking back on the church as Edward sped by down the road. I caught a glimpse of a statue of the Catholic martyr Saint Stephen in front of the red brick church and a big sign welcoming all. It was a quick blur to be investigated tomorrow.

A few more blocks and we turned south toward the Gulf of Mexico. The immediate coolness bathed my face in a layer of moist air as we bumped along the rough road. I loved sitting beside Edward in our chariot. I could ask for nothing more but this wave of love and contentment.

"Here we are," Edward said. "Your castle awaits, my lady."

Before me I saw the most charming cottage, the blue water of the Gulf enticing me behind it. Its weathered white walls were peppered with RAF blue shutters. Palm trees offered shade as we parked the borrowed jeep and crossed the way to the large screened-in porch.

Inside, a huge white ceiling fan moved the hot air lazily as we stepped into a parlor outfitted in white wicker furniture with cushions embroidered with bluebells. Framed photos of military men and their girls smiled from the walls. An RAF serviceman and his lady sat on one couch. Not wishing to intrude, I hurried by, but stopped when I heard my name called. Puzzled at who might know me on this beachfront, in this cottage, I turned back.

"Millie?"

"Meg?" I said, crossing the lounge. She grabbed me in a big hug. My Detroit Meg boasted a rich tan which had conquered her February pallor. I saw Mac behind her.

"Edward told me you were coming. He said I'd be a surprise for you," Meg said, standing back with Mac to get a good look at me. "I can't believe you're really here."

"I can't believe it either," I said, stepping back, admiring Meg's casual blue shorts and tropical flowered blouse. "And Mac? How long have you been here?"

Edward was at the desk, signing me in and chatting to a lady who actually had the authoritative look of a Miss Jackson about her. Her hair was brown, in a loose bob, flecked with gray, glasses hung from a thin chain on her chest. She smiled up at Edward. Okay, not so much like Miss Jackson.

"Two weeks, I've been here two weeks." Meg said.

"You'll love it here. The beach is dreamy." Mac remained silent beside her as Meg chattered away.

"Do you have a room here?" I asked Meg as Edward came into the lounge, smug that he'd pulled off this surprise greeting.

"Yes, she does," Edward said. "Meg recommended it for you. And here is your key," he added, dropping it into my outstretched hand.

"Ladies," Mac said, "go check into Millie's room, and we'll wait here for you." Tall, dark, and handsome had spoken.

Up the stairs we went to Room Four. It was small, but actually not overly hot, with walls brightened by pink roses and white forget-me-nots. Green chintz curtains buffeted by the Gulf breezes hung in the window which offered an inviting Gulf view. After two days on a train, all I wanted to do was sleep. Kicking my shoes off, I flopped across the soft mattress and fresh sheets.

"Oh, no, you don't," Meg said, turning on the fan on the wicker table by the window. "We're having a meal together to celebrate our liberation."

"At least let me wash the grime from my face and freshen up a bit," I begged Meg as she pulled me up from the bed. "Two days on a train have done me in."

"And how do you think I got here? Carrier pigeon? Bathroom's down the hall." She pointed. "I'll give you ten minutes. There are towels and soap, so don't bother to unpack yet."

"But this suit is so hot," I argued, feeling the sweat drip down my back. "You have shorts on, and look at me," I said, feeling like seaweed washed up on the beach.

"Okay, go freshen up, and I'll find you something," She pushed me out the door with a firm shove.

I walked the few steps down the hall to the bathroom. It was not too bad. Very clean with a little ledge under the mirror over the sink where I could put my ablution bits and bobs, as Edward would say. Thank goodness I was used to this shared set-up from the dorm. And there was a large clawfoot bathtub that I really had to fight the urge to jump into. Looking into the mirror, I surveyed the damage as I ran the water. Cornwall would be worth this sacrifice, I mouthed, my lips dry from the steam train. Splashing water on my face, I laughed, reaching for the cake of soap.

We enjoyed a dinner of tacos and sangria at a little Spanish restaurant not far away. I wore a light cotton plaid dress, much cooler than my suit. I made a mental note to ask Edward if he approved of shorts and then shop tomorrow. Meg and I caught up on our successful escapes from our families. I was amazed she'd been here two weeks, and the bridge club had not discovered her absence. Her mother must have been "too ill" to attend the last gatherings.

As the warm night wore on, we made plans. We would marry. We would move to England. We would have a good war and babies. It seemed so simple. The men remained mostly silent as we conjured up our futures with them, chattering away a mile a minute.

Back at the boarding house, we took to separate couches to say goodnight as men were only allowed upstairs when both man and woman were man and wife. The wicker groaned under our weight, its couch legs uneven on the floor, shifting us back and forth. Edward begged to go outside for a knee-trembler, but I thought it would be rude to Meg and Mac, who seemed content on their couch. I reminded him of his promise for a backrub, so he had to be content with that. At eleven, Mary, our keeper, flashed the lights in the lounge, officially telling us to knock our sweet nothings off. I had not left the dorm after all. A Miss Jackson still ruled. Edward had to get the jeep back to the base anyway, so Meg and I waved them off into the night and then made a beeline for the stairs. Meg was in Room Two, one door away from me. With a goodnight hug, I opened the door to my honeymoon suite. Only problem, the groom was missing, but not for long.

I dropped into my lumpy bed a few minutes later, too tired to try out the bathtub, no matter how tempting. That luxurious soak would have to wait. I was asleep at once. No dreams. Just a deep, deep sleep.

****

I was on my own the next morning, after that promised lush soak in the tub, to explore the city. With a few tips from Mary, and sunglasses in place, floppy hat on my head, I greeted the warm Pensacola air. I decided to double back down the road and visit St. Stephen's Church. It was a ten-minute walk in the sun, a warm contrast to my leap across to the hospital in February Detroit. As I approached the church entrance, I saw a young man in shorts, hosing down a car in the parking lot near what I assumed was the church rectory.

"Hello," I said, standing back from the spray of the stream of water he aimed at the car windshield. "Are you washing Father's car for him?"

Seeing me, he hurried over to the water tap on the rectory wall and turned the water off.

"I'd shake hands with you, but..." He laughed,

holding up his wet, dirty hands.

"You're forgiven," I said, asking, "Is Father around?"

"Believe it or not, I'm Father," he said, wiping his hands on his shorts, and holding one out to me. "Father Mike."

"Oh, I'm so sorry," I said, blushing. "I'm used to older priests." My thoughts turned back to ancient Father Champion. I hadn't even considered his reaction to my flight from Detroit. He would be glad I was taking to a priest.

"The crusty old ancients?" he asked. "They do know their Latin."

"You bet," I agreed, thinking back to years of Latin chants every Sunday as I grew up.

"Come into the rectory, and we can talk." Father Mike gestured for me to come with him. Nervous, I told myself at least I'd be out of the heat.

Following him across the lawn and up the steps, I felt more at ease. Maybe this man would understand Edward and me and help us. He ushered me into a parlor, quite Victorian in style, a contrast to the Spanish styles around me on Garden Street.

"Does this musty velvet make you feel more at home in this church?" he asked, gesturing for me to sit down. "Senora?" he called down the hall. "Some tea, please?"

He sank into an old but comfy armchair across from me, oblivious to his wet shorts and bare feet. "How can I help?"

"I just arrived yesterday," I started my story, filling him in on the whirlwind last month of my life with Edward and just how I'd arrived at the Frisco train station last night, how I'd abandoned my family and profession, the two letters I'd written. I was confessing to this young priest, atoning for my sins, and it felt so good to get it all off my chest.

"Well," he said when I had finished my tale, "I'm not going to try and talk you out of marrying your pilot. I'm sure you've been warned off him by everyone. War seems to speed everything up. You grab at chances like gold rings on a merry-go-round."

My mind flashed back to my nightmare on the carousel, losing Gary and then finding him. I had put him in a terrible position with my family—his family, too—with that letter.

"You say Edward is not a Catholic?" Father Mike asked, sipping his second cup of tea.

"No, Church of England, and he's from a prominent British family who would never…"

"There's another couple marrying soon. From Michigan, actually. Maybe you know them? Meg and Mac?"

I laughed. "She's only my best friend. We had dinner together last night."

"Did they tell you that he is converting to Catholicism?"

Surprised, I said, "No, they didn't." Why hadn't Meg told me this? Maybe to spare my feelings?

"They will be able to marry in the church building itself, as I am moving heaven and earth to speed up his conversion. We meet every Tuesday and Wednesday night to study Catholic beliefs."

"That won't happen with Edward," I said. For some reason, I told this priest about Edward's disillusionment with the war. About Dunkirk. About the

Battle of Britain. And about his abandonment of all friendships.

Leaning forward in his chair, the priest asked, "So he's not that close to Mac?"

"No," I said, "he actually makes fun of him." I felt I was betraying Edward by confiding in this stranger, but somehow I knew his Roman collar would mandate he keep my secrets.

"Well," Father Mike said, standing up and stretching, "I can marry you two, in this rectory, in this parlor, once I have Edward's paperwork. You are of age, so you need no permission."

My dreams of a white gown, bridesmaids, flowers, and my family throwing rice washed out on the waves into the Gulf, thudding back on the sand, drenched in a wave of sadness.

Sensing my feelings, Father Mike took my arm as I stood on the dark carpet. "I'd make up with your family before you go overseas, Millie. They must be heartbroken and afraid for you."

"Thank you so much, Father. I feel lighter, as if I'd been to confession," I said, walking to the door with him, braced to face the noonday sun.

"In that case, let me give you my blessing, Millie," he said. I bowed my head as he made the sign of the cross, intoning the Latin words. I again fought back tears. "Come back with Edward, and we'll set the date, Millie. Go with God. Your pilot needs you."

"I know," I said, stiffening my spine, resolving to soldier on with Edward.

"Maybe you could hook up with the local USO chapter here in Pensacola," Father Mike said as I maneuvered down the stairs. "They need you, too."

Chapter 16

The days passed. Whimsical, tropical days spent at the beach, sunning myself in my new swimsuit. I took great pleasure in buying it, imagining Aunt Lill's horror at its two pieces, its bra and skirt bursting with loud coral hibiscus blooms, painted on lime green, all the rage. I laughed as I recalled the first trousers I was allowed to purchase. The three old gals had shopped with me and made me buy a pair three sizes too big so they did not cling to my legs obscenely. Now I could dress as I chose, mostly to please Edward. The flash of his blue eyes was all the approval I needed. And he did like me in shorts. It was all about the legs, he said. I had brought all my savings with me so I could revel in shopping. It was not a fortune, but enough to tide me over until Cornwall. As Meg said, we were liberated. Praise be.

Meg and Mac had set their date. They would be married in the church on April 22nd. Her mother and father were coming for the occasion, and Edward and I would be the witnesses. She had told her parents before she left Ecorse, and they had seen her off on the train with their blessing, reassured by Mac's agreeing to convert to Catholicism. There would be no blessing for me, ever. This I knew. Meg had an engagement ring. A blessing. A wedding date. I had Edward, and I told myself he was all I needed.

Meg and I had begun volunteering at the USO. Their quarters were just outside the base in an old Spanish style building they called the Cantina. Decorated in vivid turquoise and orange, the walls covered in Mexican tapestries, it was a most welcoming drinking hole for the pilots. I switched from my usual Tom Collins to sipping tall cold glasses of red sangria with slices of lime, lemon, and orange squeezed in and covered with ice. I spent my afternoons at the Cantina being useful, making sandwiches, dancing, and playing cards. The old gramophone needle ground the records down as the guys danced and sang. Lena Horne was the current favorite. Her hit record of "Stormy Weather" played over and over. "When he went away the blues walked in and met me," we'd sing together. "Can't go on, everything I had is gone…"

My mornings were my beach time. No more than an hour, I'd been warned, unless I wanted lobster skin. I'd lie on my towel and then dip into the water, reveling in the waves as they spilled against my hot body, my hair loose and damp. I felt so free. Later in the evening Mac and Edward would often join us, Mac absent those two nights a week for his lessons with Father Mike. Meg and I sat at a table under an orange umbrella, watching our men swim as we refreshed ourselves with cool drinks. Sometimes we dipped our toes in the surf, only to have our pilots rush us, hurling us into the waves as we gasped, pleading for our lives. One evening Mary came down to the beach and sat with us under our umbrella. She had her camera and offered to snap us together. We posed, two young loving couples in the sand. Edward lay with his head in my lap. Mac and Meg sat close together, arms around each other.

Without uniforms, casual in our swimsuits, we seemed to all the world carefree and gay. We would carry that moment of happiness with us throughout our individual wars as Mary gave us all copies of her photo. She also framed one for herself and surprised us by hanging it in her collection on the lounge wall. I wonder if it still hangs there. If she shares our story with the new brides-to-be who come to stay at her boarding house.

****

It was time for Edward and me to talk with Father Mike. Edward had completed all the paperwork, and we were all set. All we needed was the date. I knew the RAF imposed a waiting period except in times of crisis. That we would discuss with Father Mike.

Edward appeared again in the mysterious jeep, and after a morning swim, we piled in for the ride to the church. Edward was very quiet, his usual charm hidden.

"Are you nervous?" I asked, trying to keep my hair in some semblance of a coiffure as we flew along, the wind whipping. Miss Georgette, back in Detroit, would be appalled at my loose curls, encouraged by the Florida humidity.

"Of course not," Edward lied, eyes straight ahead on the bumpy road.

My own stomach was flipping a bit, but I chalked it up to all the Mexican food I was trying to get used to eating at just about every meal. I'd also been drinking more alcohol than usual. The only drinks ever served by my mother were the sweet red wine reserved for the annual visit of her cousin, Father Fabian. He would sit in the sun parlor, sipping the wine with a slice of cake as Mom beside him tried to make conversation. Lill and Stell in hats for the occasion sat across from them.

Mostly Gary and I would hide. Dad usually had an emergency at the hospital.

We were there, and Edward pulled into the parking lot of the church.

"I think I should teach you how to drive," Edward said, braking the jeep. "You never know when it might be useful. If Princess Elizabeth can learn to be a car mechanic, you can learn to shift gears. But then I'd not like to give you a means of escape from me."

Saying nothing, terrified at the thought of driving this jeep but more scared of the words from *Rebecca*, "I fled" washing over me, I opened the door and reached down to the pavement. Edward and I headed over to the rectory. Edward stopped by the statue of St. Stephen, pulling me back with his hand. "So tell me about this chap," he asked.

"This guy," I said, "is the first martyr of the Catholic Church. You see," I pointed, "he carries a palm frond and three stones."

Edward looked up at the statue, squinting in the sun, "Yes. I see."

"He was put on trial and didn't have the sense to keep his mouth shut. So he went on and on about his Jewish judges." This bit of Catholic martyrdom was calming us both down.

"Poor old bugger." Edward laughed.

"Yes, because the crowd got so riled up they stoned him to death."

"Thus the stones," Edward said. "Do you think the old Catholic gals back in Ecorse would be impressed if I gave you a ring right here in front of a saint? Just think how the bridge club would quack."

He reached into his pocket before I could get a

word out. He held a small velvet box out to me and knelt down before St. Stephen.

"Open it, please," I said, tears already making their way down my tanned cheeks.

"Millie, my love, my heart," Edward said, matching my tears with his, "marry me."

He opened the box, took the ring, and placed it on my trembling left-hand ring finger.

"Oh, yes," I said, looking down at the ring. I didn't get a good look though, because Edward tipped my chin up and gave me the softest, most elegant kiss ever.

"I'm sorry I took so long, but I wrote to Mum and asked her to send a ring from the family collection. It arrived yesterday."

"So your mother approves?" I asked, holding my hand up so the sun caught the ring's sparkle.

"Of course. Mum trusts my judgment." He was smiling, nodding as if talking to her.

"I've been proposed to twice," I marveled. "And now I have a beautiful ring."

"The sapphire is not that large, but the setting is platinum and..."

"Please, Edward, I love this ring." It was a single sapphire in an ornate platinum setting. The metal curled all around the stone in a gentle touch of silver filigree. Almost like a fine French lace.

"Mum says it goes back many generations to an eighteenth-century mistress of Sand Castles, related to King George the Third. Of course he was quite daft, but..."

"Perfect." I laughed. "Everyone says I'm daft, too. To have run off with a..."

Before I could go on, Edward kissed me again,

apologized to St. Stephen, and took my hand. "You've done a runner with Edward Owen. What could go wrong?"

And together, arm in arm, we walked up the steps, and Edward rang the rectory bell. The door opened, and Senora gestured for us to wait in the parlor, the parlor where we would soon be married.

March 15th. March 15th would be our wedding day. Father Mike had pointed out that it was the day known as The Ides of March to the Romans. Edward had remembered it as the day Julius Caesar was done in by his senators. So that, along with a dead martyr outside the church, and of course, the war, could make one pause. Not us. Despite all the nightmares, all the warnings, all my doubts, I was ready to marry Edward.

As we walked down the steps of the rectory, Edward paused and sat down on the third step, staring out at the traffic on Garden Street.

"Edward," I asked, sitting down next to him, "are you okay?"

"Yes, just need a few minutes," he said, and then fell silent, deadly silent.

I waited, watching a sole ant hobble across the bottom step, weighed down by a dark crumb, perhaps from an Oreo. It disappeared into a crack.

"I have something else for you," Edward said, diving into his pocket again.

He held out a letter to me. "It's from Gary, addressed to you, so I haven't opened it. He sent it to the base to me."

Now my stomach was flipping. The sun had its rays gripping me, making me nauseous. "Let's go back to the cottage, please. I'll read it there."

"I'm sorry you're giving up so much for me," he said, taking my hand. "Are you sure?"

We stood up together and walked back over to the parking lot, this time ignoring St. Stephen. Sobered by Edward's uncertainty, I walked beside him, the cement swimming erratically beneath me in the heat. Racking my brain for words of assurance, I could offer him, I said simply, "I love you, Edward, forever."

****

Dear Mumu,

As you will know, your elopement has been a shock to everyone. It is a good thing you did not let me know your address down there as I don't know if I could have stood up under the interrogation by the old gals. I probably would have spilled my guts as they pulled out my fingernails. You were right in your timing of the letters. Dad had read his and broken your news to the family before Miss Jackson called, and all hell broke loose. The bridge club bats are teeming with gossip, most saying you must be with child. Of course they now say they never liked Edward, and he probably sold the layette they embroidered on the black market in England because of the severe rationing. They imagine he has you tied to the bed in some hellhole in Mexico and just may sell you into slavery.

Dad is more rational, of course. He has stopped Mom from hiring a detective to find you, or worse yet, traveling to Pensacola and stalking you on the streets and right into the Gulf, paddling furiously and probably drowning, as you know she can't swim.

If you write back, as I hope you will, send the letter to Andy's house. He gets the mail from the porch every day so he should be able to intercept your letter and hand it over to me.

Miss you, sis. Say hello to that bastard, Edward.

Love, Gary

I finished reading the letter aloud to Edward and broke into tears. We were at the beach, having shaken off Meg and Mac's company after showing her my ring. My head on Edward's chest, I sobbed for the first time since my brave escape. He held me and cooed into my ear, telling me over and over it would be all right. I stroked my ring, his words soothing me. He was my future. Detroit was my past, but a past more difficult to let go of than I'd expected.

****

That night I dreamed I was on trial. It was ancient Rome, and I stood before the mob, asked to defend my actions. Saint Stephen stood beside me accused of his crimes against Rome. I wore my flowered swimsuit, frightfully underdressed for this event. The hibiscus on the bra seemed to fade and droop as I stood there waiting for judgment. My judges were the ladies of the bridge club, my family nowhere in sight. I cowered on a plinth of marble, cold in my inappropriate suit as winds whistled through the crowd, kicking up sand. The bridge club all wore their minks. Beady eyes came alive as the minks squirmed on their shoulders, some sliding to the ground and attacking bare ankles around them, nibbling and gnawing.

"Stephen," I said, whispering to the man in the soiled toga, "You will not survive the day, but you will be blessed as a saint."

"How do you know?" he asked, shaking in anger.

"Because you stand in marble outside the church I will be married in on March 15th."

191

"The Ides of March?"

"Yes."

"You will burn in hell for what you have done," he spit back at me.

The bridge club ladies moved forward, hissing and pointing at me, their hats awry, their minks flailing. In their hands they carried chicken pot pies and stones. Suddenly Miss Jackson pushed her way through the crowd. She threw the first stone.

****

March 15th dawned with a very unusual rain in a slow drip across the city. We were to be at the rectory at one in our finery. I had written back to Gary through Andy, as instructed, but had not told him of the wedding. It was a risk I could not take.

Edward and I traveled in style in Mary's sedan to the rectory. In my pocketbook, I carried a ten-dollar bill for Father Mike to thank him for all his help and his refraining from judging this poor sinner. I wore a simple lilac dress of wool crepe with a matching purple hat and lilac veil I'd bought at a local shop. Arriving in the parking lot, we met Mac and Meg, who were only a month away from their own wedding. Meg carried a small orchid, which she offered to me. It was a perfect match for my dress. "For you, Millie," she said and hugged me. We both had tears in our eyes, but I had resolved not to cry ever again after my sobbing fit against poor Edward's chest.

The four of us walked over to the rectory and up the now-familiar steps. Senora as usual answered the door and welcomed us in. She wore a very nice flowered dress, not her usual uniform.

Father Mike greeted us in the parlor, not in his

shorts but in a dark suit with his white collar. He asked Edward and me to stand facing him, and for Mac and Meg to stand behind us. I honestly do not remember one word of the ceremony except for the "I do's" and the rings. My ring only, as Edward refused to wear one. Holding Edward's gaze, I pronounced my vows with all the sincerity I could muster and then helped him when he had trouble sliding the ring on my finger, swollen in the humid air. And I watched him commit to me with his ocean-blue eyes offering a dose of hope to my butterfly stomach. An embarrassed kiss in front of this priest, no matter how young, and it was over. Father Mike got his money. We got his blessing.

When we walked out of the rectory, a plane buzzed low over us. Edward looked to the sky, shielding his eyes and laughed. "That plane's a Yellow Peril," he said, "our own personal flypast from the base." With hugs and squeezes and kisses thrown in from Mac and Meg and even Senora, we were off to the Cantina for a celebration put on by the USO. But not before Meg pelted us with the rice she had helped herself to from the cantina.

We partied away the afternoon, dancing to our favorite tunes. Mary came, and even Father Mike showed up for a twirl around the makeshift dance floor. I had to admit, for a priest he sure could dance.

Edward was dancing with Meg as I slipped out the door for some fresh air, even if it was hot, humid air. Mac was outside, too, puffing on a forbidden cigarette.

"Would you like a drag?" he asked, leaning back against the wall of the cantina.

"No, thanks," I said, sighing in the quiet alleyway, taking deep breaths.

"Who'd have thought Edward and I would marry before you and Meg?" I said, stepping back to avoid the puffs of smoke from his cigarette.

"His request was expedited. Surely he told you that?" Mac said, flicking ashes to the ground.

"But why?" I asked, suddenly exhausted in the afternoon heat.

"Because he got you up the duff, of course," Mac said, finishing his smoke, flipping it to the cement, and rubbing it into the ground with his dress shoe.

"He what?" I asked, shocked, but hoping I had heard him wrong.

"Got you pregnant," he said.

Chapter 17

"How could you have lied like that?"

Edward was sprawled on my bed, "our" bed now, laughing at me. "Don't get your knickers in a twist, wife," he said. "You know what Cockney slang is for 'wife'? 'Trouble and strife.' "

"Don't. Your charm won't get you out of this one. I couldn't even go back into the cantina. Not knowing everyone thought I was…" I stood cooling off by the fan, pretending to be interested in something out the window. I couldn't even say the word.

"Come here, love." Edward cooed, "It's time for us to get loved up, not fight."

"Maybe I should sleep with Meg tonight." I was shaking, humiliated.

"Meg? You should hear how that twit Mac brags about her. Claims he was in her pants the first night they met." Edward had lit up a cigarette as he leaned against the headboard.

"Well, that's not true," I said, indignant all over again for Meg.

"What the bloody hell are you playing at?" Edward asked, taking a long drag on his cigarette.

I grabbed my robe and the plainest nightgown I could find and headed for the bathroom. This bride was in no mood to look her best for this groom. After all, I had to be feeling very queasy in my condition.

I brushed my teeth and stared at my pale face in the old mirror. All of Ecorse seemed to be looking back, clucking at me with I-told-you-so nods. Taking up a washcloth, I rinsed it and rubbed it across my face. If only I had some bright red lipstick. I'd made my bed, now it was time to lie in it.

I opened the bedroom door. Edward still lay there, a light sheet over his naked body. I'd seen the male body, of course, for three years now, and before that in my dad's office, but I'd never really seen it "function." Once in a while, a man would become excited during a sponge bath, but now I was about to finish my anatomy lessons. "St. Stephen," I whispered, "Pray for me."

Standing in the doorway, I waited.

"Millie," he said, in his most loving voice, low and sexy, "I had to create an emergency or we'd have had to wait weeks, even months. Saying you were up the duff was the first thing I thought of. I knew another bloke who got away with it, so I tried it."

I was speechless at this confession. He rose from the bed and came over to me, closing the door behind us. "Let's get rid of Aunt Lill's robe," he said. "This outfit is enough punishment for any husband."

Still silent as the robe dropped to the floor, I did smile at the mention of Lill. She was the last person I wanted here with me tonight.

"Made you smile, Millie. What would I have to do to make you speak? Maybe this?" He bent his head down, tucked it under my chin, and kissed me on the neck. "No? Then how about this?" He moved his hand to my breast, rubbing against the rough cotton nightgown, his eyes on my face searching for a reaction.

I gasped, my silent resolve gone.

"That's the ticket." He laughed. "Come to bed, darling." With a giant swoop, he picked me up in his arms and deposited me on the bed. It wasn't till then I realized he was naked as a babe. But a babe he was not. "Can we get rid of this armored nightie? Is it Stell's?"

I sat up and let him pull the nightgown over my head. It was his turn to gasp as he saw me, all of me. "You are lovely, Millie," he said. "And you are mine."

"I married you," I said, "for better or worse."

"Don't be daft." He laughed. "The better will always outweigh the worse."

"Promise?"

"Enough talking. I'm due back at the base at eight sharp."

I lay down, and he crushed me with his body, his mouth on mine, and the anatomy exam began.

****

Edward made it back to the base on time. I had tried to get up in the early morning to find us some breakfast, but he preferred to stay in bed and give me a proper goodbye, as he called it. He left in time to hitchhike his way back. I was a lazy lady, sleeping another hour and then drawing a luxurious bubble bath down the hall. I had a new relationship with my body. The nuns be damned.

As I soaked, I reviewed my life. The last six weeks had been a corny whirlwind, a cliché, really. I was now Mrs. Edward Sebastian Christian Owen, Mistress-to-be of Sand Castles. I had no idea when I would see Edward again. He had explained that he had been given a lot of time off his duties once our wedding was approved. His mates had filled in for him, but now it was time to get back to work.

"When will I see you again?" I had asked him as he opened the hallway door to leave.

"No idea, Mrs. Owen," he had replied, grinning. "But you'll have plenty of time to work on that tan. We just may make love in the sand."

"Oh, Edward. No." I had felt the blush spreading up my body.

"See you at the cantina. And the beach. You'll love snogging in the sand." He had crossed back over to the bed for one last kiss, and then he was gone.

The week passed. I was at the beach. I was at the USO. I shopped with Meg. I did not see Edward. I did, though, write a letter, two letters actually. The first:

Dear Mom and Dad,

It is with great happiness that I announce to you that Saturday, March 15, 1941, I became Mrs. Edward Sebastian Christian Owen, future Mistress of Sand Castles Hall, Cornwall. We were married at the rectory of St. Stephen's Catholic Church with Meg and Mac as our witnesses. The priest is a young guy who asks us to call him Father Mike. I first met him when he was hosing down his old jalopy in the church driveway. I mistook him for a teen washing the real priest's car. He is someone I can talk to, and he has urged me to write this letter.

I am so sorry that my marriage took place in secret, and that you were both not there. Edward and I are currently renting a room at a delightful cottage that sits right on the Gulf of Mexico beach. I have quite a tan. Meg lives here, too. She and Mac plan to marry at St. Stephen's in April. I am also volunteering every day in the afternoon at the local chapter of the USO housed in a building near the base called The Cantina.

When Edward ships out to England, I will follow him, as I am his wife and that is my duty. I can't wait to roam the beach at Sand Castles and prance with the peacocks even though I will miss you all terribly, as I do now.

I have read that there was a terrible blizzard in North Dakota and Minnesota on the day we were married, and that over a thousand people were killed. I hope your winter is not as extreme as that. I am aware that we were married on the Ides of March and although it was good luck for us, for others it was not. I hope you are not among those with ill luck, and that you will grow to regard my marriage as a good sign, not an evil omen.

If you choose, you may reply to this letter through Edward at the Pensacola Base. Please give my love to Stell and Lill. Also much love to Gary. And to Bartholomew many kitty kisses.

Love, Millie.

The second:

Dear Miss Jackson,

It is with apprehension that I write to you, as I know you must be furious with me. Please forgive me for having embarrassed you and Grace Hospital by bolting with my Edward. The war has changed us all, I fear. You must all be shaking your heads, saying that I was so foolish to leave when I had but a few weeks to complete my studies and graduate. But I ask you to look at what I have done from my point of view and Edward's. The war has a way of accelerating all our actions and decisions. Mine, especially.

Edward has survived both Dunkirk and the Battle

of Britain. I fear for his life. After Pensacola, he will return to England and more conflict. I want to spend as much time with him as possible as his wife. Yes, his wife. We were married March 15th at St. Stephen's Catholic Church here in Pensacola by a young priest, Father Mike. At this time, Edward does not have a date for his return to England. But when he does know, I will follow him by ship, as I am Mrs. Edward Owen.

Thank you for your guidance for almost three years of my life. Please be forgiving when you think of me, for when this war is over, I will visit Detroit and my family again.

Sincerely,

Mildred Owen

I posted the letters at the local post office and felt a certain finality as I walked away. I sent Gary a funny postcard of a donkey on the beach, too. I didn't expect to hear back. I had steeled myself for their silence. Edward returned with no notice on Saturday, finding me on the beach at sunset. And yes, we did move to a secluded area and make love in the sand and surf.

"I have a date when the squadron is moving out," he said, after we'd moved to a table and sat quietly together in our damp swimsuits.

"When?" I asked, dreading the day he'd return to the night skies.

He took my hand, leaned down, and kissed it. "April the first," he whispered, looking up at me in the twilight.

"So soon," I said, tears filling my eyes. "And on April Fool's Day?"

"Don't cry," he said, wiping one cheek with his finger, then the other.

"But I don't want to lose you." I stared out at the water, fearful for my Edward.

"You'll be at risk, too, love. The ship voyage will be dangerous for you. The day we were married the Germans sank fifteen ships in the North Atlantic."

"Oh, no."

"You'll be fine. Nothing can hurt us."

"Promise?"

"Promise. It should be about a five-day trip for you to Liverpool. You'll need to take a train up to New York City, and then board the ship. America is not at war. The Germans should leave you alone."

"Famous last words," I said, struggling to let his words bring me peace.

He leaned in and kissed me, then sat back, smiling a mischievous smile. "Besides…"

"Besides what?" I ventured, planting another kiss on his mouth.

"I just got you pregnant. This baby will have sand in its hair. Just you wait and see."

"Oh, Edward. Oh, Edward."

Chapter 18

I dreamed that night with Edward beside me in the little cottage with the RAF blue shutters. In the dream I was in New York City at the dock. I carried a baby girl in my arms as I waited to board the ship bound for Liverpool. I cradled the baby as she screwed up her tiny face and cried, screaming in hunger. It was no use. I could not feed her here. She would have to cry.

More and more people were arriving at the pier as a gentle spring rain began to fall. I covered the baby with her light blanket, one I'd knit for her myself. How sad her grandparents knew nothing of this little babe, so sweet and good-tempered. The patter of the rain had quieted her and lulled her to sleep.

I moved toward the cover of the gangplank as the soldiers motioned for us to board. Baby and I were pushed and pulled as I shoved my way up toward the first deck. My luggage had been stowed, so baby was my only burden as I maneuvered the steep angle upwards. She was silent, snuggled against me. I had overdressed in wool for the crossing, and I could feel the sweat on my back. The humidity of the rain curled my damp hair under my hat. I knew I looked a mess. At the top at last, I stepped carefully onto the ship as the gangway swayed. Clutching baby to me, I turned right and stopped cold. Before me stood the captain, greeting passengers. I gasped as I identified his uniform and its

Nazi insignia. I was on a German ship, headed for hell.
****

I did not tell Edward about my nightmare. I wanted to spare him my worries as I knew he must be terrified to be returning to his war. He made all the arrangements for me. Another two-day train trip to New York City, and then a five-day passage on the RMS *Samaria*, a British ship. It was to be its last crossing before it would be refitted as a troop ship. I had a second class ticket, and a roommate would be sharing my cabin.

"Probably another war bride," Edward said. We were on the beach, relaxed and in love, watching an incredible sunset streak purples and reds across our sky. Edward lay with his head in my lap. I stroked his brown hair, streaked blond from our days in the Gulf sun. It was so fine; almost silky curls trailed on his forehead.

"Look at those colors." He pointed. "Reds and oranges. Purple. I'd love to paint this sunset."

"Do you paint?" I asked him, my fingers twisting his hair.

"Yes, I do," he said, "in another world. That's why I love Housman's poems. He makes such beautiful scenes with his words." He sat up, and my hand dropped from his hair.

"I'd love to see your paintings, Edward." I imagined a studio at his estate, the sun streaming in, offering perfect light to the artist. My artist.
****

"War bride," I said to him again, "what a strange term."

"That's what you are, love," Edward replied, taking my hand and kissing it. We were at the cantina with Mac and Meg, sharing a table out on the patio. The night had brought in cool breezes from the Gulf. We all were sunburned from another day in the sand. My hair, still damp from swimming, curled down my neck.

"So when will your squadron leave?" I asked Mac, sipping on my sangria, crunching bits of ice between my teeth.

"Top secret," he said, "but we'll still have time for our wedding."

Meg said quietly, "We need to find new witnesses though." I looked at her sunburned cheeks, and my heart dropped, as I knew in days we would be separated for a long time.

"I'm sorry, Meg," I said, taking her hand across the table. "I so wanted to be here for you."

"That's okay," she replied. "My parents will be here. I just want you to have a safe passage." She squeezed my hand as only a dear friend could.

I had told her about my nightmare, asking her not to tell Edward. Boarding that ship would be the bravest act of my life, but I had to put on a good face for my Edward.

"I imagine you will have escort ships now that FDR has signed the Lend-Lease Act," Mac offered, trying to calm my fears. Mac was sweet that way even if Edward called him a poof.

"That liner is fast enough to outrun U-boats," Edward said. "Let's not argue the toss," he added. "You will be safe or I wouldn't ask you to cross the Atlantic."

"Of course you'll be safe," Meg said, but the tears streaming down her red face belied her cover-up.

"Will you dance with me?" Edward asked as a pilot dropped the needle on a new popular record, "Frenesi."

He was irritated at both Mac and Meg and wanted me to himself.

He stood up and took my hand, and we danced away in each other's arms, aware that Mac and Meg were watching us. Edward held me tighter than ever before, gripping me to him, his face buried in my damp curls. The cantina was filling up with airmen and their ladies. Maybe they would be lasting loves. Maybe they would be casual relationships. Maybe they were just meeting, but for this evening, they were not alone.

"You will be fine," he said, almost pleading with me. "I can't lose you."

"And I must never lose you."

****

The days passed all too quickly. Days of sun and sangria, nights of love-making and low voices. The RAF kept its cards close to its chest, not revealing any departure dates. All Meg and I knew was that our pilots would not leave the same day, and that she would be here for her wedding.

"Tomorrow I leave," Edward said that last night at the beach. We had just made love in our secluded spot and were spooning, my body tucked into his long legs.

"So soon?" I asked, fighting back tears, hiding them at all costs. I had to spare Edward my fears. It seemed there would always be tears between us.

"Yes, I can't tell you how or what time, but it is tomorrow." He sat up, staring out at the Gulf. "I shall so miss this lovely spot. When I am flying in a bloody bomber over Germany, I shall think back to this, and what we had here."

"And that will keep you sane until we meet again," I said, reaching out my hand to stroke his back as he continued to stare into the water.

"I have something for you," he said, reaching over me into his jacket pocket. "Keep this with you to remember me by." He handed me a miniature oil painting. I recognized it at once as our Gulf sunset. There was a tiny couple painted on the sand, looking out to the water, the gorgeous hues of the sunset ahead of them. The sun itself, a dark orange halfway sunken into the water. In the bottom right corner the initials EO appeared.

"But how? When?" I was so touched my words wouldn't come together in a coherent question.

"The USO set me up with oils, brushes, and this tiny canvas. Meg helped." He looked into my eyes, searching for approval of his gift.

I started to cry, and he took the painting back in his hand, reaching for me with the other. "You'll ruin it with sodding tears," he said, rocking me back and forth. "Stop," he begged. "I don't want to remember you having a weep."

I took the painting back and smiled through my tears. "I love you, my pilot. Forever."

****

And he was gone. I had no time to weep over him; there was barely time to miss him as I prepared for my own voyage. Meg bustled around, helping me pack, making the most of our last hours together. She was the sister I'd never had, and I had no idea when I'd see her again.

Mac helped me get the precious travel documents I would need. Father Mike made sure I had all the proof of marriage papers I would have to show. I already had a passport, but I had to change the name on it as fast as possible. The RAF worked with speed and understanding to get me on that train to New York, and then that ship bound for Liverpool.

At our last dinner together, Mac and Meg worked hard to soothe my fears. Mac was realistic about what I would find once landed in Liverpool.

"As a port," he said, "the city has been heavily bombed. The Blitz was not just over London. Both Southampton and Liverpool were hit night after night."

"How awful," I said, fearful, yet determined. "Are they rebuilding?"

"The docks must be kept up," he said seriously, as serious as I'd ever seen Mac. "They are the gateway for the ships waging the battle in the Atlantic."

"Which I'll be sailing through," I said, my resolution waning. Meg reached for my hand, her words reassuring, her eyes giving her away. She was terrified for me, especially when she gripped my icy hand.

"A toast," she offered, "To Edward and Millie."

"Thank you," I mumbled, my voice quaking. To calm myself, I finished my sangria in one gulp. "Another pitcher, please," I yelled over to the bar.

The next morning, hung over, or "pissed" as my husband the pilot would say, Meg and I made our way to the station. Mac, back on duty, had insisted on treating me to a taxi for the short drive. Once at the platform bound for New York City, Meg and I stood awkwardly, afraid to cry.

"Do you have your coat?" she asked. "It'll be colder in New York, and the ship will be an icebox on the Atlantic."

"Yes, Mother," I responded, showing her the coat thrown over my suitcase. I had decided to wear my wool trousers for this leg of the journey. Edward would never know. I had packed a good supply of silk hose for my future life of rationing. Perhaps I could give Edward's mother a pair, although she might have connections for that sort of purchase. I knew there was a flourishing black market for such luxuries in England.

"All aboard." We both heard the summons. I picked up my coat and stepped toward the coach. Meg followed behind with my suitcase, staggering under its weight.

"Let me get that," a man said behind us. He stepped forward, took the suitcase from Meg, and easily hoisted it up the steps. He carried no luggage himself. He was an older man about my dad's age, with the same wire-rim glasses.

I felt the tug of missing my dad as I hurried up the steps behind him. I found my seat, and he lifted my suitcase above to the rack.

"There you go," he said. "I have a daughter about your age. Let me know if I can help you in anyway."

I started to sit down when I remembered poor Meg. I'd forgotten her on the platform. I lifted the window and stuck my head out. There she was. "Meg, I forgot you."

She was crying now full force, her shoulders shaking like a jackhammer. "Meg, don't cry. You'll make me cry."

"I can't help it," she said, her voice shaking. "I will miss you so, you ninny."

"I never thanked you for getting Edward the oils, Meg. I so love his sunset."

This helped, as a smile broke through her tears just as the train started steaming up.

"I love you, Meg," I called as the whistle blew to send us north.

"Me, too, Millie. Forever."

Chapter 19

The train tracks led my heart on a trouble-free journey. All day I watched out the window, sitting alone, not caring what towns we passed through, my only interest in New York City. I had been there several times, always with my family. In fact, we'd been there to see a play and shop in the fall of 1939. I would never forget seeing newspapers on stands with headlines about war in Europe, not knowing then that I would be drawn into the conflict before America was. That same year we had also traveled to Canada to catch a glimpse of King George and Queen Elizabeth on their royal tour, which climaxed in their visit to Washington, D.C. They had waved to us from the caboose of their special train. Lill and Stell could not get over the Queen's most stylish pale blue suit and lovely matching hat. They were certain she was waving just to us, although we were in a crush of hundreds of royalty enthusiasts.

Occasionally, I glanced across the aisle at the man who had helped me with my suitcase, but he had fallen asleep soon after we left Pensacola. If he were a doctor like my dad, I was glad for his nap, knowing he must be overworked and in need of sleep. Meg had packed me sandwiches and cookies, which I ate along the way, later buying a cola from the dining car. As the train rumbled on, I saw another beautiful sunset, pulling Edward's oil from my pocketbook to make a comparison. It was nowhere near as gorgeous as our sunset had been, of course. I touched the couple on the sand in the painting. No matter what was in store for us we would always have those moments in the sand as the sun set. I settled into my sleep position, my head leaning against the now closed window, sure that I would dream of the passage to come.

I awoke to someone shaking my shoulder. Looking up, I saw it was the conductor. "Breakfast is being served in the dining car," he half-whispered. "It is complimentary for you. A gift paid ahead."

"Thank you," I said, sitting up straight. "I'll be along soon." I stretched and yawned, knowing this must be a Mac and Meg gift. I needed to find a bathroom to freshen up, pour water on my grimy face, and brush my teeth. I stood up, hesitantly grabbing on to the back of the seat next to mine. I was fortunate that no one had bought a ticket for that seat. Or maybe Edward had bought two to give me privacy. The man across the aisle smiled at me.

"Going to breakfast, I hear," he said. "A nice gift for you."

"Yes, my friends, I suppose, or maybe my husband," I answered, moving out into the aisle.

"You married to one of those RAF airmen?" he asked, obviously intrigued.

"You bet," I said, flashing my widest smile possible.

"Go ahead," he said. "I've already eaten. I'll keep an eye on your suitcase." He was so much like my dad. A kind, kind man.

Down the aisle and two cars further, I sat myself in a comfy booth and proceeded to gorge on a fantastic breakfast. The waiter informed me that I was eating what the British called a "Full English." Fried eggs, sausage, potatoes, baked beans, bacon, and biscuits. And steaming hot tea. I felt guilty, as I knew not many in England could be enjoying this meal today. They'd be lucky if their ration books allowed them a bowl of porridge and toast. I sat back, savoring a second cuppa before I returned to my car. The waiter came by and handed me a note. "For you," he said.

My darling,

I hope you loved your Full English as much as you fancy this Englishman.

Your Edward.

He had painted a cup of steaming tea in the corner of the card. I laughed and clutched the small card to my heart. I tucked it into my pocketbook. My Edward's collection of art was growing.

The day crawled by and "Dad" slept through it again. It was getting colder, my tan somehow out of place now. I only ate a few more of Meg's cookies the rest of the day, stuffed with Edward's breakfast treat. I slept on and off myself, storing energy for the transfer from train to ship.

Around seven, people began to wake up and chatter. "Dad" informed me we were coming into Grand Central Station in New York City. He reminded me of his offer to help me with my luggage. I was glued to the window, watching the city as we approached it. This had been exactly the route we'd taken a few years back.

"New York City. Grand Central Station," the conductor bellowed as he walked down the aisle. "Please check you have all your luggage and belongings." He stopped and reached up to the rack above me and lifted my suitcase down to me.

"Thank you," I said, looking over to my adopted sleepy dad, who seemed crestfallen.

"I'll need help getting it off the train," I said, hoping to cheer the Boy Scout in him.

So off we went down the aisle to the open door. He did help me down with my suitcase.

"Will you be all right on your own?" he asked. I must have looked forlorn, so I mentally pinched myself to perk up.

"I'll be fine," I promised. "I'm off on a wonderful adventure."

With that assurance, he was swallowed up in the moving crowd in this busy New York evening. I was alone. "Millie?" I heard my name. Then again. "Millie?"

I turned around and around again. Ladies and men were rushing by me, leaving me behind. They seemed so sure of their destinations. Women in their veiled hats, men in their business suits. Children being dragged along by their hands, some protesting, some laughing. "Millie." I felt a hand on my shoulder spinning me around, and I was hugged into a chest I knew at once.

"Gary?" I broke away, looking up at him. "What are you doing here? How did you know?" Then I noticed his co-conspirator, Andy, standing behind him.

"Mumu," he said, "we couldn't let you sail to England without a proper send off." He pushed me back and eyed me up and down. "You look great, sis. That tan suits you."

"Look at Gary and me," Andy said. "Pale as

ghosts."

"Boo," Gary cried, grabbing my arms again.

"You're not here to talk me out of it? To kidnap me back to Ecorse?" I asked, hoping they were not here to "argue the toss" as Edward would say. That was all I needed, to spend my last minutes on shore arguing.

"Honest, Millie, no." Gary raised his right hand in a solemn pledge. "Andy, get your hand up."

"Yes, sir," Andy said, raising his hand, too. "Swear on the Bible and Aunt Lill's chicken."

"We've got a cab waiting, sis," Gary said, grabbing my suitcase and pointing to an exit near a cab stand.

"To the pier," Andy called out, grabbing my arm.

"To England," Gary shouted above the crowd, who were going about their business of this night oblivious to the gigantic step I was taking in my own life.

Once settled in the back seat of the cab, I began my questions. We were squished together like marshmallows in our winter coats.

"Slow down, sis." Gary laughed. "Edward and Meg have been in touch with me, I mean us, through Andy, here. Say thank you to Andy."

"Thank you, Andy. Do Mom and Dad know you're here?"

"The old gals and your dad and my parents think we're in Chicago having a high old time," Andy added. I thought about Andy's parents, first generation off the boat from France. His mother was one of the local seamstresses, so deft with a needle. She had made my mother's wedding dress for her, a beautiful concoction of lace and satin in the 1920 flapper style. They must be horrified by what had happened to their beautiful city of Paris when it fell to the Nazis.

Married, did Gary know?

"Do you know we're married?" I asked, pushing forward to see Gary's face better.

"For goodness' sake, why get hitched on the Ides of March?" Gary asked. "That's seriously tempting fate."

So if he knew, Mom and Dad must know. And Lill and Stell. And the bridge club. And all of Ecorse.

As we approached the pier, I became more and more aware of my brother and his friend beside me. My courage was sagging. I needed their support, but I would not show weakness to them. They had to give a good report back to Ecorse, as I knew they would eventually.

The cab pulled up to the building where I would check in for my journey. Gary got out first and leaned into the driver's window to pay the fare, plus tip, while Andy helped me with my suitcase.

"Come on, sis," Gary encouraged me. "Let's get you on that ship."

We entered the crowded building, where I found the right line for RMS *Samaria* and checked in. The man very formally asked me for my papers. I fumbled through my pocketbook and produced my documents, trying to read his reaction as he read through it all. He stamped my passport and the letters from Edward and Father Mike. Looking at me, he said, "Approved for sailing, Miss. That way." He pointed to the right entryway, finally half-smiling. "You two can accompany her to the pier, but not onto the ship," he warned, his attempt at a smile having misfired. "Wartime regulations. Check your luggage on the pier."

"Yes, sir," Gary said in his sternest voice from

behind me. He grabbed my suitcase and pushed me to the doorway, Andy following along.

My first glimpse of the ship took my breath away. What a daunting sight. It loomed above us, five decks high. How could a German U-boat touch this beauty? I had read that last fall this ship had arrived in America, its decks filled with children being evacuated from Europe. Some were accompanied by their mothers. Some had made this journey alone, as I was prepared to do. But I was a woman. Thinking of those young souls buoyed my own courage. If they could do it, so would I.

Gary had checked my suitcase in while I had been lost in thought about my voyage. He and Andy now stood forlorn, and it was up to me to buck up their spirits. "So," I said, "when I am Lady Dunnabunk of Sand Castles Hall, I shall reward you by inviting you to my estate. You could tend the peacocks to earn your keep."

No response. They both stood there. Gary began to cry. I had seldom seen him cry, ever.

"Come on, Gary," I begged. "I haven't seen you cry since Aunt Lill made you wear those girlish Mary Jane shoes when you were five."

That got a laugh, well, more of a smile from him. The ship whistle blasted, welcoming passengers aboard.

"Come on, you two," Andy said. "Hug and let her go on board before she misses her ride."

Gary stepped forward and kissed me on the forehead, then hugged me one last time. I turned and pulled Andy into a hug, then stepped back. "I'll never forget what you did today," I said, turning toward the gangplank. I started up, gripping the railing as it swung slightly. A gorgeous sunset was playing out along the horizon, but it was blocked as I climbed higher. Turning back one last time and letting others pass by, I saw Gary and Andy still watching me from the pier, waving and whistling. I waved back one last time and blew them a kiss. Tears were streaming down my tanned cheeks as I continued my climb, now so unsure of what lay ahead for me, for my Edward. I crossed onto the deck, at once pulled to the railing. They were still there, my dear brother and his loyal friend.

****

I looked across at James and was surprised to see he was awake. How long had I been daydreaming?

"Are you okay?" he asked me, his brow furrowed in concern.

"Fine, just anxious to get this journey over. And stop all this crying."

Chapter 20

I forced myself to wave one last time, and then I moved away from the railing. A gentleman in uniform stepped up and asked to see my papers and boarding pass.

"Welcome aboard, Mildred," he said, smiling and handing my papers back. Checking his roster, he continued, "You are assigned to cabin 232, second class, on the deck above us. Your cabin mate has already checked in with us. I hope you have a most pleasant crossing."

"Thank you," I answered, grateful for the formality after the emotional farewell I'd just been through.

"American?" he asked.

"A war bride," I said, blushing in the evening breeze.

"So soon?" He laughed. "No flies on our boys."

Not sure what I was laughing at, I turned away from him and walked through the gangway to the other side of the ship just to get away from the throng of passengers boarding. I was not prepared for the sight I saw as I peered out into the harbor. For there, docked in great majesty, the queens of the ocean ruled the still water. I grabbed the railing, afraid I would cry again.

"Quite a sight, isn't it?"

I jumped at this comment, which came at me from behind. Then she moved beside me at the railing.

"Those are three great liners. RMS *Queen Mary,* SS *Ile de France,* and SS *Normandie.*" She pointed at each one with her gloved hand. "They're here to be refitted as troop ships. Something sad about that."

"Yes, but there is so much sadness about this war," I said, my chin trembling in spite of my best efforts at composure.

"I'm Constance," she said. "Constance Childs, Connie for short. And you are?"

"Mildred Beaubien. Millie to everyone," I responded.

"I figured as much," she said. "There aren't many of us war brides on board. Looks like you're stuck with me as a cabin mate for the crossing."

I turned to look her full in the face. She was about my size, a little heavier maybe. Dark brown eyes and blond hair, a brassy blond Aunt Lill would say. She hugged her wool tweed cape around her with one hand and held a cigarette in the other.

"Don't worry," she said. "Promise I won't smoke in the cabin. It's very small."

"I'm sure we'll get along just fine," I said confidently, my thoughts going back to Carol at the dorm, who was now enjoying a single room without me and probably furious at my desertion.

"I was told there was tea in the main lounge," she said. "Shall we be veddy British and have a cuppa?"

"Of course," I said, quite grateful for the company. "But where is the bloody lounge?"

"That's my girl," she said. "Let me lead the way."

We took our time over tea, as the ship seemed to linger in port. It would be a blackout departure after dark, Connie informed me. And our luggage would take a while to be sorted and placed in our cabins anyway, so why not get acquainted.

Connie's story was like mine. She had met a handsome pilot in Toronto while visiting her aunt. He had been there training for six weeks. Her one-week trip had extended to six with her aunt's permission. She had returned to Cleveland, Ohio, her pilot in tow.

I poured my story out to her as she nodded over her tea and scones. It all sounded familiar. Friends warning both of us off our pilots. Our parents apoplectic. Our siblings' secret support. Even one cat named Christopher and another named Bartholomew. But she had defied them all, and with her sister Janet as one witness and the reverend's wife as another, they had married here in New York last week. Then he had returned to England to drop bombs, and she, Mrs. Harry Childs, was now the cabin mate of Mrs. Edward Owen, as we both risked the Atlantic crossing to Liverpool. By the end of our tea, we were both in tears and fast friends.

An announcement came over the loudspeaker inviting us to visit our cabins, as the ship would be departing soon. We were also advised to read the announcements left in our cabins. So off we went up the stairs to the deck above. Our cabin was about midway down the hallway. It was an inside cabin, which was fine with me. I had no wish to see what was out there in the ocean as we sailed. The cabin was small but just fine for a five-day voyage. Our suitcases had been delivered, so we unpacked, sharing the little closet and dresser. I placed the beach photo of us with Mac and Meg on the table. Connie put a similar photo of her with Harry building a snowman in Toronto, her aunt on the porch laughing at them. Whether on a Pensacola beach or in a Toronto front yard, we were both war brides sailing into the night for our airmen. Exhausted, we fell into our bunks, unaware of the dangers lurking as the ship set sail in the cover of night.

****

"We made it through the night," Connie said, shaking me awake. She was already dressed, her hair pulled back behind her ears, and very red lipstick on her lips. She wore black trousers and a red sweater as she reached into the closet for her cape. "Rise and shine. Breakfast is served, I'm sure."

I grumbled a good morning of sorts and got my legs over the side of the bed. It was chilly, the floor cold under my feet. "Give me five minutes," I begged, my eyes adjusting. I knew she must be dying for a cigarette.

"I'll be out on deck by the dining area," she said.

I could feel the rocking of the boat, tolerable, but I knew I would fare better with some food in my stomach. A quick visit to our tiny bathroom and a splash of water on my face brought me to full consciousness. Pulling on my trousers again, but with a pale green sweater this time, I ran a comb through my hair, grabbed my jacket, and headed for the deck below.

I found Connie smoking her cigarette and looking out on the ocean. "Will you look at that," she said pointing, her hair blowing in wisps across her face.

Alongside of the ship, not too far distant, sailed a destroyer. Edward had been right. We did have an escort. "Part of FDR's Lend-Lease Act, I imagine," I said, relieved to be able to tell Connie, as she always seemed to be teaching me something.

"Makes me feel safer, somehow." She sighed. "Let's eat," she said as she casually dropped her cigarette over the side of the ship.

After breakfast, we went our separate ways to explore the ship. In our rooms last night before we had collapsed, we had read over the information left for us. One sheet had been a Menu of Events, beautifully engraved in a lavish scroll. It had listed religious services. I had been so far away from religion in my last Florida days, except for Father Mike, that I had completely forgotten that Easter Sunday was coming up soon. I would be in England by then. Edward had told me there was a chapel at Sand Castles. It sounded so beautiful the way he described it, with a stained glass window of a peacock and the family crest. Perhaps there would be an Easter service there. The Menu had continued, listing a series of lectures on England and the war, covering topics like rationing and air raids. How to cope with our new lives in a strange country at war. There were also available for our cruising entertainment gramophone concerts, knitting classes, deck games, and movies. We were also urged to visit the ship's library. Three movies were scheduled for the crossing: *Backstreet*, a drama starring Charles Boyer and Margaret Sullavan; *Andy Hardy's Private Secretary,* a comedy with Mickey Rooney and Kathryn Grayson; and *The Lady Eve*, a romance with Henry Fonda and Barbara Stanwyck. I put them all on my mental schedule, mostly to take up time, but especially the Andy Hardy picture because I loved Kathryn Grayson's beautiful coloratura soprano voice.

A lifeboat drill was scheduled at ten that next morning. I would usually have groaned and complained about a drill like this, but not now, not on this ship, not in these waters. But first, I wanted to visit the library. I'd been meaning to look up a certain author but hadn't had the time.

The library was on the same deck as our cabin so I headed back that way, hoping I would be able to find my way there quickly. Back past my cabin, I traveled on to the end of the corridor. To my left I found an open room, its walls shelved with books.

"Come in," a lady called to me, seeing me hesitate at the door.

I could see from her uniform that she was a member of the Red Cross. "Hello," I said, marveling at such a well-stocked library on a ship. "I'm Millie Owen."

"Jane Reid," she said, turning and reaching her hand out to me. "The Red Cross is stepping forward to outfit libraries with the help of the government so soldiers can have access to books," she said, holding up a few she was shelving. "This ship will be refitted as a troop ship soon."

"How wonderful," I said. "I am—was—a member of the USO."

"Was?" she asked. "Don't tell me, you're one of our war brides on this ship."

"How many of us are there?" I asked, curious to know who else dared to cross the ocean besides Connie and me.

"Just fifteen," she said. "Can I help you with a book or two?" She waved around the room at the assortment.

Fifteen, I thought. Maybe we could all knit together or maybe catch a movie together. As if reading my mind, she said, "You might meet the other war brides at the lectures on life in England. Perhaps I could organize a literary tea. Maybe…" Her voice petered out as if she were aware she might be overstepping her boundaries.

"I'll check that out, but right now, I'm looking for an author, a poet really, Jane," I said, wondering how much poetry they stocked here.

"What poet, Millie?" she asked, eager to help. She probably did not have many customers on the ship, at least not yet.

"Wilfred Owen, a poet of the Great…"

She interrupted me. "War. Over here." She gestured for me to follow her, and reaching up to the top shelf of books on tiptoes, she pulled a slim volume down and gave it to me. "He's rather a sad case, as he was killed before the end of the war, when he was quite disillusioned with it all. I expect the brass may want this one hidden from the troops, as it would kill morale. Why don't you take it for yourself?"

"Are you sure?" I asked, running my hand over the green leather volume.

"Yes, very. Read his poem 'Dulce et Decorum Est,' and you'll see what I mean."

My four years of Latin with the nuns translated the title for me. "It is sweet and right?" I asked.

"It continues, 'Pro Patria Mori,'" Jane added, frowning in a very serious way.

"To die for your country," I translated, my voice hushed, my fingers trembling as I opened the small book. I turned to the index, skimmed my finger down the page, found the title, and leafed through the pages until I found this poem. I read aloud:

"Bent double, like old beggars under sacks,
Knock kneed, coughing like hags, we cursed
through sludge,
Till on the haunting flares we turned our backs
And toward our distant rest began to trudge..."

I stopped. "How awful," I said, my heart sinking at the thought that this was Edward's relative, writing about the hell of his own war twenty years ago. "And he died?" I asked.

"Just before the end," she said, seeing how upset I was. "At one point he was hospitalized suffering from what they called 'shell shock' back then. He's writing about the mustard gas attacks in the opening of this poem."

"Oh, all this, and then he died." I closed the book, voice hushed, a now-familiar fear rising in my chest. "Thank you for the book," I said, turning to leave before I completely fell apart.

"Wait," Jane said, coming toward me, "maybe you shouldn't finish reading that poem if it's too upsetting. You must be so worried about your husband." She put her arm around me and asked if I'd like a cup of tea. I was learning that putting the kettle on solved so many temporary problems for the British. "We just have time before the drill, if you like," she said putting her small kettle on a hot plate on her desk.

And so I shared a pot of tea with this kind lady from the Red Cross. I poured out my story again, but this time adding that my Edward Sebastian Christian was also a member of the Owen family. A cousin of Wilfred Owen. "So you see," I told her, "I must read all of this poem."

****

225

The lifeboat drill went well. No one joked or even smiled, let alone laughed. This was very serious business. We did not actually get into the boats, but stood beside them in our lifejackets, listening to the clipped instructions of the crew members. Looking around, shivering in apprehension, I played a calming game of guessing who the war brides were. Connie was standing behind me, so I sought out thirteen more on the deck. I assumed they would be all around me, as our cabins were near each other so we should be near the same rescue boats. One lady stood apart, dressed in black from head to toe, brightened only by her drab life vest, her head down, shaking slightly. When she raised her eyes, I could see tears streaming down her face, ruining her powder. Connie moved in front of me and crossed over to her, taking her arm and smiling at her. "This is Barbara. One of us," she whispered to me. I smiled my best back at this terrified waif in black.

"There's three more over there," Barbara said in hushed tones, pointing to the railing. I saw them, huddled together against the Atlantic winds, bent over, arms around each other. One of them for some reason wore a red hat with a black wispy veil. I was sure at any moment that hat would blow off into oblivion. And it did as we watched, a tiny red dot sinking into the sea. The dark owner of the improbable hat began to sob at her loss.

So that made six war brides I could see. *Get it together, ladies. You've come this far.* "Pull your finger out," as Edward would say. And where were the rest of us hiding anyway?

****

Jane wasted no time in hosting a tea as she had

suggested. That afternoon, fifteen brides of the air gathered in the small salon off the dining room. We had all dressed for the occasion; we all wore hats, save one who had watched hers blow away earlier in the day. We showed off our fine silk stockings, knowing we would soon lose this luxury, among many others. Jane had ordered the fine china and silver tea service with a spread of pâté and cucumber finger sandwiches, scones, and strawberry tarts. She played Mother, pouring tea into Spode blue and gold china cups. It was a lovely tea. We chatted lightly at first until Connie dove deeper by telling her marriage story. Then one by one we heard each other's tale. We were from Michigan, Ohio, New York, Florida, Pennsylvania, Iowa, even California. We were from farms, factories, offices, libraries, shops, schools, and even hospitals. We were diverse in home and career, yet united in our love for British airmen. It was a glorious afternoon, and we were relaxed and laughing by the time the sun began to drop to the horizon. Reinvigorated, we left the salon, thanking Jane profusely and once again on course for our goal, Liverpool, our tears exchanged for smiles.

****

Several of us met up again for the last dinner sitting at seven. It was so good to have friends on this ship. Friends who understood each other. We decided as a group to take in the showing of *Andy Hardy* that night, knowing Mickey Rooney's antics would keep our spirits up.

****

That night back in my cabin, I dreamed. It was a mad dream of bizarre hats flying at me from nowhere. I was alone on deck, in a chair, in my nightdress, the one

I had refused to wear my wedding night when I was so angry with Edward. It did me no good now either, a thin armor against the gusts of wind that buffeted me about in the wooden chair. I felt for my hat, but instead my fingers touched rough canvas across my face. I realized that I wore a gas mask tightened by a strap around the back of my head. The apparatus had a long nose, like an aardvark that slumped down onto my chest. I felt further up my forehead and was relieved to feel the weave of a lacy veil over my mask. I was dressed properly for tea.

A steward appeared with a tray of sandwiches and a mug of tea. He was blind, his eyes covered with a cloth tied behind his head. Groping for the table and depositing the food, he felt for my face with his fingers and lowered my mask. "The sandwiches are very tasty today," he said, shouting over the wind, "especially the mustard egg."

"Thank you," I said, struggling with the bulky mask. "What is your name?" I asked, being polite and not really caring who he was.

"My name is Wilfred Owen," he replied, his mouth nowhere near a smile, his eyes covered.

"The poet?" I asked, sitting up straight, chewing on a sandwich.

"Don't bother," he said. "My eyes are as dead as I am."

"I'm so sorry," I said, not knowing what else I could say to comfort him.

"Don't worry," he intoned. "Dulce Et Decorum Est. End of."

He disappeared as he had appeared, and I was alone again. As I reached for a sandwich, a great swoosh took the entire table, tray, sandwiches, and tea and tossed it overboard into the ocean. My hat followed, sailing into the air, the gas mask right behind.

****

Early the next morning, I dressed in my sea-going trousers and sweater, grabbed a jacket, and faced the fresh air breezes coming off the Atlantic. Standing alone, squinting at the horizon, I so hoped to hear a sailor yell, "Land ho!" just like in the movies. Instead, I jumped as someone touched my hand and slipped an arm through mine. Assuming it must be one of the brave fifteen war brides, I continued to take in the sea air in quiet contemplation. "Nothing like the sea air." I jumped again, startled by the deep male voice beside me. Turning to him, I recognized his Roman collar and knew he must be the ship chaplain. Recovering from the surprise, I stammered out a good morning.

"You must be one of the war brides," he said. "The ship is abuzz with your courage."

"Yes, I'm Millie Owen," I said, blushing even deeper than my already ruddy complexion, my tanned face further roughened by the sea breezes. He was a middle-aged man, with the beginnings of chubby jowls lapping over his priestly collar. His warm brown eyes rested under bushy eyebrows which were flecked with gray. He wore wire-rim glasses much like my father's. His warmth took me home to Ecorse as I fought back tears.

"I'm Father Joe. And where is Millie Owen from?" he asked, his eyes taking in the blush and the hesitation in speech.

"Michigan," I answered, pulling myself together. I would not cry. "Ecorse, Michigan, outside of Detroit."

"Catholic?"

"Yes, Father." Now I was embarrassed that I'd not sought him out earlier in the voyage.

"You've not been to see me yet, my child." Maybe it was my good old Catholic guilt, but his eyes grew colder and seemed to bore into mine.

"I meant to, but…"

"You must keep your faith strong, especially once you have arrived in England. Your life will not be easy."

"I know, Father. I did not leave my home easily." The tears were welling again, and I wiped them away with my glove. "I meant to confess to you, but…" I was crying now, too hard for the wind off the ocean to hide my tears anymore.

"Come. Come, Millie," the priest soothed. "Just tell me about your family and what is making you so sad when you should be so joyful for your new life." He took my gloved hand and waited for me to tell my story.

This time my story emphasized my family. Edward took a back seat to my guilt, my pain at deceiving them. I spoke of the letters I had written to my family and Miss Jackson. I told him of abandoning my nursing. I condemned myself for breaking the commandment, of failing to honor my mother and my father. I berated myself for involving Gary, Andy, and Meg in my deception. Their complicity weighed heavily on my heart. Even the usually jovial Andy had been so serious and uncharacteristically quiet at the pier in New York. I was a terrible person, selfish as selfish could be.

"Whoa, Millie," Father Joe said, having listened to my story as it tumbled nonstop from me as I gazed out to the water, never taking my eyes off the horizon, never slowing down, just talking full speed ahead. "You have been through so much, but you must let me help you take this heavy burden of loss from your shoulders or you will carry it with you, and it will destroy your new life."

"But Father, how do I do that?" I turned to him, seeking absolution in his face. I shivered in my jacket, waiting for the miracle cure for my guilt.

"You must write to your parents again as soon as you are settled. Show them your new life is a good one, in spite of the war. Relieve their worries. They have lost a daughter to a pilot they barely met and need to know you have not made a foolish mistake."

"Yes, Father, I will do that soon. I promise." I turned back to the water, feeling it wash over me, cleansing me, forgiving me.

"Millie," he said, touching my arm again. "Let me give you my blessing."

I knelt on the deck of the ship, my head bowed as Father Joe made the sign of the cross, blessing me. How many blessings from how many priests had I welcomed in my life? The tears came again as he helped me to my feet. I swayed in the breezes, regaining my balance.

"Millie, above all, do not let your pride come first. In what lies ahead and behind, go first with your heart and be humbled by love. Lead with the compassion you felt as you nursed your patients. Remember your father's example, what you saw in his office. His acceptance of a chicken in payment for his services."

"Thank you, Father," I said, humbled indeed by this conversation and smiling, remembering my mother handing off the payment chicken to Aunt Lill to be plucked and dressed.

"Go with God," he said, hugging me. "And go to mass once in a while, too. Or just pray in that ancient chapel at Sand Castles. Don't forget us. Keep the faith." Then he walked away, and I was alone with the sea, yet somehow buoyed for the future.

****

The rest of the crossing was uneventful. The lifeboats were never needed. If we ever were in danger, it was kept from us. We knew of no torpedoes threatening the ship. No planes buzzed us. The destroyer did its job, shepherding us to the port of Liverpool. The movies were entertaining, as were the lectures on England and the war. I managed one early morning mass just for Father Joe. A handful of passengers and two other war brides knelt for one last blessing, and I took communion.

As we approached Liverpool, we were ready. We understood the rationing system. We knew about the Women's Land Army, tending crops and livestock. We knew about the Blitz-bombed ruins of cities across the country. We knew about the bravery of King George and Queen Elizabeth as they refused to leave London. We knew about the courage of the British people as they lost homes and family. We knew about the children evacuated to the country for safety. We knew about Prime Minister Winston Churchill and his words that so inspired his countrymen. But most of all, we loved and feared for our airmen, who were the few owed so much by so many.

****

"We're bonkers, you know?" I said that last night in our cabin.

"Naïve, I would say." Connie stood to stretch her bones, finishing up her packing.

"What lies ahead?" Connie asked.

"Love, I hope."

"Promise me one thing, kiddo. If things ever get rough, Millie, you know, if things don't pan out like they do in your romance novels, don't forget I won't be far away. Promise me."

I looked into her very serious face and promised. But nothing could have prepared me for what I was about to face.

Chapter 20

The ship arrived safely in Liverpool. All fifteen of us were on deck at the railing in the dim light of twilight, dressed in our Sunday best, our hats and veils pinned in place. A light rain was falling. We were not prepared for what we saw. We had heard in a special lecture on Liverpool how it had been severely bombed right before last Christmas. As the main port for ships to embark for the never-ending Battle of the Atlantic, it was a major target for German bombs. RAF fighter planes defended the city. Women and children had been evacuated in 1939, but when no bombs fell at first, in the Phony War, they had returned only to leave again in late 1940. The Christmas raids had taken almost four hundred lives here. It was also a port where fuel, food, and raw materials arrived. We would be one of the last passenger ships allowed to dock, we were told. Peering out into the growing darkness, we could see the large barrage balloons which kept bombers from flying below five thousand feet. We could also spot the decoy fires on the River Dee. The city itself was wearing black for the occasion of our arrival as night fell. A shiver ran down my spine as I looked out, very unsure of my decision to come here. A tugboat pulled up alongside of us to guide the ship into the dock area.

"Ladies, please step back for your own safety while the ship slips into the pier."

We waited for what seemed forever, but we were soon in place, the gangplank was lowered, and we were told it was safe to come forward. It was time for last-minute hugs and goodbyes. Jane had typed a list of all our names and British addresses for us. She had raised her eyebrows, very impressed with my Sand Castles Hall home. Connie and I promised to be in touch. She was headed for Somerset, which was not that far from Cornwall she assured me. She would be living on the Childs cider farm. I had no idea then how important a role she would play in my life. For some of the ladies, like me, we were fortunate to be met by our pilots at the pier. Others had family coming to meet and welcome them. Two were on their own to find their ways. The captain wished us well, and off we went, stepping carefully in the dim light. Connie and I were holding hands as we descended the wobbly gangplank.

"I so need a cigarette," she said, sighing in the near-darkness. Her Harry was to meet her here in Liverpool. "Is my lipstick presentable?"

"You want a beauty critique in this bad light?" I asked, laughing at her, shaking my head.

"Good point," she agreed. "We all look just damn fine in this light. What a blessing."

Stepping off the gangplank, we crossed gingerly onto the cement of the pier, gripping each other for support as we exchanged our sea legs for land legs. Around us was the debris of war, crumbled piles of bricks and cement and hastily rebuilt structures in order to keep the port operational. A single spotlight, beam low, marked our way. The odor of something burning permeated our senses as we stood, not knowing quite what to do except keep moving along with the other passengers.

"Connie!" A young man in blue uniform pushed his way through the crowd, rushing to us. He grabbed Connie in a huge bear hug and twirled her around, almost knocking down a little boy behind her. Planting a firm kiss on her mouth, he swung her around once more.

"Harry," she gasped, "put me down. You'll hurt yourself."

I stood awkwardly, scanning the crowd for my pilot as Connie scrambled to introduce me to hers.

"Harry, this is Millie, my cabin mate for one hell of a crossing," she said, pushing me toward Harry. He was gorgeous, of course, with that wonderful British accent. He was a mechanic by trade, with dark green eyes that shone even in this dim light. He was a ginger, as the Brits say, red hair curling around his face in the damp misty rain.

"Millie," he said, bowing slightly, "welcome to the old sod."

I had no chance to respond as I was grabbed from behind, spun around, and smacked with a deep kiss. Coming up for air, I stepped back, my heart racing to the moon.

"You had better be Edward," Connie said, holding her hand out. "I'm Connie, cabin mate to your wife, Millie."

"Welcome, Connie. I hope you took good care of my wife," Edward said, reaching around me and shaking Connie's hand and then Harry's.

After one more farewell hug, Connie and her pilot disappeared into the crush of people, leaving Edward and me alone. I had promised Connie to keep in touch.

That would happen.

"My darling," Edward asked, "Is this all too dreadful for you? Liverpool is a shambles."

"Shocking, but your kiss has lifted me above it," I said, searching for his blue eyes in the growing darkness.

"Plenty later. I've found us a room in a pub away from the docks, near the train station. It'll be safer there. Let's see if your luggage is anywhere to be found."

"I can get it in the morning," I said, hoping I didn't sound too eager. "I have all I need for the night with me."

"You tart." Edward laughed. "I've taught you too well. We can come back here tomorrow morning before we catch the train for Penzance. That will be a daylong journey, I'm afraid."

He took my hand, kissed me once more, and we were off to start our married life in England. The crowd on the dock had dispersed. All the war brides were gone. Fifteen women were beginning their new lives in a very old, courageous land.

We walked along the road from the port, arm in arm, passing so many other couples, happy to be reunited with their servicemen. Edward was quiet, but I talked a mile a minute detailing the crossing. One by one I introduced him to all the war brides, my priest, my librarian, and of course, the movies we'd seen, the lectures we'd heard, the meals we'd shared. Edward laughed at my enthusiasm, mostly hugging me as if to make sure I was really there and safe after an Atlantic journey that had been perilous, to say the least.

"Here we are," he said, stopping in front of an old

stone pub called the Duke of Wellington. It seemed to be unscathed by war. There was little light, as I could see the blackout curtains had been closed tight. The moonlight guided us along the path. "It's a bomber's moon," Edward whispered.

"Is that good or bad?" I asked.

"That depends where the moon is shining and which side of the war you're flying for," Edward said, staring upwards to the night sky.

"I could murder a shandy," I said, laughing as I forged ahead to the wooden door.

"I think you've grown accustomed to more than tea on that boat," he called after me as I towed him by the hand.

"Ship, darling," I corrected him as he opened the heavy door, and we entered our temporary housing. A roaring fire greeted us as Edward talked to the barkeep and got our room key. I realized we were very lucky to have this room.

"Sit down over there," Edward called back at me. "I'll get us drinks."

I fell into an old soft leather chair by the fire. It was good to be out of the rainy damp. Edward came and plopped our drinks on the small wooden table that separated the two old armchairs. The table was carved with names and initials, rough testimonies to other lives, other times. Evidence that A.L. or M.R. had sipped ale here as we did now. Edward told me about the Eagle Pub in Cambridge. It was famous for its ceilings covered with the names and initials of pilots who hung out there. He said he had climbed on the shoulders of airmen to paint our initials in a silly heart on that ceiling. He'd take me there he promised. We nursed our drinks as we fell into staring at each other, still finding it hard to believe we were both here together in this ancient stone inn. We had made it. We reveled in this silence by this fire. The odds were in our favor for this night anyway.

Drinks finished and empty mugs deposited on the table, we said good night to the barkeep, Paul, who supplied us with a candle to light our way. Thoughts of Bella and her Paul shivered down my spine. I had never been able to shake that movie, *Gaslight*. We climbed the stone steps arm in arm to our room just to the left of the stairs. Once inside, we found another candle already lighting the room with a soft glow. Two pink hot water bottles had been filled and placed on our pillows. "Woman," Edward commanded, "get undressed and into bed."

"I might want to keep my coat on," I warned, contradicting myself as I unbuttoned it.

"Not tonight," Edward said, already out of his uniform and into the bed. "Tonight we keep each other warm."

I took a candle and found a bathroom down the hall. It had a toilet like I'd never seen, with a large overhead tank and a chain to flush. I ran the tap water in the sink and of course, it was icy cold. I splashed my face with it anyway and shivered my way back to the room. Edward was nestled under the down quilt, but he flung it back open and gestured me inside. Crawling onto the lumpy mattress, I snuggled up to him as he pulled the cover over us both.

"If you get caught short during the night," he said, "there's a chamber pot under the bed."

"Stop the sweet nothings in my ear," I said.

"Enough charm."

"But not enough of this," Edward said, his voice lowered to a sexy purr and his hand moving up under my nightie. "Let's get rid of this."

With one pull, I was nude and shivering either from the frigid air or Edward's wandering fingers. I couldn't tell which, and for the moment I didn't care. Edward moved on top of me, the quilt over us. Heat began to rise through me as we moved together, closer than usual just to stay warm. A sweaty film seemed like glue between us as we rocked the old mattress, keeping our language low, sure the rooms around us could hear. Edward gripped me closer, his mouth covering mine, his tongue darting, lifting himself enough to touch my breast. Then it was over, and we huddled together until Edward broke the lock between us to reach over to the chair where his jacket hung. "I need a fag," he said, coming up from the chair with his cigarettes and lighter. A blast of cold air froze my breasts as he leaned away, pulling the cover down with him.

Propping himself up against the bedframe, he positioned me against his chest and then lit up his cigarette, covering us with the quilt again.

"You know," he said, "you're a pitiful shag."

"What?" I laughed, using my British slang. "Are you winding me up?" My head was buried in his chest as I felt the blush start its rise to my cheeks.

"Do you know," he asked, "when you Catholic girls were busy making sandwiches at the Olds house on Grosse Ile what was going on upstairs on the second floor? Any idea?"

I lifted my head and looked up at him, puzzled. "No, what?"

"It was a brothel, my darling Millie. USO ladies gave us whatever we wanted to keep our spirits up. And our spirits weren't the only things up." Edward took a drag on his cigarette and with his other hand moved mine down under the covers.

"But Father Champion?" I asked, pulling my hand back up.

"Not sure if the old papist knew or not. There were definitely religious experiences going on up there though."

I was hurt at this change in Edward. Not knowing what to say, I turned over and reached for the hot water bottle. Tucking it to my tummy, I faced away from him, hoping sleep would come. Edward reached back over and pulled me to him, his cigarette butt in the ashtray on the table. "I'll teach you, my trouble and strife." I remained silent, tears wetting the pillowcase. "I'll have to teach you to love me up, or else I'll see other women. Why, within two weeks, I'll move another woman into Sand Castles. Someone who knows her tricks. And mine. Maybe a Land Girl."

With that he turned away from me, reaching for his hot water bottle. I was Bella.

Chapter 21

I awoke early that next cold morning. My hot water bottle now useless, I found my nightie and robe and went to the bathroom. Edward's demands of the night before were real, I told myself. They had been no dream. And he was right, I knew. He had married a sheltered virgin. I had no idea how to please him, but it certainly was not lying there expecting him to do all the work. I would be his willing pupil. I would learn how to please him. I would do tricks the nuns would blush over. But I could not live with his cruelty. I would not be his Bella. Slapping cold water on my face, I toweled off and tried to put light powder on with a coat of pink lipstick. I pulled on a skirt and blouse over my silk undies and took a deep breath as I crossed back to the room.

Edward was also dressed and sitting on the bed. He said little as he took my arm and escorted me down the steps for breakfast. The fire was again stoked, and we took our same chairs as the night before.

"Paul," Edward called, "what's for breakfast?"

Paul came over to our table and recited a very short menu. "Rationing allows a bowl of porridge and tea and toast. I'm afraid that's all. Sorry. Yanks aren't used to that."

"That's fine," I replied, embarrassed to seem a glutton.

"I can give you a dollop of milk for your porridge and tea. Homemade marmalade for your toast," he continued, wiping his hands nervously on his apron.

"That'll be fine, Paul," Edward said, lighting up a cigarette. "We have three Land Girls at the estate, so there will be more fresh vegetables in Cornwall," Edward said to me after Paul had hurried to the kitchen.

Land Girls? I wondered. Did they know Edward's tricks? Did he know theirs?

"You're quiet this morning," Edward said, blowing smoke rings into the air, relaxed in his chair,

What could I say? "I'm sorry about last night." I stared into the fire, for the first time not wanting to look at him.

"Whatever for? Look at me, you ninny." Edward asked, putting out his cigarette and looking me straight in the eye as I raised my head to him.

"For not being enough for you...you know, in bed."

"You silly goose," he said in his best Maxim de Winter impersonation. "It can only improve."

"Teach me," I begged, my lip trembling, "but respect me."

"We have a saying over here for wives. 'Just close your eyes and think of England.' A sacrifice of sorts. Your war effort."

I was blushing red now. Not knowing where to train my eyes, I looked down.

"You're as red as the beetroot our Land Girls weed." He laughed, leaning over and lifting my chin as Paul arrived with a tray of our steaming bowls of porridge, a teapot and cups, and a jam jar. "Let me play Mother," Edward said. "As long as you play wife. Then

I will respect you for many reasons."

****

After breakfast we walked down to the port again to pick up my luggage. It was just a single suitcase. I had packed light again. But now with the first taste of rationing, I wondered if that had been wise. The port was a different sight in the daylight. The damage was more apparent. It was as if Edward's behavior of the night before and the bleak images of Liverpool this morning were combining to belt me with a good dose of reality. I waited by the pier while Edward sought out the office for my suitcase. The ocean breeze took me back to conversations with the war brides and Father Joe and the compassion he had urged I show. If war was distressing Edward, I would be his oasis no matter what. I saw him coming out of the office with my luggage and hurried to him with a big smile and planted a kiss on his cheek. "I love you," I said, stepping back and framing him against the sea. He didn't reply.

We set off for the Liverpool Central Station where we found our train already chugging, waiting for us. The Salvation Army was waiting, too, with cheese and pickle sandwiches and tea and biscuits for our journey. We found our seats on a rear car, noting the troops crowding the train, boarding with raucous shouts as they grabbed seats. I would be far outnumbered by men on this journey.

Balancing our tea and food, I sat down while Edward placed my suitcase above us. He had only a small kit he kept with him. He sat next to me, several airmen across from us.

"This is a long journey," Edward said into my ear, grabbing his cup of tea. "We've got at least twenty stops until Penzance, but you'll get to see the country this way."

"What cities?" I asked, remembering our lecture on the great cities of England.

"You American, ma'am?" asked one of the servicemen sitting across from us.

"Yes, I am," I admitted somewhat unsure of myself, squeezing closer to Edward and sipping my tea.

"My wife," Edward said, hopefully proud of me.

"Well, ducks," the man continued, "you're about to get a scenic tour of merry old England. Birmingham. Exeter, Plymouth, Truro."

"That's if she can see what the Blitz has left beneath the skies," the pilot next to him said, shaking his head.

"Listen, mates," Edward interrupted, "she's just arrived here by ship."

"Welcome," they both said at once. "We will be silent." With that they both leaned back into their seats, closed their eyes, and I knew they would be no bother at all. I remember my dad saying that a soldier could sleep anywhere at all at any time.

With that the train began the journey from the first station. Edward was also soon asleep, having trusted me with the sandwiches and biscuits. He leaned against the window, slumped and uncomfortable, but I knew he was feeling no pain. And me, I watched over my husband and peered around him out the window, anxious to see my newly adopted country as it passed by.

****

The conductor yelled, "Plymouth," as the train slowed. Edward roused and sat up, stretching his arm across me. The two airmen stood, gathering their belongings, and prepared to leave the train.

"Plymouth has been hit hard," one of them said to me. "The Germans love to blitz our ports."

"You can't see the damage from here," Edward said. "The docks are bad though. It'll be better as we go further west. You lads are off then?" he asked.

"Yes," the airman replied. "Sorry we didn't talk much. We needed our kip." With that the two were gone to their war, and Edward and I faced ours.

"Ships in the night," Edward mused, putting his arm around me. "I'll never see them again."

"Sandwich?" I asked him, handing him a cheese and pickle.

He smiled and took the brown bag from me. "Won't be long now," he said. "Let's hope Cook has a decent supper for us."

We had the coach to ourselves, so Edward stretched out, his legs spanning the aisle to the opposite seats. I curled up against his chest, my legs tucked under my skirt.

"Time for a quickie?" he asked, slipping his hand under my blouse, holding his sandwich with his other hand. We were interrupted by the tea lady knocking on the door. I sat up, but Edward remained in his casual pose, legs up on the seat.

"Tea?" she asked. She was one of those nondescript volunteers doing her bit for King and country. She noticed Edward's feet, but said nothing. A uniform gave you a lot of privileges it seemed.

"Yes, please," I answered. "One white, the other white with two sugars."

"Here you go," she said, handing over two cups.

"And here are biscuits, too."

Edward put his feet down and reached for one cup. He smiled his best smile and gave her a gracious "Ta." I grabbed the other cup, and she left us alone again.

The train began its journey again, headed to Penzance with just a few stops in between. Edward and I drank our tea together, the quickie forgotten for the moment. Cup emptied, Edward moved across to the other seat to stretch out for the last leg of the ride. I moved to the window as we left Plymouth. I felt like a little child with her nose pressed against the glass of J.L. Hudson's windows at Christmas time. They were famous for their festive window designs. It was a family tradition each year to go see the new designs. Santa was available for consultations, of course, on the floor that was a wonderland of toy trains and baby dolls. Children would wait in line, some patient, some crying to whisper in Santa's ears what they wanted under their tree that year. Another tradition was the Thanksgiving parade of floats and huge balloons that meandered down Woodward every year. The climax was always Santa in his sleigh with his helper, Christmas Carol. What would happen if America entered the war? Would these traditions continue or would blackout curtains shutter the Detroit avenues like the streets of England?

"Wait till you see St. Michael's Mount," Edward said. "When the tide is out, one may walk the sand, but one has to go by boat when the tide is in. And you will love Truro Cathedral." He was awake now, and who knew how long he had been watching me in my reverie of Detroit and Santa. "If it weren't for this damn war, I would love to escort you to all the sights. Instead you will see abandoned roads, for lack of petrol, and military pillboxes on the cliffs. War sucks the beauty out of everything." Sadness enveloped him, passing over his face, dulling his blue eyes, and I was struck again by Father Joe's admonition to listen and show compassion for this man.

"But Sand Castles must be beautiful sitting above the cove," I suggested, hoping to see the cloud lift.

"Yes, if you ignore the Land Girls weeding in government allotments. And the blackout curtains in fifty windows. And soon, Mother tells me, the house will be requisitioned as a convalescent home for soldiers."

"Perhaps I could be of help," I said, trying to find a purpose for me in all this.

"What? Getting dirt under your varnished nails, digging potatoes, or weeding beetroot?" His mood was past sadness and into bitter sarcasm now.

"I'm sure I can be useful here," I persisted, half-wishing he'd go back to sleep. He sighed and smiled, just staring at me as if he had checked out for another planet. A peaceful one.

"End of," he said, stretching out again. My wish was granted as he drifted off again.

I drifted off, curling up on the seat alone. I don't know how long I slept only to wake with a hand shaking me. I peered into Edward's face leaning over me. "Wake up, darling," he said gently. "We're in Penzance."

"What time is it?" I asked, sitting up and straightening the wrinkles from my skirt as best I could.

"Just after seven. Let me get your suitcase, sleepyhead," he offered. "I've been watching you sleep through the last few stops. You looked so peaceful I hated to wake you." He was cheerful, supportive Edward again as he retrieved my bag from the overhead rack. He must be happy to be home with a new American wife to show off. Maybe the sight of Sand Castles would even out his mercurial temperament.

"Penzance, like the pirates?" I asked, finding his mood contagious.

"Ah, so you know your Gilbert and Sullivan operettas," he said, impressed.

"My dad loves them," I replied, standing firmly, my imaginary cutlass drawn. I was ready to face Penzance and the pirates.

We stepped off the train and into a really tiny station. It was not very crowded, and I could feel the rise in temperature after the coolness of Liverpool. We walked together, Edward carrying my suitcase, hand in hand. I hoped I didn't look too crumpled, with my hair all stringy after an all-day train ride. Before we approached the exit, I spotted a young girl sitting alone on a bench across the track. She was crying and pulling at her leg. A small bag sat at her feet, and she clutched a small box in her lap.

"Oh, look," I said to Edward. "That little girl. Alone." Before he could reply, I walked around the front of the train, up the stairs and over the overpass. He caught up with me as I descended the steps on the other side and hurried over to her.

"Are you all right?" I asked her, looking into green eyes below scruffy irregular bangs. Tears smudged her face, clotting the steamy humidity with the dirt on her face. As she scratched at her leg, I could see a heavy brace on her right leg.

"I come from London," she said, reaching for my hand. I saw a badge pinned on her coat that said "Maisie Rice."

"Maisie?" I asked. "Why are you here?" I sat down next to her and put my arm around her. Edward remained standing, silent.

"I come on the train." She sobbed. "There was ten of us. I couldn't come before because I had a sickness." She poked at her leg and cried even harder.

"And you've been sitting here all day?" I was shocked. I had heard about the evacuees, known about the ship bringing thousands of mums and their children to Canada and the USA, but those stories did not prepare me for the sight of this waif in this station alone.

She couldn't talk. She was convulsed in sobs, burrowing into my coat. "Maisie, Maisie," I soothed her and rocked her in my arms.

Edward spoke up. "Where have all the other children gone?" He had knelt down in front of her and taken her hand in his.

"They got chose," she said, hiccupping between sobs.

"Chose?" I asked, my eyes seeking answers from Edward.

"When the evacuees arrive here, the locals come and pick and choose among them. They are looking for healthy children and sometimes set them to work," he said softly so as not to further upset Maisie.

"This is crazy," I said. "Is there no one in charge here?"

"Probably took the train back to London earlier," Edward surmised. "I'm not proud of this system, don't get me wrong." His brow furrowed as he stood up. "Let me see if I can find someone."

He left us alone, and it was then that I determined Maisie's fate. She would come with us to Sand Castles Hall.

"Maisie," I whispered leaning over her as she clutched my coat, "is your sickness polio?"

"Yes, ma'am," she said. "Mum says I'll be all right. She says I should be proud because Mr. Roosevelt has the same sickness."

"Why, yes, he does," I agreed. "He is our president, you know, and he can do anything."

"Does he have a brace?" she asked, turning her tearstained face up to mine.

My heart stolen, I answered, "Yes, I believe he does."

Maisie smiled at me, reaching to touch my hair. "You're beautiful," she said. "I have a gas mask right here." She held up her box to me. "In case there are bombs like in London."

Edward returned, reporting that he had found a lady from the Red Cross who said that Maisie was due to be put back on the train and returned to London as no one here wanted the responsibility of taking care of her.

"I do," I said in a firm way, echoing my wedding vows. I stood up, releasing my arm from Maisie, and said, "We have to take her. I can't leave her here."

As we discussed the decision, Edward none too keen, the Red Cross volunteer approached us. Seeing how distressed the little girl was, she offered her a biscuit and a small cup of milk, kneeling down before her.

"My wife is keen to help her," Edward said,

reaching down to stroke Maisie's hair.

"Yes, please." I reinforced Edward's offer, hoping it was just that, an offer. I stood next to him, the two of us a united front.

"It's not up to me," the volunteer stated, standing up and facing us, "but there doesn't seem to be anyone else around in charge."

"The townspeople don't treat these children well," Edward added. "They even run a second shift at the local school for them so they don't mingle with their children."

"That settles it," I said. "We will take her."

"And you are?" she asked, looking us up and down.

From behind me, I felt a little hand reach out and grip mine. I squeezed it tight.

"Flight Sergeant Edward Sebastian Christian Owen, and this is my wife, Mildred," Edward replied, in a pompous tone. "We live at Sand Castles Hall. We can offer this child the best."

"Very well," she said, taking a notepad and pen from her pocket. "Please write your name and address here. Maisie…"

"Maisie Rice, that's me," the little girl said as she stood up between Edward and me, and found her balance, and even smiled.

Chapter 22

We walked out into the Cornish early evening breezes aware that our plan to take the paths along the cliff to the hall were now undone. Maisie would have to be carried, and that wouldn't do.

"Is there a bus?" I asked Edward as we stopped on the road, Maisie between us. She still looked very uncertain as she clutched both our hands, her gas mask hung around her neck. She seemed ready to erupt into tears again staring up at us, her head moving back and forth, first locking on me, then on Edward.

"What's a bus?" she asked, leaning on her strong leg.

"What we call a coach," Edward responded, hoisting her up in his arms. "But I doubt if there is one running this late in the day."

"Edward!" His name rang out in the country air, and we all turned to watch a man pull up beside us on the road, yelling a "whoa" to the two horses who towed his cart. He was a middle-aged man, his skin weathered and lined by outdoor chores. His fingers on the reins showed grime under his nails. His rough clothes fit snugly around his chubby body. A tan dog with hair covering its eyes plopped next to him and barked at Edward.

"Brian," Edward replied, "you're a godsend. Can you give us a ride up to the hall? Quiet, Dodgy,"

Edward said. "No need to scare the women."

"This is Dodgy, ladies. No worries. He's the kindest dog in the world. A mutt, though of curious lineage. So I christened him Dodgy." His skin crinkled around his eyes as he smiled. "Of course, Teddy boy. You and the lady hop on."

He held the horses still as Edward first put the luggage on board, then lifted me up and into the cart.

"And who is this wee pisky?" Brian asked, nodding at Maisie as she looked up at him from the side of the cart, wondering where she would sit. "There's room beside me and Dodgy up front, if she likes. She can ride in style like the royal princesses themselves."

"Oh, yes, please," she called out, smiling broadly at the thought of prancing horses.

"Very well," Edward agreed, walking around and lifting her up to Brian. "This is Maisie," he said. "She's all the way from London."

"So pleased to meet you, Maisie," Brian said. "Just sit tight." Maisie laughed as Dodgy attacked her with sloppy kisses.

Edward climbed into the cart across from me. "Brian is the head gardener at the hall," he explained. "A good chap."

With a lurch we were off. I could hear Maisie so excited ahead of us, giggling and laughing as Brian would lean over to talk to her, revealing secrets along the journey as he pointed here and there. She clung tightly as Brian had asked, her little hands gripping the hard seat on either side of her, Dodgy on the floor at her feet. Once we hit a rut on the dirt path, and Edward jumped up to secure her from behind in her seat, putting his arm around her. I was seeing a new Edward with

Maisie. Caring. Compassionate. I could see he would make a wonderful father.

The countryside was beautiful as we passed along the road. Centuries old trees bent to our little cart, welcoming us. Willows stretched down to the shrubs, nettles warned us away. Wild flowers scented our path in hues of yellow and red. No more snowy roads of Detroit. No cars buzzed by. Edward had told me most cars had been covered and stored away for lack of petrol. We were climbing up the road away from the sea, and I could feel the humidity wringing my clothes out, my back wet. We could never have walked this stretch with Maisie. I was learning that when a Brit told you a destination was just up the road, it would be a good mile at least.

"We'll be there soon," Edward said, moving across the cart to sit by me. "We'll come up by way of the back gates. Then you can look down the lawn to the cove."

"And we'll see the peacocks?" I asked, sure that Maisie would love the colorful birds prancing with pride.

"Yes," Edward said quietly, putting his arm around me. "You'll love me, won't you? No matter what?"

"What a strange thing to say. Of course." I became in my mind the second Mrs. de Winter on her first ride up the long sweeping road to Manderley. So unsure of herself as she faced her new role as mistress of the great estate. How odd for Edward to be the one hesitating and not me. I squeezed his hand that hung limply over my shoulder and turned to give him a reassuring kiss, but he was staring over my head at a huge spindly tree across the road. A lone black cat paced beneath it, yapping at us as we passed by, anxious to cross the road.

We rounded a bend and I saw the wrought iron gates ahead of us. Brian stopped the horses and turned around to us. "The gates are open for you; I'll lift Maisie down to you."

Edward hopped off the cart and grabbed Maisie as Brian hoisted her into the air. Then securing her away from the road by the gates, he returned for me and the luggage.

"Where's my gas mask?" she asked, pointing toward the pinkish sky. She had spotted in the distance a huge barrage balloon. I remembered from a lecture on the ship that the people of Cornwall have always feared a German invasion on their shores.

"No flies on you, Maisie," Edward said, ruffling her hair. "There are pillboxes along the cliffs also. Cornwall is not immune from the war," he said to me in a low voice. "We call that old balloon in the sky Belinda."

"The gate, Maisie," he said, pushing the iron latticework inwards as Brian pulled away with the cart, obviously headed to another entrance. "Just up this path." He pointed the way for us. The gate was an elaborate grill of a family crest, a peacock at its center. We traveled the path, tall trees our sentries. Yews, beeches, and oaks. Ancient soldiers saluting us. Brambles and nettles crept along beneath them. And then an unending carpet of bluebells. Entrancing. It was cooler in this shelter. The last trees parted for us, and I stopped, enchanted instantly by the shower of flowers all white and salmon. Rhododendrons high over my head. Hydrangeas at my waist. Azaleas enveloping me in sweet scent. All in pastels, none jarring. What a glorious welcome. Then Edward grasped my shoulders and, without saying a word, turned me to look down the lawn to the cliffs and beyond them to the sea. A peacock strutted into my view as I blocked the sun from my eyes. It was picture perfect. And well worth every trial I'd survived to see this. To breathe in ancient Cornwall at last.

"Oh, Edward," I said, "How perfect, even with the war." I reached for his hand. And the three of us stood silent, just taking it all in.

"There's an old stone boathouse down there." He dropped my hand and pointed. "It's built from the stones along the cove. We call it Serenity Cove."

"And the boat?" I asked, peering down the lawn, imagining the boathouse, hoping there had been no murders there, thinking back to Rebecca's boathouse.

"She's called the *Bluebell*," Edward said, picking up Maisie.

"Can we go on the boat?" she asked. "Please. Please."

I was just realizing how different Maisie's life in Cornwall was going to be. Maybe she would become a robust little girl away from the Blitz of London and its ashen smoking remains.

Just then Brian walked across the lawn closer down to the sea, pointing out the vegetable gardens that lay to the left of the lawn. We could see three girls bent over in the cool of the evening, one on her knees weeding, one bent, hoeing. The third walked over to talk to Brian.

"Those are the Land Girls," I explained to Maisie. They've come from cities to do the farming the men who are fighting in the war usually do."

"Are they from London?" she asked. "I could help," she said, twisting in Edward's arms, wanting to touch down on land again.

"You'll meet them later," he said, placing her back down on the green lawn. "Time to go meet the house staff. We'll go back around to the kitchen to surprise them."

Edward led the way as we walked back through the flowers and toward the house. It was majestic, two floors of rooms with more windows than I could count. As I watched, I saw the windows one by one become dark. Cornwall was no escape from blackouts. I knew behind these walls was a conservatory and a spectacular library. Many well-appointed bedrooms. And there would be the grand hall and staircase where all the descendants posed, painted in oils on the silken walls. In the salon would be tapestries from centuries back, depicting battles or outings on the lawn; peacocks, I'm sure would take part. Walking around the back of the house, we saw ivy creeping up the walls and an open courtyard, stables across the way. An old lady in faded uniform and apron was tossing a bowl of water on a small patch of vegetables. She ignored us as we crossed the courtyard and entered the kitchen. It was the kitchen you see in books, one wall a huge fireplace, large enough to walk right into. The stone walls were cut with window casings covered with chintz curtains. A large wooden table, scratched and battered, swallowed up the room. Truly, ten could be seated there. On the table were three mounds covered by cotton cloths, perhaps hiding bread dough as it rose. A bouquet of fresh flowers sat on the end of the table. Pots and pans hung from copper racks overhead. A hutch filled with dishes and cups sat across from the fireplace. This kitchen was somebody's home. That was obvious.

The three of us stood together in the doorway of the vacant kitchen. "Tickety-boo, wouldn't you say, Maisie?" Edward asked.

She just nodded, smiling, lost for words.

"Teddy?" The old lady pushed past me and grabbed Edward in a bear hug, rocking him back and forth. "Why didn't you say you were coming? You'll give me a fright, you will." She spoke in a distinct Cornish accent, much like Brian's. "And who is this pisky?" she asked, ignoring me for the moment.

"Maisie," he said, "an evacuee from London."

She stooped and gave her a hug and then stood and turned to me with a quick smile which revealed a missing tooth right up front. "And you, dearie?"

Edward stepped in and said softly, "This is my wife, Millie." Dead silence greeted his admission.

The old woman moved to the table without acknowledging me in any way. Pulling the cloth off one of the mounds of dough, she began to knead in a rocking manner as if holding on to something for strength. Then she started to punch the dough. Hard. Better it than me. She spoke, her eyes locking on Edward. "You married overseas, you damn fool. And to this daft American cow? What were you thinking? What were you thinking?"

Confused, I moved closer to Edward, reaching for his hand, but he pulled away. "I have to get back to the base," he said. "There's a coach at twenty-one hours."

With that he was out the door, leaving the pisky and me to fend for ourselves. I was stunned.

The pounding continued from the table as Maisie and I stood awkwardly. I could see the little girl's tears beginning, the joy of our arrival bleeding away.

"Sit yourselves down," she said at last, gesturing to the chairs across from her. "Would you like a drink? You must be parched."

"Yes, please," Maisie said, fearful of making her angry again. Cook, as I assumed she was called, moved to get a jug off the shelf by the window. Moving to the hutch, she filled two mugs and put them down on the table in front of us. I sipped first, and then Maisie copied me. It was water, but could have been champagne as it trickled down our parched throats.

"So," Cook said, staring me down as I put the mug back on the table, "I don't know what Edward has told you, so I'll just ask. Do you know who I am?"

"I assume you are the cook here at Sand Castles Hall," I said, staring right back at her. I didn't understand her attitude, rather haughty for a cook.

"Yes, I am that," she said, returning to beating her dough with a puzzling force.

Maisie had finished her water and watched the dough flatten. "Are you his mum?" she asked. "Is this your house?"

"Yes, dearie, I am his mum, but this is not my house." She laughed. Her eyes seemed to reach out and hook mine, dragging my heart from my chest. The water churned in my stomach as I jumped up, frantic to be rid of her. I crossed the kitchen to the door and ran into the courtyard, making it to the garden, leaning over and vomiting into the vegetables. What had I done? How could he lie to me? And compound his lies with taking on Maisie? Was he mad? I felt an arm around my legs and knew it was Maisie come to comfort me. I turned to her and drew her to me, my tears letting loose into her little shirt.

"Edward's mum has gone to find the lady," she said. "It'll be tickety-boo. Just wait."

Chapter 23

My dreams abandoned me that night, probably at odds with me as I had failed to take in any of their warnings of the disaster I now found myself in. Besides, I had far too little sleep to dream anything. I was living my nightmares now. The night before I had been summoned to the salon for tea with Lady Anna Renfrew, who was no relation to Edward at all I learned. I had found her sitting in an aristocratic pose on the settee, a young lady beside her. This was her daughter, Emily, who would have been Edward's sister if there were an inch of truth to his story. She gestured for me to sit across from them near the unlit fireplace. Edward's real mother, the cook, soon arrived with an elegant silver tray of tea and sandwiches, which she placed on the table before the two women. She left immediately, as she had charge of Maisie for the duration of this meeting. She seemed for all purposes a stranger with nothing to do with this crisis her son had manufactured.

"Shall I pour, Mother?" said Emily, reaching for a cup and saucer. She was a slight girl of about thirty or so, her blond hair loose around her shoulders, her casual blue summer dress flared about her on the couch. A thick belt emphasized her tiny waist. Her elegant hands with nails clear of varnish signaled to me that she had never done a true day's work in her life.

"Indeed." Lady Renfrew nodded. She seemed quite austere, a dead ringer for Queen Mary, her gray hair curled toward her eyes, her ears bared by tresses in a bun at the nape of her neck. She wore wire rims as if she had been reading. Dressed all in lavender wool crepe, she seemed out of another century, another time when pirates still roamed the Cornwall coves. Serenity Cove Edward had called it. Serenity, indeed. She pulled her glasses off and laid them on the side table and turned back to me.

"So, my dear, it seems our Edward has lied to you about his circumstances and then abandoned you here in my kitchen."

Taken aback by her honesty, I searched for words to match her boldness. "Spot on," was all I could come up with. I stared into her dark eyes, determined not to cry or appear the daft cow she must think I was.

"Here is my proposal," Lady Renfrew continued. "You seem to have compounded your mistake by acquiring the child, Maisie, at the train station."

"Edward said it would be all right," I interrupted. "She had spent the entire day in the station watching all the other children chosen but herself. It broke my heart."

"Yes," Emily said, "your heart is unquestionably well-intended, but perhaps it also leads you to be gullible to liars." She smiled and handed me a cup of tea across the table. I felt about six inches tall as she served my tea with cream and a lump of naiveté.

"Very well, we shall take on the responsibility for the child for the time being," Lady Renfrew continued, sipping her tea. "What to do with you is the question."

"Sandwich?" Emily asked, offering me a plate.

"No, thank you," I said, somehow sure they had heard of my vomit spewed across the vegetable patch. I didn't dare eat anything else. I sipped at my tea, waiting for the verdict. What would they "do" with me?

"I understand Edward has bolted, returning back to his base, leaving Cook to set you straight and that then you were sick in the garden," Lady Renfrew continued, drinking down her own tea and replacing the cup and saucer on the tray.

"I'm sorry," I said, so embarrassed that I might cry. I kept my head down, eyes averted. Emily giggled, but stopped abruptly as if remembering her superior standing in life.

"We have three Land Girls here working in our gardens," she went on. "You could join them until you decide what to do next. They sleep in a large suite on the second floor. There is room for you there with them. As for Maisie, she could stay with Cook for the time being." She sat back on the couch, having delivered the verdict, satisfied with herself. Very cold.

I was to be a farm laborer, digging in the dirt for beetroot and onions. The tears came then. Silent streams down my face. We stared at each other across the table. A man appeared at the doorway of the room and stood waiting.

"Albert," Lady Renfrew said, "please show Mrs. Owen to the Land Girls' suite. And make sure she has the proper uniform to begin work tomorrow. Now Millie, go along with him. Your belongings are already taken care of." She stood and dismissed me with a gesture toward the door and the awaiting Albert.

And I followed Albert from the salon into the grand hall and up the staircase I had envisioned before.

The Renfrew portraits lining the red silken walls sneered at me, deriding me for my stupidity. "Land Girl!" they seemed to call out at me. Compassion, Father Joe had advised. But where was the compassion for me? What kind of monster had I married?

The three Land Girls were already in the suite, which amounted to two sets of bunk beds and a bathroom off the main room. No better than the set-up in the boarding house in Pensacola. The only good thing was the breathtaking view from the suite down across the lawn to Serenity Cove, and beyond that the sea. I could lose myself in that, I knew, when I calmed down. If I ever did.

"So you're Millie," the first girl said. "You'll sleep up there." She pointed out the top bunk above a messy lower bed. "I'm Sophie."

"And I'm Judy. And this is Martine." She poked the girl on the other top bunk, who groaned and rolled over, facing the wall.

I surveyed the room and my new workmates. Sophie was a brunette with very dark eyes. Judy had the greenest eyes I'd ever seen, bordered by red bangs. Actually, I thought the British called them fringe. Martine was a lump facing away from me. I walked over to the one chair in the room and sagged my body across it, my spirits so far down they seemed to ooze onto the bare floor at my feet.

"Is it true you were sick in the vegetable patch?" Judy asked, crossing the room and standing over me, her eyebrows raised in expectation. "Old misery guts must have loved that."

"Let the kid alone," Martine mumbled, rolling over in her bunk and looking over at me. "Can't you see she's been crying?" Her dark eyes snapped at the other girls.

"She looks like a dog's dinner. I hope they don't expect us to clean up the sick," Judy protested, not willing to let my shame go.

"If it's any consolation, dearie," Sophie said, trying to console me, "Edward has tried it out on all three of us." She stood at the window, gazing out.

"The bugger played us all against each other. Snogged us all," Judy said, a look of disgust on her face.

"God's gift to women, that's our Teddy," Sophie said, "but we done him in when we found out."

"Plunked him down in that chair you're sitting in and told him off," Martine said, climbing down from the bunk. She was the beauty of the trio, her hazel eyes framed by a beautiful mane of auburn hair. She was movie star material.

"We tore a strip off that lad," Judy said.

I sat, more tears filling my eyes. What a fool I was. I opened my purse to retrieve a hankie, but was waylaid and began to search for my passport. Where was it? I tipped out my purse in my lap and sifted through lipsticks, change purse, hankies, comb, the RAF compact, the brooch. No passport. Panicked, I pawed the pile again.

"What are you looking for, love?" Sophie asked, crossing the room and kneeling beside me.

"My passport. It's gone." I began to sob now, pushing everything from my lap to the floor. My shoulders shook as I gave in to a torrent of tears.

"Go ahead and have a good weep, Millie," Sophie said. "We'll take care of you."

All three girls gathered around me in a show of solidarity. On her knees, Judy began to scoop up the contents of my purse from the floor. She held up the RAF compact. "Girls, will you look at this?" Martine got up and crossed the room to the desk. Opening the top draw, she picked through its contents and held up a similar compact. "Why it looks just like mine," she said, laughing. Then she dove into the drawer again. "And Judy, isn't this yours? And crikey, here's another one. Yours, Sophie?"

"Bloody bastard," Judy said. "Bloody bastard."

****

James leaned across the small aisle, smiling. "You're so deep in thought."

"Yes, I'm a million miles away. Sorry to be such poor company," I said.

"Just wanted to say that the Sally Ann lady says we're about an hour out of Liverpool."

"Thank you, James." But I was really back at Sand Castles, reliving my nightmare.

****

The days dragged on. I saw little of Cook. Perhaps that was best. I felt shame. For my utter stupidity in trusting him. I had no idea what she was feeling. Did she support her son at all costs? Had she no pity for me at all?

I ate meals with the Land Girls in a room off the kitchen. They did their best to cheer me up, introducing me to the radio programs they loved, their favorite, *It's that Man Again,* detailing the war adventures of Colonel Chinstrap and Mrs. Mopp. They explained to me that the RAF pilots had adopted the characters' famous lines, "After you, Claude. No, after you, Cecil," during aerial attacks to decide the order they would proceed. They lent me novels and took me on walks into the village. They did my hair and polished my toenails. They just tried to bring me back to life. I also spent more evenings with Maisie at the boathouse, guilty I had gotten her into this prison. At night I would flop into bed in the suite, ready for an exhausted, troubled sleep. Lady Renfrew was a ghost, only seen through a window, or getting into her car, or greeting guests on the steps. Emily picked flowers from the garden some days, her cotton summer dresses billowing around her hips. She did allow me to choose books from the magnificent library to read. Her first suggestion for me had been that best seller everyone loved, *Rebecca*. Apparently, there was no Earl Renfrew on the estate. No one knew his story or if they did, they kept it to themselves. And Charles, the true heir to Sand Castles, was off fighting his own war in the Atlantic. No, there would be no more teas with the likes of them. The lines were drawn. I was not of their class. Instead Brian sometimes invited me back to his cottage behind the main house. He watched over me in the fields as my skin reddened, wrinkled, and peeled in the blistering Cornish sun, kindly providing me with a salve for my hands when the hoe blistered them, and finding me an old straw hat to shade my eyes. He would puff on his pipe by the fire, Dodgy lounging at his feet, and tell Maisie and me the tales of old Cornwall. By day I wore the required uniform of corduroy breeches and rough shirt. When the inspector visited, I was told to hide in the boathouse, as I was not officially assigned and as an American would not be wanted anyway. I had to laugh at the permanent dirt under my nails. No, Edward, there was no varnish on these nails at all, only a layer of yellowish grime that defied removal by the strongest soap Brian could find.

****

One day when the weeding was finished, Brian said he had a special treat for us. Lady Renfrew had given her permission for us to take the *Bluebell* for a sail. Maisie and I watched as Brian lowered the boat into the water from beneath the boathouse. Down the lawn came Sophie, carrying a picnic basket, and Judy behind her with mugs and a thermos, no doubt tea. Martine, they said, was staying behind due to her fear of a touch of seasickness. It was a glorious afternoon, the wind whipping our hair and faces as we seemed to fly from the cove onto the sea. Maisie was the happiest I'd seen her, her worries dissolved in the spray.

I was working in the garden the next morning when he reappeared. I was wiping the sweat from my brow, shaking out my damp hair, leaning on my rake, when I saw Edward walking down the lawn toward us.

"Bastard on the lawn," Martine hissed, coming across to stand by me, waving at the other girls to join us in a protective wall. Together all four of us faced him as he approached.

"Ladies," Edward said, "if I might have a word in private with my wife."

"Thankless job that is," Sophie said, spitting in the dirt.

"Please, girls," I said, so angry with myself that my knees even now were weakened to their usual state when my husband was around.

"You call us if you need us," Judy said, looking Edward up and down with distaste. "Brian is right over there. Don't fall for his porkies." She pointed across the lawn to the shed where Brian lurked, waiting.

"Yes," Martine called back, "we'll be powdering our noses with our shiny compacts."

Edward and I walked away from the garden. I had no idea what he would say to me. What he could say to me. We walked on, not touching at all, not even a finger brushing a hand.

"Go change your clothes," he said abruptly. "You know I dislike you in casual trousers. I want to take you somewhere."

"Where?" I asked, staring out to the cove, still at a distance from him, both physical and mental.

"Just change," he repeated. "I'll wait round the back." We started up the lawn, still apart.

"Don't be daft, Millie," Martine called after us, shielding her eyes from the sun and raising her voice. "Stay with us. Don't fall for another load of codswallop."

Dangling like a marionette by my husband, I ignored her. I went upstairs to our room and changed into a green gingham cotton skirt and pale pink blouse, grabbing a sweater, too. I splashed water on my face and had time just to apply a bit of pale lipstick. My hair was beyond hope, curly and damp from my digging in the garden. I was so confused and angry with myself for once more giving in to his demands. But I argued that I had to get answers from Edward. Surely I was in no danger from my own husband.

As I headed back down the stairs, scenes from *Gaslight* flooded my mind, but I pushed them away as I entered the kitchen. Edward was seated at the table, his feet up on another chair, chatting with his mum, puffing on a cigarette. She was laughing at him, looking across the table as she kneaded dough, her hands pounding. She adored Edward, that was obvious. Silence cut their chin wag short as I walked in.

"That's better," Edward said, approving my wardrobe change. "I like you in green. We're going to the Mount, Mum," he said, standing and pushing the chair under the table.

"Will you be home for your tea?" she asked, kneading and ignoring me.

"Not sure. Not sure," he said, finally touching me as he took my arm and led me to the door.

We caught the coach down the road in front of the pub. Not a word had passed between us. Edward stood back and let me board first. I found a seat toward the middle, and Edward sat down beside me. He put an arm around the back of the seat, almost but not quite touching me.

I stared out through the window at the people passing by, even more confused now. My heart said to show compassion. Listen to Father Mike and Father Joe. My mind warned me off this man sitting so close to me yet so far away. The silence grew louder as everyone else chattered away. Soon we arrived in the town of Marazion. And across the causeway, I could see St. Michael's Mount. The ancient castle perched at the top of the mount. For centuries people had made this pilgrimage to the saint. It was stunning.

"Here we are," Edward said. "You will love this place. It's the stuff knightly tales are made of."

We climbed down from the coach and walked down to the beach. The tide was in, so we would need to take a boat out to the Mount. The breeze on my face was a refreshing respite from the strong sun of the potato patch. I reached for my sweater I had tucked over my arm, and Edward helped me on with it. "Would you like an ice cream?" he asked as casually as if we were on the Pensacola Beach and he was still the heir to Sand Castles.

"Maybe on the way back," I said, treading along the sand, my head down.

"Edward, my boy," a fisherman called out, "over here if you want a ride out."

"Yes," Edward waved and called back. "Come on," he said, taking my arm and hurrying me along. "I've known Neil since I was in breeches." We walked along the causeway as far as we could to the boat. Edward helped me in, and Neil caught me and spun me onto the boat as if I weighed nothing.

"Who's the young miss, Teddy?" he asked, eyeing me as I sat down, pulling my billowing skirt around my legs.

"She's my wife, Neil," Edward said, proud as one of the peacocks on the lawn. Maybe he did love me. Or had loved me.

"Your wife?"

"Yes," I spoke up, "from America."

"A flippin' war bride," Neil exclaimed into the wind. "What have you done, Teddy?"

The boat took us on the short ride to the Mount, Edward shouting against the wind, telling me that in the fifth century the Archangel Michael himself had appeared to fishermen on the Mount. He hugged me close as he gave me a history lesson. When we arrived, we clambered out of the boat, said goodbye to Neil, who refused any fare, and began to climb up to the castle.

My shoes were not exactly meant for climbing mounts, but I knew I could make it if I really concentrated, putting one foot after the other, ever climbing upwards. Perhaps my marriage could survive such a climb, also. Halfway up, we came upon a little niche on the path, a stone bench sheltered by trees and scarlet rhododendrons.

"Sit with me," Edward asked, reaching for my hand as he sat down on the ancient bench. I joined him, sitting halfway up this sacred Mount, praying silently for help. *St. Michael, please.*

Edward leaned in and kissed me on the cheek, and then his lips moved to mine. "I've missed you," he murmured, his fingers straying across my blouse.

"No," I said, pushing his hand away. "I need answers."

"Answers?" he asked, pulling back, reaching into his pocket for a cigarette and his lighter.

"Edward," I said, panic rising in my voice, "who are you?"

"I'm the bloke you married," he said, lighting his cigarette. "End of."

"You are the son of a cook," I continued, determined to know the truth. "You are not the godson of the Duke of Windsor. Not the cousin of Wilfred Owen. Not the heir to Sand Castles Hall. Am I correct?"

"What difference does that make?" he said, leaning back against the bench, his long legs extended before us in a casual stance, drawing in smoke from his cigarette. "I suppose you think I've gaslighted you, my darling."

"Am I in danger?" I asked, gaining courage as I

looked at him. Remembering Bella's words, I lost it, pounding on his chest, frantic, shouting, "Hit me. Hurt me. How can you torture me like this?"

"Another load of guff. Yes, yes," he said, exasperated. "Now my lines are supposed to be that I knew a girl who died in an asylum and how the eyes give madness away. Right? Go ahead, Bella, my dear, do tell me I tried to kill your mind."

I turned away from him. So lost in his cruel, mocking words, I could not watch. Had he killed my mind? My heart? There was no love coming from him. Just pain.

"I may not have a pot to piss in, my darling, but I am not a murderer," he said, crushing his half-smoked cigarette under his polished shoe. He stood and turned to me. "I'm going back to the base. Find your own way home. Go read another bloody book. Find true love in its pages." With that dismissal, he started back down the path, abandoning me once more. I waited with what little pride I had left forbidding me to run after him. He turned back and shouted, "Oh, that sapphire family ring? I bought it in a pawnshop in Pensacola, you little fool. Enjoy the beetroot."

He was gone…again. I continued the pilgrimage up the Mount in tears, praying to St. Michael for courage. I put one foot in front of the other, my throat dry from the exertion. I climbed and climbed, stumbling, unaware of what I must look like to those who passed by me on their way back down to the boats. My hair was blown wild, my face moist with sobbing, and my eyes swollen. Once at the top I stood, the breezes whipping my skirt around me, alone, confused, yet somehow closer to the truth.

****

It was at night when I could forget the drudgery of the day that I truly loved this place. Cornwall had seeped into my blood even under these dire conditions. The boathouse was cool in the evening, its stone walls keeping out the sinking sun's last weak onslaught of the day. Inside was a couch covered with several old musty quilts, comfy enough for naps. A scarred desk sat by a window looking out to sea, carved with initials of bygone sailors. A kerosene lamp hung by the door. Old fishing nets tumbled together in a heap by a rusty sink in the corner opposite the window. The *Bluebell* was stored beneath the floor. The water lapped against her hull as if pushing her out to play. No one took the boat out except Brian, but I understood Edward as a boy loved to sail. It was a quick walk from the boathouse to the sandy beach of Serenity Cove. The water was cold to the toes at first, but a soothing respite from the hours weeding in the gardens. I could forget the barrage balloons as I waded in the cove. Maisie was able to flail about in my arms in the water, her brace left behind on the sands. It was all magic to this London child. It could have been magic to me, too. There could have been "magic abroad in the air."

I had lost track of the time after the confrontation at the Mount, resigned to spending the remainder of the war as a Land Girl at Sand Castles Hall. It was just another evening in the boathouse. I was writing a letter while Maisie napped on the couch, Dodgy snoozing beside her. Before falling asleep, she had related to me in her breathless way the latest Cornish tale Brian had told her. It seemed a certain Parson Densham, who was so mad he drove his parishioners away from his church at Warleggan on the moors, had been found dead on the steps of his derelict parsonage. His vicious pack of dogs had vanished. And today his ghost paced the overgrown gardens of his parish. Of course, Maisie had begged Brian to take her to the wild moors to no avail. Her eyes had grown as wide and dark as those of the mad yapping dogs as she told me this gruesome bedtime story. She seemed to have acquired a new rather morbid fascination with death and murder, a legacy of her time in Cornwall with Brian.

****

And then he was there in the doorway. My stomach did its familiar flip at the sight of Edward in his blues. But this time the flip signaled a strange new mixture of fear, then love. The Cornwall myths of murder were getting to me, too.

"Writing to your family?" Edward asked, walking over and standing above me.

"No, to Meg," I said, trying hard to control my quaking voice. "I'm not sure where she is." I kept my eyes on the paper.

"Still in Pensacola," Edward said, reaching over and crumbling my letter and tossing it into the pile of nets. He ran his fingers up my arm, leaning over to buss my neck. Twisting, I pushed him away and got up from the desk. "Still wearing the sapphire?" he asked.

"Yes," I replied, twisting the ring around my finger. "It doesn't matter to me where it came from." And it just might find its way back to another pawnshop someday, I thought.

Maisie awoke then. Seeing Edward, she pushed the covers aside and stood, wobbling without her brace. Edward crossed the cold floor to her and knelt, steadying her. I watched, tension growing and curling up my back.

"Maisie," I said, "go up to the house and see if Cook has a biscuit for you. Take Dodgy with you."

"You made Millie sad," Maisie said, shaking her finger in Edward's face. "You make her cry. There are ghosts who can haunt you, you know. Big ghosts."

Edward laughed and said, "Brian telling you porkies?"

"No," she said, her voice rising to an eerie shriek, her hands in the air. "The parson will get you. And his pack of wild dogs."

"Maisie, please go," I repeated, worried for her more than myself. Surely Edward had stopped to see his mother first, so they must know where I was. Dodgy barked and snapped at Edward's ankle.

"Dodgy don't like you," Maisie cried. "Brian says animals are frightfully clever and know who's a blighter."

Edward remained silent as Maisie limped to the door and began her trek up the lawn, Dodgy yapping behind her. He closed the door and sat down on the couch. He pulled his pack of cigarettes from his pocket, lit one, and sat back, drawing his breath in as cool as if he'd done nothing wrong. As cool as if he'd never lied. As cool as if he'd never deserted me.

"I've had the best time," he said. "There's this delightful lady, Lucy Boston, who owns an extraordinary old Norman house near our base. She is holding gramophone concerts weekly. The base lays on a coach to take us there, and we listen to Chopin and Elgar. She covers the floor of the Music Room with mattresses and covers the windows, too, to keep us safe.

And we sit and have tea and listen. Glorious." He closed his eyes and took another drag on his cigarette, then, raising his hands, conducted a classical tune that played only in his mind, his cigarette ashes dropping to the floor. "Can we stay here tonight?" he asked, eyes still closed.

"What?" I said, shocked at his suggestion.

"Don't play the virgin with me," he sneered. "You are my wife whether I own a hall or a pisspot." His eyes were wide open now. I saw for the first time a wildness in him. He was Heathcliff. This boathouse had become a cottage on the moors in *Wuthering Heights,* and I was afraid. I knew I had to get out of this boathouse. "You were after my fortune from the first time I met you. From that first dance at the USO," he accused.

"I didn't know you had a fortune. I mean, there is no fortune." Confused, I moved to the door. My head was swimming with his accusations. With his lies and deception. Had I asked for this?

"You're not going anywhere. Sit down, my darling." He was a man I'd never seen nor heard before.

"What do you want?" I asked, crossing to the desk again. I looked about the room for a weapon, a way to defend myself.

"Oh, of course," he laughed, mocking me, "you're Rebecca at the boathouse. Are you afraid I'm going to kill you? Shoot you? Push you against the nets so you crack your lovely head?"

"How can you be so cruel?" I asked. I would not cry. I would not cry. The sun was setting now, and darkness crawled across the room.

"Don't you want to call me Maxim?" Edward asked, leaning to put out his cigarette on the floor, squashing it with his foot. "Mustn't start a fire. What a daft cow you are. In love with books and movies with no idea of real life. Of war. Of bombs. And planes exploding. And the smell of burning flesh."

"Edward, how could I know?" My heart was responding to his pain, and I watched him, desperate to help, fighting back Father Joe's compassion, so confused.

"You were an easy mark," he said. "From my first years here as a child, watching Emily and Charles grow up in posh style, my only thoughts were to someday get out of here. To go to a new country where one is not judged by one's father's name," he said, pitching his voice high in an exaggerated mockery of the upper class. "Father? What father? I never knew mine. I grew up with whispers behind my back that perhaps Earl Renfrew had fathered a bastard with Cook."

"Edward, is that true?" Shocked, I listened as he poured out his past to me. I stood and edged my way to the door.

"So I joined the RAF to escape, and mission accomplished, damned if I didn't come in on a wing and a prayer to blessed Grosse Ile, Michigan." He crossed himself as he spoke, his eyes looking heavenward.

"But you loved me. I know you did," I argued, softening to his words, searching my heart, which was now bereft of love.

"Yes, I love you now, but not the way you want me to, you ninny. I am no good for any one woman." He lit another cigarette, and his face was for a moment intensified in the light. I could see tears on his cheeks.

"But we could try again," I suggested, rising, my

inclination to go to him. My mind and heart were struggling now, at war for my life.

"You're like shit I've trod in with my boot in your vegetable allotment, and I can't scrape you off." He was mocking me now with a fierce cruelty. "You may think these Land Girls common, but they know how to please a man." His eyes were dark in the dim light. Furious at me. At everyone.

"I know they all have matching RAF compacts. Payment for their services?" I asked.

"How you Land Girls do whinge, stroppy cows, all of you," Edward said, rising from the couch, blocking my escape. "I have your passport. Or rather I burned it. If you flee, I will follow you."

"Why?" I asked, knowing full well the response. His words baffled me. I couldn't tell what he wanted. For me to stay? Or go? He was beside me now, looming over me. He had never seemed so tall and imposing. Reaching for my hand, he looked at my nails, then dropped it in disgust.

"You've let yourself become common," he said. "You're nothing. I can't bring myself to even touch you. If you had any pride, you would kill yourself." And with that he was out the door.

I collapsed on the couch, crying and pounding my fists against the quilts and pillows. I knew I was not safe here, but I was afraid to leave. I saw him through the window on the beach, smoking and looking out to sea. Then by the bomber's moonlight, I watched as he stripped naked, his uniform strewn along the sand. I watched mesmerized as he waded into Serenity Cove, his pale thin flesh bathed by the moon and the sea. Startling back to reality, I knew this was my chance. I ran, tugged open the door, and was away up the back path, hurrying, yet picking my way as best as I could in the darkness, avoiding brambles, knowing I would be safest with the Land Girls in our suite. Yes, *I fled him*, and somewhere I heard an owl screech. Owls were evil omens Maisie had said. Cook had told her.

Chapter 24

The girls were already asleep when I tiptoed up the stairs and into the suite. I was so exhausted I climbed up into the top bunk in my clothes and fell into a deep coma of sleep. No dreams. I'd already lived through my nightmare. I had no energy to worry about the pilot who had just walked into the sea. Not even enough strength to peek around the blackout curtain and see for myself if he had returned to the sand from the water or if perhaps he had allowed himself to be washed out to sea. I was beyond saving him. It was time to save myself.

I awoke with the sun streaming across the room. The girls were up, dressed, and gone. For a moment, fuzzy with sleep, I forgot about last night's scene. Panic washed over me when I remembered Edward's dark eyes and cruel words. Hauling myself out of bed, I changed from my trousers and blouse to my Land Girl uniform. No time for breakfast, I hurried downstairs and out the front door. I stopped cold. Edward was in the garden, smoking and chatting with the three girls. He was out of uniform in trousers and a light blue sweater. Sophie had her hand on his arm, leaning on her hoe. Martine sat on the lawn, looking up at him while Judy beside her sipped on a mug of tea. He had a willing audience for his charm. Were they laughing at me? Exchanging stories at my expense? No. Those girls were like sisters to me.

Then I saw Brian coming up the lawn toward me. Before I could come down the steps, he reached me and pulled me back into the grand hall. "We need to get you and Maisie away from Sand Castles," he said, taking my arm. "He's down there with the girls making some wild talk about you both."

"But where can we go?" I asked. "He's burned my passport." Panicked, I felt the tears coming.

"There is a couple who runs a local pub called the Punch & Peacock, very near here. He'll think you've gone as far as possible from here, not stayed so close." Brian leaned over toward me and whispered, "Pack your things and Maisie's. Tell no one. Not a soul. The spirits will be listening. Say nothing aloud. Meet me out back in an hour."

"Near the stable?" I asked. That was too near the kitchen. Cook would see.

"No, near the gates. I'll get Maisie there." Brian turned and started singing a Cornish tune as he walked back out the door down the lawn to Edward and his Land Girls. I wasted no time in bolting up the stairs and packing. *I fled him.* At last.

An hour later, I was at the gate. Brian was already there in the cart. He had wooden crates of vegetables and a blanket in the cart. Maisie was not in sight. "Let me help you into the cart," he offered, taking my arm. Up I went, and he gestured to the blanket. "Cover yourself." He lifted my suitcase up next to the crates. I could see Maisie's bag and gas mask near it.

Pulling the blanket up, I heard a squeal and a giggle from Maisie as I uncovered her. Snuggling down next to her, I listened as she announced in hushed tones that we were Cornish ladies hiding from dastardly pirates come up from the coves to hide their stolen brandy in tin mines and pilchard caves. I shook my head and shushed her with a finger across her mouth. The cover over us, we felt Brian turn the horses with the words, "Ride on." The trip would not be long. Curled up with Maisie tucked into my arms, I said a prayer to St. Jude. The nuns had always told us to pray to him when we were in dire need. My prayers to St. Michael had gone unanswered.

We traveled along the rutted road, each bump jarring our bones. I tried to pull Maisie's crippled leg over mine to cushion it, but I think I did more harm than good as she whimpered into my ear. To calm her I said, "Tell me another story about old Cornwall. I love your tales."

"Swell," she said. She had announced that Sophie had taught her that word, and it was now her favorite. "Swell," she repeated, deciding what story to tell me. "In old Penzance there was an evil woman who poisoned her own husband with snic," she began.

"Snic?" I said. "Do you mean arsenic?"

"Very well," she said in her scariest voice. "Arsenic with an 'a' just like in Maisie." She said Cook had been helping her learn her letters.

"Go on," I urged, amused at the seriousness of this small child as she wove her tale of murder and mayhem.

"The police thought she had done the old man in, slipping the poison in his tea day after day, so they dug up his body, and they did find the poison rotting his bones. Enough to kill three strong men they said. So they hanged the evil wife and to this very day her ghost walks the cemetery on stormy nights, her neck all swelled up from the noose."

"My goodness," I said, "Cornwall can be a scary place."

Maisie hugged me and again whispered, "Don't be scared. I'm here. Brian says I got to watch over you." I turned my face away so she could not see me tearing up again. Someday I promised myself there would be no more tears. It was time I protected myself.

I could hear voices now on both sides of the cart, so I knew we must be coming into civilization. I whispered to Maisie to stay very still. I had time for one more prayer, this time a Hail Mary, before the cart stopped. "Stay still," I said.

Then there was sunlight on us as Brian pulled the blanket away. We both sat up, hot, with our wet hair flattened against our brows. We were stopped around the back of a very old stone inn. As Brian lifted Maisie up and to the ground, a smiling woman hurried out the door.

"You must be Maisie," she said, picking her up and swinging her around in her arms. Just then a man came out the door and reached over to help me down from the cart. "This is my husband, Ian, the best innkeeper in Cornwall," she said.

"And me wife here is called Bette," Ian added, grinning proudly. "Welcome to the Punch & Peacock, called thus for the very peacocks that roam the great lawn of Sand Castles."

"Just swell," Maisie said, checking her brace. "I had polio, just like Mr. Roosevelt in America."

Ian and Bette exchanged tender looks, and I knew they would love Maisie as their own.

"Come in, all you travelers, and rest your weary

souls by the fireplace," Bette said, gesturing for us to follow her. Brian carried our bags behind as we entered the doorway. Ian had to duck his head to fit through the ancient doorway. Inside we found two chairs by the fireplace unlit in the warm spring. We sat as Brian spoke with Ian and Bette in low voices.

"What a swell fireplace," Maisie said. "I could fit right inside it. Do you think ghosts walk here at night? Have there been unholy murders here?" She crossed her throat with her hand, slicing it with an imaginary dagger, and then changing it to a hangman's noose jerking her neck.

"I'm sure we'll be safe here," I said, more afraid of the living than the dead. This chair was so comfortable I could just curl up and sleep forever. My stomach was churning and growling, of course, as I'd had no breakfast, not even a cuppa.

Bette left the conversation and came over to us. "Can I get you a drink? Or a sandwich? We've cut back our bill of fare because of rationing, but we still offer good Cornish food."

"Maisie," I asked, "are you hungry?" She came over and climbed up onto my lap, her brace clunking against the old wood of the chair.

"I could do a sandwich, cheese and chutney?" Maisie asked.

"And tea?" Bette suggested.

"Swell," she said, sitting up and smiling.

"That's her new favorite word," I explained, and we laughed together. The tension was gone for just a moment.

"Come sit over here," Brian said, so we crossed to a booth and sat down opposite him. I sank into the leather cushions, the fear receding from my mind and heart. "You'll be fine here. Just stay off the road and keep in the back of the inn. And maybe help Bette out with the cooking or tidying up," Brian suggested. He was such a kind man. I would do what he wanted me to, of course.

Bette brought our sandwiches, big thick homemade bread with slabs of cheddar cheese and chutney she had made herself. Ian carried over a pot of tea. "Tuck in," Bette said, "and then you can see your room and maybe have a lie-down."

I poured tea for us all, then bit into my sandwich, looked about my new home, breathing easy for the first time since I had arrived in Cornwall.

Chapter 25

That peace stayed with me for a few days until Lady Renfrew stormed through the pub doorway early in May, demanding that Maisie return to Sand Castles with her.

Maisie shed a few tears, but in the end pronounced it "swell" to return to the hall, especially to be with Brian and hear more ghost stories. We hadn't realized that a little girl with a brace would gather attention from the villagers.

It was just me at the inn. Lady Renfrew told me Edward was back to flying missions over Germany, or so they surmised. But I would make one more attempt at escape, not trusting Edward. The Land Girls showed up at the pub a few days later. They ordered a round of punch and settled in to kick back and relax. I was anxious to hear how Maisie was working out, but they assured me she was fine. Sophie told me that Cook had been intercepting any mail I had received and destroying it in the kitchen fireplace. I couldn't imagine who had written to me, but Martine gave me a letter she had managed to save from Cook. It was from Connie Childs, the war bride from the ship, inviting me to come visit her on the cider farm near Taunton in Somerset where her Harry's family lived.

The girls and Brian put their coins together and booked me a train ticket for Taunton. It would be a four-hour journey, and the train would depart that afternoon, late. I was moved by their concern and kindness. Ian gave me a few more coins, spending money, he said, and Bette packed me sandwiches.

I fled him again. Ian had already sent a telegram to Connie advising her of my arrival time. Bette had packed my bag, and I left for the station on foot alone, not wishing to draw attention with a send-off crowd of friends. The trip was uneventful. Connie was there when I arrived. I felt safer than I had in days.

Connie and I walked along the path to the cider farm, passing the defensive pillboxes on the cliffs. By the time we had reached the apple orchards, I had spit out my story to her. I was ashamed of my naiveté, but still unable to totally blame Edward, knowing full well the toll the war was taking on him. Connie pointed out that her Harry had not had an easy war, that he'd even been wounded, but he was still a decent bloke. Not a liar. Not cruel.

"He said I was an easy mark," I confided to Connie.

"But what did he want from you?"

"I think he wanted to eventually emigrate to America and live off my dad. He thought in America he could get away from the class restrictions that would hold him back. But how are you doing here with a new family?" I asked her as we headed back to the farmhouse.

Connie told me she was getting along okay with her in-laws. She was helping out in the orchards, and her nails had also taken a beating and her hands roughened, but she had been used to her life in Ohio, which was much like Somerset. She had not seen her husband, Harry, since he had brought her to Somerset from Liverpool.

I never saw Harry again. I met his parents, Rose and Ron, and we sat at the big table in their kitchen, the aroma of baking bread warming us. Rose, in her country clothes and stained apron, kept shaking her head as I told her my tale, finally pronouncing Edward a dreadful bugger. I was right to do a runner, Ron told me, assuring me I was welcome as long as I needed to stay. He was a big man, with a dark mustache, his face toughened in the sun of a farmer's life. These were good people. I must admit the jug of cider brandy we kept pouring from soothed my nerves and opened my tongue. And the warm bread that Rose eventually added to our plates, drenched in fresh butter and clotted cream, was divine. A fire burned down to ashes in the huge fireplace as I talked and talked, safe and sound while the stars came out. I had arrived in Cornwall a stranger and was leaving on the wings of so many angels who had supported me.

I tumbled into another strange bed that night, ready to rise early and help in the orchards. I was asleep at once, the cider soothing me. No dreams. Just a tentative peace.

The next morning, after working in the orchards, watering and weeding, we returned to the farmhouse kitchen for lunch, and there by my plate was a shocking telegram. Edward was dead, drowned in the cove. The tears came again, my swollen eyes overflowing. Perhaps in the end Edward had fled me. My decision now was whether to travel back for the funeral or stay with Connie. Would I even be allowed to attend the service in the old chapel?

I didn't want him to die. Not like that. Was it suicide? Had he had enough? I decided to return and honor Edward in death. I was his wife. I shook my head, reasoning with myself that it was my duty. My goodbye. I went back up to the bedroom and began to pack. I had brought the Renfrew copy of *Rebecca* with me. A secret thrill that I had stolen something from that Great Hall. I flipped it open to a back page and read aloud, "It was going to be very different in the future…there were heaps of things that I could do, little by little."

Little by little. Step by step. I just wanted to go home to everything I had so foolishly deserted.

****

The door to the coach slid open. Looking up, I recognized Barbara, the woman who stood there as the Red Cross lady from the Penzance station. She must have heard all the gossip that had so enraptured the old town. I had no desire to be pitied. It was too late to pretend I was sleeping. James stood up and offered her his seat. "Please sit here," he said. "I'm off to find a few mates for a card game."

"Look," she said, crossing the coach and pulling the blackout curtain away from the train window. We both peered out to see what looked to me to be a fireworks display from the sky to the ground off in the distance. Brilliant flashes against a dark sky.

"That must be Liverpool in flames," James said, whistling a low sad reaction as he left the coach.

It wasn't Manderley burning. This was not a scene from a novel. Mrs. Danvers had not set this fire at Rebecca's beloved estate. Edward was right. I could no longer live through novels or movies, ignoring the

291

reality of war and its effects on cities, on hearts and minds.

"It's the seventh night of bombing," she said. "The train will make a final stop at the next station, not Liverpool," she said. "If you were hoping to get a ship out of Liverpool, I'm sure there will be none sailing for some time, my dear."

Wondering how she knew my plans, but remembering the gossip of the folks of Penzance, I asked, "What can I do?" I was determined not to cry again in front of her. She obviously knew my story. Penzance was a small town, though idyllic, also a nest for gossip.

"Sit down, my dear. How are you coping? When I met you and Edward at the station in Penzance you seemed so happy. About to start a marvelous new life. And you were so kind to take in Maisie."

"Maisie will be fine at Sand Castles. They all love her," I answered uneasily.

"But you? I heard about the inquest."

Yes, there had been an inquest, hastily held in the library at Sand Castles. "I was not called to testify," I told her. "I was there though." I shuddered as I recalled the excruciating hours I spent in the library, listening, muzzled.

"Strange that they did not ask you," Barbara mused.

"It was a hurried affair, rigged from the start. Hushed up to quell the gossip." I didn't know if I could go over it all again.

"If you don't mind my sticking my oar in, who were the witnesses?" Barbara asked, intrigued now.

I took a deep breath, knowing I had to tell the rest

of this story aloud, not just in my mind. "Let me see, there was the Earl Renfrew, whom I didn't even know existed. He was never about nor did anyone talk about him. He was commanding in his depiction of Edward as a lad who had grown up at the hall and only wanted to serve his country. His word went a long way as he is part of Churchill's war council at 10 Downing in London."

"Impressive. I saw the Earl and Lady Renfrew at a Red Cross function once," Barbara said, watching me closely as I revealed more. "Much too posh for me."

"There was an officer from the RAF who talked about Edward's exemplary service record. One with no blemishes or signs of inner turmoil. He spoke of our hasty marriage as detrimental to Edward, a distraction."

"That must have been quite the natter party while they began to point the finger at you, the American wife." She looked worried for me across the aisle. I wished I had known her while I was in Penzance. She could have been an ally.

"Yes, I began to feel that I was on trial," I said as she came and sat by me. "Next up was Cook, Edward's mum. She put on quite a show. Hysterical. Pointing directly at me. Accusing me of killing her son."

"And you sat there? With no recourse?" She seemed more indignant now than I had been at the time.

"But as I said it was a foregone conclusion what the verdict would be. It only took minutes for the coroner to announce accidental drowning as the cause of death. I left the library and turned down the hall to the stairs. I felt a hand on my shoulder and spun around, hoping to see a friendly smile. Instead I was staring into the distorted raging face of Cook. She had aged years in hours. Her deeply creased cheeks seemed to sag in grief. I almost felt sorry for her. 'You slag,' she shrieked at me. 'You American whore. You have robbed me of a good boy, my Edward. I have lost two sons now. Gerald over Germany, I could accept. He died for England. But *Edward.*'

"I was speechless. Torn between her anger and grief. I tried to just walk away, but she pulled me back by my arm. 'Here,' she spat out as she slapped me across the cheek with something. 'Be gone!' As it slipped to the ground, I recognized my passport. In her hatred, she was releasing me, helping me travel back to America. I later learned the RAF had sent me his effects, and she had kept all but my passport. I stooped to pick up the passport and backed away from her in silence. Edward had not told me of his brother's death."

Barbara hugged me, but I would not cry. The tears were over. It was time to think about that "different future."

"Your husband told me you had almost finished your nursing studies stateside when we first met at the train station," she said, taking my hand.

"Yes, I was three months away from finishing. I was doing my last rotation on the cardiac unit," I said, refraining from adding what a fool I had been to walk away from it all.

"The Red Cross needs what we call volunteer aides," she said. "There will be a car waiting for me at the next station if you want to come with me. You are certainly overqualified, but we can put you to work until a passage on a ship opens up for America."

"Yes, oh, yes," I said, "please let me help, Barbara." I held out my other hand to her.

Just then James returned to the coach. He was grumpy, as he'd lost a few quid playing cards. He slumped down across from us. "So have you ladies had a good natter?" He tossed a magazine to me, one he had found in the other car. "You might find this interesting reading," he said.

I looked quickly at the cover to see "Are You Being Gaslighted?" as a feature article. Later, I thought.

"You've missed my future," I said. "I'm volunteering to work with the Red Cross here in Liverpool until I can book passage home."

"Good on you, Millie," he said, perking up from his loss at cards.

"Yes, she'll be a welcome addition to our group," Barbara said. "We'll be leaving the train at the next stop, one before Liverpool."

"And what about you, James? Your escort duties are finished," I said, thanking him.

"I'll be on my way back to Cambridge," he said, leaning back in repose.

Barbara fell quiet, too, so I picked up the magazine and turned to the feature article. I became engrossed at once as I read. Dr. Stearn, a psychiatrist, had laid out for the reader several examples of harmful relationships he had encountered in his practice. Gaslighters, he explained could be of three types. The Glamorous. The Good Guy. The Intimidator. They all had two things in common. First, the need to control. But secondly and more shocking to me, they needed a willing gaslightee. I could see all three types of gaslighter in Edward. But it was much harder to recognize myself as a willing participant to all he had inflicted on me. I closed the magazine, unable to read on. I thought ahead to my future, leaving Edward behind. Firmly.

As the train pulled into our station, I stood and hugged James goodbye. He retrieved my suitcase and shook my hand, laughing that he would never forget the stargazy pie nor the quid he'd lost at cards. Strange that I knew we'd never meet again, yet he'd been there at a very low time in my life.

Stepping off into the night, deadly dark in its blackout, I took a deep breath and followed Barbara to my future. Little by little.

****

Later that night, in a hotel outside of Liverpool that had been requisitioned by the military, I signed the papers to become a voluntary aide. I was shown to the ballroom, which had been refitted with rows of cots. I sat down on the one assigned to me, my suitcase by my feet. A monkish life awaited me. On the wall across from my cot, a poster had been tacked to the wall. On it was a sepia photo of St. Michael's Mount, and beside that landmark was the following poem:

Hymn for the RAF

Lord, hold them in thy mighty hand
Above the ocean and the land.
Like wings of eagles mounting high
Along the pathways of the sky.

Immortal is the name they bear.
And high the honour that they share.
Until a thousand years have rolled
Their deeds of valour shall be told

In dark of night and light of day.
God speed and bless them on their way,

And homeward safely guide each one
With glory gained and duty done.

I knew then that I would stay in Liverpool and care for the wounded of this war, those wounded physically and those wounded in their hearts and souls. Someday I would return to my home, to America. But for now I would be the war widow of a decorated airman, his duty done but mine just beginning.

Epilogue

March 29, 1970
Dear Mum,

Funny, I haven't called you Mum in years, not since we both left England after the war, when I was four. British enough to speak with an accent when I started kindergarten. Here I am, sitting in the Punch & Peacock Inn in Cornwall on a glorious Easter Sunday. I'm alone, waiting. You'll never guess who I've been able to dig up from our past? Maisie Rice. She's to meet me here soon.

I haven't been successful in finding many other characters in your life from the war. I did see a procession of snooty-looking bluebloods snaking its way to the small chapel. All decked out in flowered hats of varied shapes and sizes. Pristine in their suits and dresses, clutching their prayer books. The children in their matching blue coats, no doubt sneaking Easter eggs in their pockets, dawdled behind the adults. I must confess I peeked into the chapel a bit before the family began their parade to the old stone church, curious to see where you had said goodbye to Daddy so many years ago. You never told me much about him, only how brave he'd been during the war. So I have come to discover both England and Daddy on my own.

The inn is under new ownership. Only a photo remains on the wall behind the bar of Ian and Bette,

298

your friends. The next generation, Charles and Emily, lord over Sand Castles. They are not very popular with the villagers, I gather. There certainly was no one standing along the path to the chapel to greet them.

I have you to thank for my life, Mom. You stuck out the war in Liverpool, finishing your nursing studies while working with the Red Cross, pregnant with me. That could not have been easy. A young widow with so many responsibilities. Postwar Britain was a mess. Cities were in ruins. Rationing continued for years. But you did so well. You rose through the nursing ranks to supervisor, always watching out for that American soldier who entered your wards, hoping to give him just a touch of home as the USO had set out to do.

Then came that evening in 1946 when your friends Meg and Mac knocked on our door. They were off to America, and would we come, too? Over the years you smoothed things over with family. Uncle Gary wrote often after he was drafted and sent to fight the war in Burma. Aunt Lill was the lone holdout and the only cold shoulder when we arrived back in Ecorse. You found us an upper flat nearby in Wyandotte. You started as a managing nurse at the local hospital where Grandpa was in charge. Gary followed the family tradition and became a doctor, too. An obstetrician. As if that were not enough, I got the medical bug, too. I pushed the boat out, as the Brits say. I reached beyond being a nurse. I became a psychologist, finishing my studies just last month. But with all of these medical professionals in the family, we could not heal your lungs so affected by the fires of the war. You were not even fifty when we said goodbye. It was always just you and me; for that reason and this new loneliness, I want the truth about my dad.

A woman has just entered the inn. She walks with a slight limp. Yes, that must be Maisie. Gotta go. Looking forward to the specialty, stargazy pie.

Love you, Mom, Mum, Millie. Thank you.

Christine

A Note from the Author...

A big thank you to my family, who have been so supportive of me during the writing of this book. It has its roots in the beginning of the wartime courtship and marriage of my parents. I hope my mother's family will enjoy seeing their dad and his antics. I salute my niece, Bridgette, and my nephew, Sam, who serve in the military today. I also give thanks to my auntie Jean, the last remaining member of the WWII generation in our family. Her story of being evacuated to Cornwall during the war is the basis for Maisie's plight at the Penzance Station. She was able to read the evacuation excerpt in her last weeks and had a big smile on her face I am told.

I thank Daphne du Maurier and her classic, *Rebecca,* which has enthralled me since I first read it when I was thirteen. I used both the Lux Radio Play and the original movie version of the book in preparation. I found invaluable psychological information in *The Gaslight Effect* by Dr. Robin Stern. I also drew on the British movie *Gaslight* from 1940 and the novel *Before the Fact*, the basis for the film *Suspicion.*

And many thanks to my sister and class valedictorian Carol Rebbeck, who attended nursing training in Detroit and filled me in on her course and patient work. She even brought her nurse's cap and explained how they starched them and slapped them on the refrigerator to dry.

About the author...

Barbara J. Rebbeck is a teacher and writer who lives in Royal Oak, Michigan. She has published poetry, essay, and professional articles. In 2015 she published her YA novel *NOLA Gals*. Since then she has been an author-in-residence and visited many classrooms of students who have read her novel.

She is a past president of Michigan Council for Teachers of English and a former Director of the Oakland Writing Project. Currently she is Program Chair for the Detroit Working Writers and a member of Sisters in Crime.

Barb's dad was born in England and met her mother, a USO hostess during WWII, when he came to America for flight training with the RAF. Their whirlwind courtship is the basis for the Detroit chapters of *The Girl from the USO*. Barbara is very proud of her British ancestry and has traveled there often.

Visit her at:

http://www.nolagals.com

Thank you for purchasing
this publication of The Wild Rose Press, Inc.

For questions or more information
contact us at
info@thewildrosepress.com.

The Wild Rose Press, Inc.
www.thewildrosepress.com

CPSIA information can be obtained
at www.ICGtesting.com
Printed in the USA
LVHW051656101220
673847LV00013B/1328